RED MEANS RUN

MEANS

RUN

A NOVEL

BRAD SMITH

SCRIBNER

New York   London   Toronto   Sydney   New Delhi

SCRIBNER
A Division of Simon & Schuster, Inc.
1230 Avenue of the Americas
New York, NY 10020

First Scribner trade paperback edition January 2012

SCRIBNER and design are registered trademarks of The Gale Group, Inc.
used under license by Simon & Schuster, Inc., the publisher of this work.

For information about special discounts for bulk purchases,
please contact Simon & Schuster Special Sales at 1-866-506-1949
or business@simonandschuster.com.

The Simon & Schuster Speakers Bureau can bring authors to your live event.
For more information or to book an event contact the Simon & Schuster Speakers Bureau
at 866-248-3049 or visit our website at www.simonspeakers.com.

DESIGNED BY ERICH HOBBING

Manufactured in the United States of America

1   3   5   7   9   10   8   6   4   2

Library of Congress Cataloging-in-Publication Data is available.

ISBN: 978-1-4516-4551-4
ISBN: 978-1-4516-4642-9 (ebook)

"It is easier to stay out than to get out."

—MARK TWAIN

RED
MEANS
RUN

ONE

The rain that had threatened all day finally retreated without delivering a single drop; the heavy clouds scattered to the east and the late afternoon sun breached the tall windows in the office, banking off the bookshelves on the wall opposite where Mickey Dupree sat, leaning back in his chair, his feet up on the desk, his passive expression belying the impatience lingering within. On top of the bookshelves was gathered the usual bric-a-brac one might find in a law office—commendations from various community groups, letters of gratitude from prominent clients, declarations attesting to this accomplishment or that. Among these insignificant items was a framed certificate stating that Mickey had scored a hole in one on the sixteenth hole at the Burr Oak Golf and Country Club. Glancing at it now served only to remind him that he was at this minute supposed to be teeing off at the course, rather than sitting idly waiting for Chuck and Sally Fairchild to arrive.

The certificate in its walnut frame was coated with a thin layer of dust, as were the other items there. Mickey noticed the dust only when the sun hit the window at a certain angle late in the day, at an hour when he was usually finishing his second Rusty Nail at Harry's Pub, and he always made a note to tell the cleaning woman to take care of it, invariably forgetting about it by the following day. He'd made the hole in one in September 1989, and it had been his first and only ace to date. The year itself had held a number of firsts for Mickey, and a more sen-

1

timental individual might from time to time give pause to the memory of them. Mickey was not a man to fall victim to such whimsy, but if he were, he would recall that 1989 was the year in which he married his first wife—the former Margaret Louise Jensen—a few months after Margaret's father made him junior partner in his firm. He also bought his first new car that year—a Mercedes coupe that seated just two and, as such, Margaret insisted, was entirely impractical for a couple with a child due in the fall. Mickey ignored her, an act that did not fall into the category of firsts.

There were other firsts that year of varying degrees of significance, but only one could Mickey accurately say changed the course of his life, or at least of his career. It was in 1989 that he first successfully defended a client in a capital murder case. The accused was Ronnie Dillard, a drunkard and layabout and sometime cokehead who robbed and shot a dealer from White Plains and was found a few hours later in a stupor in a motel room outside of Coxsackie, cocaine scattered around the bathroom and the murder weapon lying on the pillow, inches from Ronnie's muddled head.

Looking back, Mickey had no business getting an acquittal for the royal mess known as Ronnie Dillard. But the local cops who found Dillard, after being tipped off by the motel's owner, bungled the arrest and the subsequent investigation in a number of ways, first denying the suspect his Miranda rights, then neglecting to secure the room before the forensics unit arrived. The coup de grâce, however, came during the actual trial, when the district attorney produced a gun designated as the murder weapon, along with a damning ballistics report. Ronnie Dillard, in a rare observant moment, noticed that the front sight was intact on the Smith & Wesson presented as evidence, whereas the one on his own revolver had been filed off.

At Mickey's request, the unit performed a new ballistics test, which showed that the prosecution had the wrong gun. It was later determined that the revolvers had been switched, quite accidentally, in the evidence room at the police station, and that the real murder weapon had since disappeared, probably taken home by a cop who'd taken a fancy to it, unaware of its role in the case. By that time it no longer mattered, as Ronnie Dillard was a free man, back on the street and headed for whatever slippery slope his moronic nature had in store for him.

And with that Mickey Dupree had his first murder acquittal. Since then, he'd added seven more to his credit, the most recent coming just ten days ago with the exoneration of Alan Comstock. He'd become the go-to guy in upstate New York when it came to murder one. However, Mickey was more than just the lawyer who had won eight capital murder cases, he was the lawyer who had never lost one.

Now he sat impatiently waiting for his meeting with the Fairchilds, a meeting he really didn't want, about a capital murder case he didn't want. The fact that the couple was keeping him from the stag nine at Burr Oak did nothing to improve his disposition.

Mickey had joined the old country club in 1987 and had managed to remain a member of good standing ever since. With the notable exception of the seventh hole, he loved everything about the club and the extended privileges that membership provided. Located a few miles south of Kingston, the course was fifteen minutes away from his home. The food in the clubhouse was good, if not inspiring, and the staff was cordial but rarely fawning. The course itself was kept in immaculate condition and had been rated one of the top twenty in the state for several years running. Not long at sixty-one hundred yards, it was nevertheless a difficult test of a demanding game.

Built in 1927 by a dipsomaniac Scotsman named McDougal, and then redesigned in the 1960s by Robert Trent Jones, it was a gorgeous layout, a meandering old-style course that featured hundreds of ancient hardwoods—huge sugar maples, black walnuts, ironwoods, and the white oaks that gave the place its name. Stands of pine and spruce had been integrated into the landscape over the decades. Gibson's Creek tumbled down from the White Mountains and crisscrossed the course in several spots, eventually pooling up in a pond in front of the eighteenth green before continuing on toward the Hudson.

Mickey was a decent golfer, better than the average duffer at Burr Oak, but not nearly as good as the best members there. The best players teed it up virtually every morning, whereas Mickey usually played on Sundays, and in the occasional Saturday tournament. And on Tuesdays, of course.

Every spring, the membership was divided by draft into four teams, which competed for a title that was significant only for the bragging rights it carried. The stag was nine holes, alternating the front and the back, every Tuesday throughout the summer. Most guys played in the afternoon and afterward had dinner and drinks in the clubhouse, and then darts and shuffleboard in the game room, the social side often lasting until the wee hours and resulting in some monumental hangovers Wednesday morning. Mickey played in the afternoon when he could, but work often made that impossible, especially if he was in court for the day. Occasionally he played the nine alone early Tuesday morning, just to get his score in, but since his last divorce he'd drifted back into his old habits, late nights at the bars on Broadway, where he would fall victim to too many drinks, too many animated conversations, and too many pretty waitresses. He rarely got out of bed before nine these days and that left no time for morning golf.

So he often played late on Tuesday, squeezing the round in on his own just before dusk. Gregarious by nature, Mickey nonetheless did not mind golfing alone. He usually had the course to himself and there was something clean and unblemished about the deserted landscape in the gloaming, stretched out before him like a fresh slate. It was a metaphor that cropped up constantly in Mickey's line of work. Everybody was deserving of a fresh slate. It was a cliché, but unlike most clichés, it was patently untrue. There were a number of people out there who were deserving of no such thing.

Par for nine holes was thirty-six, both front and back, and Mickey usually scored three or four above that. Mickey never cheated on his scorecard, even when playing alone. This wasn't due to any inherent honesty on his part—he was, in fact, an inveterate cheater in many aspects of his life, both personally and professionally. However, in the rough camaraderie of the clubhouse, where crooked lawyer jokes abounded, Mickey was not about to give his fellow members any additional ammunition to fire at his profession. Not only that, but cheating at golf when there was no money involved was like cheating at solitaire: it made no sense. So he dutifully recorded his thirty-nine or forty most weeks and handed in his card. He rarely shot higher than that.

Unless, of course, number seven got him. The seventh hole at Burr Oak had been Mickey's nemesis since his first year there. Like many a scourge in history, it was unassuming and short: a par three, a hundred and sixty yards, slightly uphill, with a long and narrow green that sloped downward to the left. At the front corner of the green was a sand trap, small and oval and very deep. An opposing trap waited at the far end, to the left. But it was the front trap that was the consistent thorn in Mickey's side these many years. Off the tee, he could not stay out of it and once in, he could not *get* out of it. On the rare occasion that he did, he usually thinned the ball, rocketing it across the green into the opposite bunker.

"You're going to find me dead in that bunker one day," he would often say in the clubhouse bar, rattling the ice in his bourbon and water. "Starved to death. When it happens, bury me where I lay. I give up."

On the first Tuesday in July, Mickey wasn't due in court so he planned to be at Burr Oak early enough to join up with some other members for the stag nine. He would have made it too, if it wasn't for Chuck and Sally Fairchild. Shortly past six, Mickey had been getting ready to leave his office when his secretary came in to tell him that the couple had called from their car on their way from the county jail and had asked if they could stop to see him. It was a meeting that Mickey had been avoiding and he was tempted to just leave, have his secretary say they had missed him, but then he said to hell with it. Might as well do it and have it done.

It wasn't Chuck Fairchild who was the problem. Chuck was a former NFL quarterback who had subsequently worked as a color man on the Jets telecast for a few years. He was retired now, an ex-jock with bad knees and nothing to do most days. He was a member at Burr Oak and Mickey liked the man. Sally was a different story; she had been a model in her twenties, a career that had been short but apparently long enough to instill in her an elevated opinion of herself. She was now a writer of lifestyle pieces and coauthor of a book on holiday entertaining. The Fairchilds had a house on five acres south of Albany, a summer place in Maine, and a condo in St. Lucia. What Chuck and Sally didn't have was the slightest notion of how much of a fuckup their only son was.

Byron Fairchild was currently sitting in the county lockup,

awaiting trial for murder one. Mickey had been working on the case for nearly eighteen months, doing whatever he could do to avoid going to trial, and the district attorney was growing impatient. He had even suggested that Mickey was deliberately delaying the matter because he had no defense for Byron Fairchild. The DA was right. Mickey needed no convincing of the fact.

But Chuck and Sally Fairchild did.

The couple arrived and sat opposite Mickey in his office, Chuck in his usual Dockers and polo shirt, Sally wearing designer jeans and T-shirt, her face still vaguely beautiful despite the surgeries and injections that conspired to steal away that beauty.

"I've been asking the DA for a year now," Mickey told them. "I've asked him when he's been sober; I've asked him when he was drunk. I asked him when he was practically doing cartwheels when the Yankees won the Series last year. I get the same answer. Second degree is the best he'll do. If he hasn't budged by now, he's not going to."

Chuck and Sally sat silent for a moment. Mickey reached over and poured himself a glass of water from a pitcher on his desk. The Fairchilds had, upon arriving, declined water, or iced tea, or anything.

"But that means fifteen years," Sally said. "That's what you said."

"Yes."

Sally glanced at her husband. He sat looking at his big hands, perhaps recalling his glory days on the gridiron, when those hands could influence the outcome of a thing. Mickey couldn't know, though. Chuck was stoic, the quiet one. Any suffering he did, he did it internally. As a football star, he was known for his ability to play hurt.

"What I don't understand . . ." Sally began slowly. "What I

don't understand is why they can't make it manslaughter. My son is not a criminal. He is only twenty-two years old. He is not some drug addict from the street who is going to re-offend. Manslaughter, you said he could be out in three years with the time he's already served."

"We've gone over this," Mickey said, speaking just as slowly. "Manslaughter is by definition death by involuntary means. Now, we know the victim here was involved with your son's ex-girlfriend. If, for instance, Byron and this fellow had a fist-fight over the girl at a bar, and the victim died from a blow to the head—*that* would be manslaughter. The intent to kill would not be there. However, that's not what happened."

Mickey opened the file on his desk while he took another drink of water.

"Your son bought a nine-millimeter Glock at a sporting goods store in Syracuse a month before the murder. He bought a silencer from a disreputable citizen named Ducky Sands here in Kingston four days later. His computer shows that he used MapQuest to find the victim's address, and his cell phone records indicate that he called the victim's place of employment several times to determine his schedule. Your son shot the man in the parking lot of his apartment building when he got home from work. When the police arrived, your son admitted to the act. And he said he was glad he did it." Mickey closed the file. "I'm really struggling to find a spot where we might make the word 'involuntary' apply here."

Sally shifted her eyes past Mickey, to the windows, and the leafy maples outside. "My son is not a criminal."

Mickey nodded after a moment, as if agreeing to the stupid statement, and then looked at Chuck. "I'm sorry, Chuck. Second is the best we can do here. Unless you want to go to trial. And then he's looking at life."

"Not if you get an acquittal," Chuck said. "I mean, that's what you do. That's what you're known for. You find a technicality, or improper police work. We're willing to pay you whatever it costs."

Mickey picked up the case file and dropped it on the desk before the Fairchilds. "I've been looking for eighteen months. It's not there."

Chuck looked at his hands again. "We just came from the jail," he said. "Byron's not interested in a plea bargain. Not for second degree, anyway. He wants a trial."

Mickey winced theatrically, as if despairing of the very notion of a trial. This was nothing but fucking nonsense, utter and complete denial. He wanted to be on the golf course, a cold Coors in his hand as he drove the cart. He wanted to be away from these disillusioned people. After a moment he nodded. "Then that's what he'll get," he said. "He is the defendant here. It's your dime, but he is the defendant." He opened up a thick leather binder in front of him. "We won't be able to delay this any longer. Unfortunately . . ." Mickey took a moment for a well-rehearsed perusal of his schedule. "Unfortunately, I'm not going to be available for the actual trial. My colleague Dan Wilson can fit it in, though. I've spoken to him, contingent on your decision."

A heavy silence fell over the room. Mickey, pretending to glance again at the ledger, took the opportunity to check his watch.

"You sonofabitch," Sally said softly. Then, upon further reflection, "You fucking asshole!"

"I beg your pardon." Mickey closed the schedule.

"We were told you would do this," she said. "You don't want to go to trial because you're afraid you'll lose. You're trying to protect your record. You don't care about my son."

"I care enough that I'm advising him not to do this," Mickey said. "But either way, my slate is full. We've dragged this out for more than a year at his insistence."

Chuck stood up. By his expression it was quite evident that he shared his wife's opinion. But he was not about to verbalize it. He was a professional athlete who had been forced to retire because of gimpy knees, and a TV talking head who had lost his job due to his increasing years and inherent blandness. Mickey suspected that he fully understood the concept of inevitability. His wife, however, had not arrived at that place yet.

"You're a self-serving little cocksucker," she told Mickey before they walked out.

By the time Mickey arrived at Burr Oak, it was nearly eight o'clock. The final few groups were just finishing the stag, which was the front nine this week. Mickey teed it up alone and set out in a cart, thinking he could just get the round in if he hurried.

Driving down the first fairway, he thought about the meeting with the Fairchilds. He was a little offended by Sally's accusation, even though it was fundamentally true. Man is prideful by nature, and, as such, Mickey was proud of his unblemished record in capital cases. But it was also true that this reputation delivered to him the highest-profile clients. These cases had netted him over two million dollars the previous year, money that he required to keep two ex-wives happy, and to maintain his home and hobbies and lifestyle. Relinquishing his perfect score would undoubtedly hurt his future business.

But there was more to it than that, in this particular instance anyway. Mickey had no desire to represent Byron Fairchild in court. The kid was a nasty little prick, a sociopath with dead eyes and a detached manner bordering at times on narcolepsy.

Mickey had no doubt he would re-offend. He had grown up alone and coddled in a rambling house in the country, where, Mickey had learned, he had begun shooting squirrels and rabbits and the neighbors' cats with his father's .22 at the age of five or six.

Mickey Dupree was not about to risk his own reputation on a punk like that. In truth, he was hardly dismayed at the prospect of the kid going upriver for life.

Mindful of the approaching dusk, he played quickly and evidently the pace was good for his game. He was even par after six holes. If he could get past the treacherous seventh, he just might post a good score and help out his team. Maybe even birdie the par five ninth and come in under par. Seven was playing short, with the pin in the right front. Mickey hit a seven iron that headed straight for the flag, landed short, bounced once toward the green, then hit something and kicked right. And into the bunker.

"Gimme a fucking break," Mickey said as he jammed the club back into the bag.

When he arrived at the green he found that the ball was on a downslope in the sand, with the pin a mere twenty feet away. It was a tough shot. Mickey got out of the cart and walked to the deep bunker, carrying his sand wedge. Other than the downslope, the ball was lying decently, sitting up in the sand. Before stepping into the bunker, Mickey thought he heard something and paused for a look around. He was the only one on the course and it was a beautiful summer evening. The setting sun threw fingers of light through the sugar maples to the west, illuminating the shallow water of Gibson's Creek where it crossed the eighth fairway. Mickey could hear the faint gurgle of the stream. To the south there was a copse of pine trees and then the iron fence, which marked the course boundary. Beyond the fence was a deep ravine. Mickey could hear the squawks of blue jays and the machine-gun rat-a-tat-tat of woodpeckers, the soft rustle of leaves in the wind. Perhaps it had been the birds he had heard. He felt a strange and uncharacteristic wave of contentment pass over him.

The news reached the maintenance barn first, and then went to the pro shop before finally whipping through the clubhouse like a prairie fire. Just before dusk, one of the grounds crew had driven a Gator out to turn on the sprinklers surrounding the seventh and eighth greens and spotted the abandoned cart. Mickey Dupree was still in the bunker. His ball, however, was on the green, roughly three feet from the pin, suggesting that Mickey had finally made a good sand shot on the hole. The par putt, however, would remain unstruck. Mickey was on his knees, bent back awkwardly, the sand wedge in his hand, a sizable welt on his cheekbone, and a look of surprise on his face.

The broken shaft of a five iron had been driven through his heart.

TWO

The rain stopped during the night and the morning dawned clear, with a drying wind rising from the southwest. After lunch, Virgil Cain walked out into the alfalfa field along the side road and decided it would be dry enough to cut by mid-afternoon. While he waited, he changed the oil in the Massey and then hooked the tractor to the mower and pulled it out of the machine shed. He greased the fittings on the mower and the Massey's front end, out of routine more than anything else; he'd serviced the mower before putting it away last summer and hadn't used it since. He climbed onto the tractor and was about to hit the starter when he heard the harsh blat of a blown muffler and looked up to see a rusty Sunfire roll to a stop in front of the house, where Kirstie's green Jeep sat on the lawn, a FOR SALE sign on the windshield.

Virgil waited until the two young guys got out of the car and started toward the Jeep before he climbed down from the tractor and headed over to meet them. He watched them circling the Jeep as he walked. They were skinny rednecks, both wearing frayed ball caps, one advertising Coors Light, the other some NASCAR star. The taller of the two wore a sleeveless T-shirt and had a thick leather wallet fastened to his belt with a chain. Each of them had the standard tattoos and piercings, proclaiming them to be the individuals they weren't. The Sunfire, parked on the shoulder of the road, was a rattletrap that might fetch a couple hundred dollars at a wrecking yard.

"Hey," the taller one said as Virgil approached.

"Hello," Virgil said.

"Year is this?"

"Oh-seven."

The other one opened the driver's door and got in behind the wheel. He glanced at the odometer; then his eyes went to the sound system. When Kirstie had bought the Jeep, she had immediately replaced the factory stereo with a fancy German setup. Virgil couldn't remember all the specs of the system—this many amps, such-and-such speakers, any and all bells and whistles available—but he did know that the package ran her around two grand. Two grand that she typically did not have but that her credit card would cover. At least temporarily.

"What're ya asking?" the taller one said.

"Twelve thousand." If these two jokers had access to twelve thousand dollars, Virgil would eat his hat.

The other one was still paying a lot of attention to the sound system.

The taller one nodded thoughtfully at the price, as if considering his current financial situation. The other one turned in the seat. "We take it for a drive?"

Virgil glanced back to the tractor and mower. He had a lot of hay to cut. But, as unlikely as these two were as buyers, he really could use the money for the Jeep. Taxes on the place were due and Kirstie had left a lot of debt behind. Kirstie had left a lot of everything behind, none of it good.

"Yeah, we can take it around the block," he said.

"You don't gotta come," the other one said. "You can get to your farmin'."

"My farming can wait. I'll go with you."

"What, you don't trust us?" the taller one said. He was close to being offended.

14

"No," Virgil said. "Why would I?"

"Dude's got a problem," the other one said.

"Actually, I don't," Virgil said. "But I don't know you."

The other one got out of the car. Apparently the notion of going for a drive had lost its appeal when Virgil became part of the bargain. The two circled the Jeep, stopping short of kicking the tires, but just. The taller one had an inspiration.

"Interested in a trade?" he asked, indicating the Sunfire.

"You a comedian?" Virgil asked.

"I can't believe this fuckin' guy," the other one said.

"I'm not interested in a trade," Virgil said.

"So you're asking twelve," the taller one said. "What'll you take?"

"Gotta get twelve."

The taller one gave the Jeep one last critical look. "I'm gonna think about it. See what I can swing."

"It'll be here," Virgil said.

He watched as they got into the Sunfire and drove off. He hoped he'd seen the last of them but he wasn't sure about that. He wasn't sure about much nowadays.

As Virgil walked back along the lane toward the tractor, the thoroughbred gelding came across the pasture field and followed him along the fence, looking for a treat. Or just company. The other eight horses were gathered beneath the hickory tree at the far end of the field, where they stood out of the sun, hip to shoulder, tails flicking flies off one another. The gelding was a sociable animal, especially for a thoroughbred, which he was finally beginning to resemble. He'd put on weight, thanks to Virgil, and seemed to have recovered from his tendon problem, courtesy of Mary Nelson. Virgil would love to sell him, but there wasn't much of a market out there for broken-down racehorses.

The gelding trailed Virgil as far as he could, stopped at the end of the field where the pasture met the barn. With his head over the fence, the horse watched as Virgil climbed back into the tractor seat, fired the engine, and drove into the front field where he began to cut hay.

Once she decided, there was nothing to do but get on with it. At times like this it was harder not to do it than to do it. The bay gelding was lying on the ground in the shade of the pole barn, and they had been unable to get him to eat or even to drink anything all morning. His organs were done, she knew. The other horses, save the half-feral mare, were all gone now, the last one loaded up twenty minutes earlier, headed for a rescue farm outside of Binghamton.

Mary walked to the F-250 and opened the back door. Pulling on a pair of surgical gloves, she loaded the syringe, guessing the emaciated horse's weight to be no more than four hundred pounds. Donald Lee held the bay as she injected him. Mary kept her hand on the animal's neck as his breath grew shallow and then shallower and then stopped altogether. The horse's bladder released and a thin stream of urine stained the dirt of the corral.

Mary got to her feet and looked at Donald, the anger rising within her.

"What did they charge him with?"

"Improper care of animals. Misdemeanor."

"And what's that going to be, a two-dollar fine?"

"First offense, it won't be much," Donald admitted.

Mary removed the gloves. "And then he'll be back here."

"Well, it's his farm."

"I'll be watching him," Mary said.

She walked to the truck and placed the syringe and gloves in a disposal bag. She heard Donald approaching behind her.

"What are we going to do about her?" Meaning the mare.

"I was hoping you might know the answer to that," Mary said without turning.

"I don't. The SPCA doesn't have any place that will take her. I think the horse is crazy."

Mary turned and walked toward the corral. The mare stood watching her, lifting her head up and down in a rhythmic tic, as if agreeing with something over and over again. Her ribs were showing and her mane and tail were matted and tangled. She was filthy from fetlock to withers and her hooves were a mess, overgrown and splayed.

"She's no crazier than you or I would be under the same conditions," Mary said.

"I suppose," Donald said. "But I don't know what we can do for her. If there's no place for her to go, I think we have to put her down."

Mary nodded slowly, still watching the mare, who stared back. Then Mary glanced at the dead bay gelding in the dirt, the animal's tongue extended, sour urine beneath the skinny body. She thought about the owner, a man named Hopman, whom the police had led away a couple of hours earlier. His snarl and his unrepentant eyes. Mary thought about loading a syringe for him, and the thought suddenly jolted her. She was seventy-one years old and had never, even for a fleeting moment, considered killing anyone before. Of course, she wouldn't do it. She couldn't do it. But apparently she had changed enough that she actually entertained the notion, even for only a moment.

She heard a noise from the mare then, a soft nicker from somewhere within, rolling up from her chest. Mary looked over. The mare was still watching her.

"Well," Donald Lee said. "If we're going to do it—"

"We're not," Mary told him.

* * *

It was late afternoon when Virgil finished cutting the ten acres. After completing the final swath at the back of the field he drove out of the side-road gate and headed back to the farm, thinking about a cold beer. From a quarter mile away, he saw Mary Nelson's F-250 parked by the barn, with the double horse trailer behind. As he drew closer he saw that Mary was leaning against the front fender, watching him come down the road. Her long gray hair was tied back and tucked beneath a straw hat, and she was wearing brown pants and a man's button-down shirt. He guessed the shirt had belonged to her husband, who had passed away a few years back, before Virgil had arrived in the area.

Virgil thought it comical that Mary had decided to buy the big F-250. She was maybe five foot three, with short legs and a bit of a belly. She practically needed a ladder to climb into the truck. He wasn't sure of her age, but she was well past retirement, he suspected, although she wasn't allowing a little thing like that to slow her down. He also knew that she had a heart about as big as the truck she was leaning against.

She removed the hat to smooth her hair back as he drove up, and he realized he was not unhappy to see her. Virgil didn't have a lot of visitors and more often than not was content with that. But now he was thinking it would be nice to have a beer with Mary. He was finished for the day, and he was thirsty. Maybe she was too.

He stopped the tractor beside her, indicating the trailer. "Don't tell me you're finally going to pick up some of your horses," he said.

"They're not my horses."

"They're not mine either," he told her.

He drove the tractor and the mower into the machine shed.

It wasn't until he walked back out that he saw the mare's rump over the trailer gate. He stopped.

"Chrissake, Mary. The answer is no."

"I didn't ask anything," she said.

"No," he said.

"Virgil—"

"Don't Virgil me, and don't snow me, and don't nothing me," he said. "I told you the last time."

She threw her hands dramatically in the air, announcing that she was giving up. "Forget about it."

"I already did. You want a beer?"

"No, I don't have time for a beer. I have to find a home for a quarter horse."

"Good luck with that."

"You don't have to be a jerk about it."

"I'm not being a jerk. Have a beer."

She stood looking at him, her lips pursed like a petulant teenager. It was a pose uncharacteristic of her, and, as if realizing this, she quickly dropped it. "All right. Give me a goddamn beer."

Virgil kept beer in a forty-year-old fridge in the old milk house built onto the end of the barn. He went inside and retrieved two bottles of Bud. Along with the beer, he brought out a couple of mismatched wooden chairs, and he and Mary sat in the shade of the barn and drank. Virgil lit a cigarette with his antique Zippo and inhaled deeply.

"Thought you quit that," Mary said.

"I did."

"Why would you start up again?"

He shrugged, pulled on the smoke, as if in defiance of something.

"Okay," she said, as if she knew why and wasn't going to make an issue of it. Not now, anyway. "How does your hay look?"

"Pretty good. I get it baled without being rained on, be all right."

"What's the weatherman saying?"

"Shit. My next life, I'm going to be a weatherman. You ever notice that we can split atoms and put men on the moon and build computers the size of your fingernail, but there's nobody out there can tell us what the weather's going to be like tomorrow? Might as well flip a coin."

"You been working on that speech?"

"Nope. I winged it."

She smiled. "So you're going to be a weatherman?"

"Why not? You get paid to be wrong half the time. I've been doing that all my life for nothing."

"Well, let me know when you start. I'll watch you."

The horses in the pasture were approaching the barn now, heading for the water tank. They came lazily, stopping now and again to pull at tufts of grass. Smoky, the black gelding who thought he was still a stallion, was in the lead, as always.

Mary had a sip of beer and stretched her stubby legs in front of her. She was looking at the horses in the field, but her mind was elsewhere; Virgil could tell.

"You'd really be helping me out if you could take this mare for even a couple weeks," she said.

"You're like the damn weatherman with your couple of weeks," Virgil told her. "That buckskin was going to be here a couple of weeks; it's been seven, eight months. That roan was going to be here a couple weeks; it's been a year at least. Don't start on me with your couple of weeks."

"All right. Geez." Mary took another drink of beer. She looked at the Jeep parked on the lawn. "That was Kirstie's, wasn't it?"

"Yeah. The cops held it in evidence until after the trial."

"Why?"

"I guess if there were any questions about the DNA samples they found or something like that. Doesn't matter now. Does it?"

"I was going to call you when I heard about the verdict," Mary said. "But I didn't know what to say."

"It wasn't going to bring her back," Virgil said.

"Were you surprised?"

"No." Virgil took a drink of beer, rubbed the back of his hand across his mouth. "The money always wins. Alan Comstock is worth what—a hundred million, two hundred million? I never thought they'd get a conviction."

"So I guess you just have to live with it," Mary said.

"I guess."

"Doesn't seem right."

"No."

She turned in the chair to look at him, but he didn't look back. The horses had reached the water trough and Smoky and the buckskin were drinking. When the thoroughbred gelding came for a drink, Smoky nipped at him to remind him who was boss.

"So what's the story with the mare?" Virgil asked, knowing he shouldn't.

"I got a call from Don Lee at the SPCA this morning. Guy named Hopman has a farm back behind here on the Irish Line. Was six months behind on his electric bill, so the county went out to cut off his power. There was nobody home and the worker noticed an illegal power line running to the barn. He checked it out, thinking the guy was running a grow-op maybe, and instead he found six starving horses and some dead pigs. No food, no potable water. Same old story."

"Dirk Hopman," Virgil said.

"You know him?"

"I sold him some hay last winter. I should say I *gave* him some hay last winter, because he never did pay me for it." Virgil tipped the bottle back. "Showed up here with a sob story, said he had money coming the end of the month. So I let him have fifty bales. I even delivered it."

"Well, he must have eaten it himself," Mary said.

Virgil drank off his beer and got up and went into the milk house for two more bottles. He handed one to Mary, even though she'd barely made a dent in the first. He didn't sit down. He had a drink and watched the horses at the water trough for a while, and then he walked to the trailer and looked through the slot at the animal inside.

"She's wired," he said.

"You'd be wired too, what she's been through." Mary came up behind him. "There was a gelding there I had to put down. Don Lee talked some people into taking the other four, but he recommended I needle this one too."

"Why didn't you?"

"Because as far as I'm concerned, Hopman was trying to kill these horses. I didn't feel like being an accomplice to a sonofabitch like him."

Virgil turned to look at her. "Fools rush in where angels fear to tread."

"You talking about me?" she asked.

"I'm talking about both of us." He shook his head and glanced at the weathervane atop the machine shed. "We'll put her in the corral behind the barn. She's not ready for that bunch in the pasture yet. I'll start her on some hay and a little bit of grain." He took a couple of steps, then turned back. "This has got to stop, Mary."

"You're right about that." Mary walked to the rear of the trailer. "Let me take her around. She knows me a little now."

They put the mare in the pen where Virgil kept the cattle during the winter. The herd was in summer pasture now, in the field by the bush lot at the back of the farm. Virgil ran the pump to fill the water trough while Mary went up into the hay-mow and threw down a bale. Virgil gave the mare a sliver off it, to see how she reacted. The horse wouldn't come near while Virgil was in the corral. She backed herself into a corner and watched him.

"She's got some trust issues," Mary said.

"Give her a few days." Virgil looked at the skinny, scared mare for a moment. "She needs to be wormed, you know."

"I know that, Virgil. Do I tell you how to cut hay?"

"Wouldn't surprise me if you did."

They walked around to the truck and trailer, hoping the mare would eat if they left her alone. Mary picked up her beer from where she'd set it on the truck bumper and had a drink, watching the horses around the water tank.

"Why would a man acquire horses and then not bother to feed them? What kind of person can do that? Can you explain that to me?"

"No," Virgil said. He was looking past her, to the roadway. "There's a lot of things I can't explain. For instance, I have no idea why the cops would be pulling in my driveway right now."

Mary turned. A dark blue sedan was approaching slowly along the lane.

"How do you know it's the cops?"

"I just do."

THREE

Joe Brady sat in the passenger side of the unmarked cruiser, attempting different variations of the name Virgil Cain in the database on his laptop. Sal Delano drove, his head finally clearing from the oversize hangover he'd awakened to that morning. Today was his first time working in plain clothes since he'd transferred to the Kingston department a year earlier, and he'd done a little too much celebrating last night.

"I got nothing on this guy," Joe said. "He had to come from somewhere."

"Is this the place?" Sal asked.

Joe looked up. "Yeah. That's the dead wife's Jeep."

They pulled in the driveway and saw a man and a woman standing beside a Ford pickup by the barn. Sal parked fifty yards back from the truck and shut off the engine. Then they sat there, at Joe's suggestion, watching for a reaction. Sal guessed the man was in his early forties, six feet tall; he was a bit of a roughneck, with a couple days' growth of beard, large hands and forearms, dressed in jeans and a worn shirt and work boots. The woman was older, short, with long gray hair.

"That him?" Sal asked.

"That's him," Joe said. "I recognize him now. From court, during the trial."

"You ready?" Sal asked, and Joe, by way of answering, opened the door and got out. Taking the lead, of course.

"Are you Virgil Cain?" he asked, approaching the man. Sal followed a few feet behind, watching closely.

"Yeah."

Joe produced his investigator's shield as he introduced himself and Sal before turning to the woman. "And you are?"

"Mary Nelson."

"And what is your relationship to Mr. Cain?"

"My relationship?"

"She's a veterinarian, here to look at a horse," Virgil said. "I don't think she's a criminal but I can't say for sure. What can I do for you boys?"

"We want to talk to you about a conversation you had with Michael Dupree ten days ago in a bar called Fat Phil's."

Virgil nodded slightly, waiting.

"Why don't you tell us about it?" Joe suggested.

"I don't remember it being much of a conversation."

"You don't remember threatening to kill Mr. Dupree?" Sal asked.

"I never threatened to kill him. Is that what he's saying?"

Sal opened his notebook. "You don't remember saying, let's see, 'Somebody ought to do the world a favor and blow your fucking head off'? You don't remember that?"

"I remember that," Virgil said. "I wouldn't call that a threat. That's more of an . . . opinion."

Sal glanced at Joe.

"Where are you from, Mr. Cain?" Joe asked. "Were you born in New York?"

"I'm Canadian."

"Canadian," Joe repeated. Which explained the futility of his Internet search. He hadn't gone international, hadn't thought about it. He asked Virgil for his date of birth and, once he had it, nodded at Sal to continue before trudging back to the car.

"I think that could be construed as a threat," Sal said. "Particularly since a few hours earlier, Mr. Dupree had managed to get an acquittal for the man charged with the murder of your wife. It's almost understandable that you would be feeling . . . vengeful."

"Is that how I was feeling?" Virgil asked. "How would you know how I was feeling?"

"You advocated blowing the man's head off."

"And you're here to arrest me for it?" Virgil asked.

"We are here to talk to you about it," Sal said.

Mary stepped forward, as if to run interference. She turned to Virgil. "Should you have a lawyer here? I can call somebody."

"For a comment I made in a bar?" Virgil asked.

"But you'll admit that you have a problem with Mr. Dupree?" Sal suggested.

"I'll admit I had a few drinks and shot my mouth off," Virgil said. "What's Dupree saying, anyway? For a guy who defends murderers for a living, sounds as if he's got pretty thin skin."

"We'll get to Mr. Dupree in a minute," Sal said. He glanced toward the car, where Joe was busy at his laptop. Then to Virgil, "Have you ever been to Burr Oak Golf and Country Club?"

"No. I'm with Mark Twain on the subject of golf."

"What does that mean?"

"It means I've never been to the . . . Burl Ives golf club."

"Burr Oak."

"Never been." Virgil indicated the surroundings, the frame house with the patched roof and the weathered barn, the ten-year-old pickup in the drive. "I look like the golf and country club type to you?"

"Have you ever been arrested?" Sal asked. From the corner of his eye he saw Joe walking over from the car.

"Sure."

"What for?"

"Lots of stuff. I was a rambunctious youth."

Joe, approaching, shot Sal a look of triumph. "Ever been arrested for attempted murder?" Joe asked.

Virgil glanced from one cop to the other. "Look, if you guys are here to charge me with threatening the lawyer, get to it. Otherwise I've got work to do."

Joe had a notebook in his hand. "In 2001 you were arrested in Quebec for the attempted murder of a man named Finley. You were convicted of aggravated assault and served time in prison. It appears you have a thing for lawyers, Mr. Cain."

"I don't know what that means."

"This Finley was a lawyer too."

"Just a coincidence. He could've been a tinker or a tailor, wouldn't have made any difference."

"Well, Mickey Dupree was no tinker," Joe said. "And you left him in a sand trap on the seventh hole at Burr Oak Golf and Country Club." He hesitated, looking over at Sal while obviously coming to a decision. Then he turned back to Virgil. "You're under arrest for the murder of Michael David Dupree. You have the right to remain silent, you have the right to an attorney, you—"

Virgil glanced at Mary while Joe read him his Miranda rights. Sal put the handcuffs on him as Joe finished.

"You look after the livestock?" Virgil asked her.

"Of course. Do you want me to call someone?"

Virgil shrugged and Sal led him to the car and opened the back door.

"Wait a minute," Virgil said as he turned back to Mary, who

hurried forward. "Can you drive that Jeep into the machine shed overnight? There were a couple morons here earlier and I think they fell in love with the sound system." He smiled, and indicated Sal and Joe Brady. "Not these guys, two other morons."

Claire had been heading out the door of the station when Marina at the front desk stopped her and said she had a phone call.

"Who is it?" she asked.

"Judge Harrison."

"Can it wait?"

Marina raised her eyebrows, as if to ask whether Claire was serious. Claire took the phone.

"Claire Marchand."

"Ms. Marchand." Claire's last name arrived in a splendid baritone; Harrison had never managed to shake his Scottish burr, despite having been in the country for over forty years now. Claire imagined she was talking to Sean Connery. "I need to see you."

"I'm just on my way to Woodstock," Claire said. "This Mickey Dupree thing."

"No, you're on your way here," Harrison said. "To talk to me about the Mickey Dupree thing."

"Now?"

"Now is perfect. Nice of you to offer."

"Shit," Claire said when she gave the phone back to Marina. "Where's Joe?"

"Said he was heading for Woodstock," Marina said. "Took Sal with him. Sal's wearing a suit."

"Did he say where he was going?"

"No. I can call him."

28

"No," Claire said. "He can chase his tail for a while, I guess. How bad can he screw that up?"

"Is that one of those questions you'd rather I didn't answer?"

Claire shot her a look before heading out the door for the courthouse. As she pulled into the parking lot, she saw Miller Boddington sitting behind the wheel of a black Maserati and talking on a cell phone. Claire parked a few feet away and got out. Miller's window was down and he watched her as she walked past. He raised his voice for her benefit.

"I'm at the courthouse right now," he said into the phone. "I've been summoned by the old Scotch man. And right this minute I'm watching the cop who arrested me walking by my car. Oh, she heard me. She's giving me a dirty look."

Claire kept walking, sorry that she had looked his way. In her opinion, Miller Boddington was a despicable piece of shit who didn't deserve a look, or a thought, or anything else from her. Unfortunately circumstances required that she did think about him. She tried to console herself by thinking about him behind bars. But even there, he would be treated better than the animals he'd abused.

She heard the car door open and then footsteps behind her. Miller kept talking into the phone.

"Gotta tell you, for a cop she looks great walking away."

Claire cut across the lawn, moving quickly, past the statues and the stone fountain in front of the courthouse. She could tell that the diminutive Miller was hustling to keep up.

"Yes, sir, she's got a great ass," she heard him say. "It's a goddamn shame she's got her head up it."

Claire stopped abruptly, turned, snatched the cell phone away from him, and tossed it into the fountain. Then she went inside.

Judge Harrison was in his chambers. District Attorney Alex Daniels was also present, looking like a high school sophomore with his cowlick and fuzzy cheeks. They were talking about their respective vacations when Claire walked in.

Miller Boddington slumped in behind her, presumably pissed that his cell phone was now wet and worthless. Claire expected him to tell Harrison about her offense but apparently the little man was keeping his grievance to himself. He sat across the room from her, his runty legs barely reaching the floor, and kept silent for the time being. He was wearing black pants and a white dress shirt but no jacket. He had taken to dyeing his hair black and combing it straight back from his forehead of late, making him look like a miniature Latin dictator in a B movie. When Claire glanced over, he tilted his head to one side and then shook it almost imperceptibly, as if he was profoundly disappointed in her.

"Investigator Marchand," Harrison said. "Did you and Mr. Boddington carpool?"

"Yeah, we're old friends," Miller said. "She's had me in handcuffs."

His tone was leering and Claire wouldn't give him the satisfaction of a response, choosing instead to look expectantly at Harrison.

"By now we have all heard the news of Michael Dupree's death," Harrison said. "And since Mr. Dupree was counsel to Mr. Boddington, we need to talk about this trial date we have set for next Friday. Obviously, we will not be proceeding at that time. However, given that this case has now dragged on longer than the War of the Roses, I thought we should have this little get-together today to lay a blueprint for the future." Harrison raised his voice for emphasis. "In other words, Mr. Boddington, I am preempting any attempt on your part to arrive in court next week, claiming ignorance of these latest developments."

"Hey, I want to get on with this," Miller said.

"You have a strange way of showing it," Harrison told him. "Obviously you will be retaining new counsel."

"I guess so," Miller said and laughed. "Apparently it's up to me to keep these slippery bastards in the upper tax brackets. I mean, if you guys insist on pushing this thing."

Claire glanced at Daniels. He was watching Miller Boddington with amusement. Miller had that effect on people, it seemed. Not Claire, though. She knew what he was, and there was nothing funny about it.

"Matter of fact," Miller went on, "I was kind of thinking you might have called me here to say you were dropping all the charges, with Mickey dead."

"Even if that suggestion had the slightest bit of logic to support it, I have a feeling that Mr. Daniels here would oppose the notion," Harrison said. "And Ms. Marchand too."

"What do you think, Alex?" Claire asked. "Do we want to push this? Do we really care about some guy who treated a couple dozen thoroughbreds like they were Civil War POWs?"

"I never mistreated a horse in my life," Miller said.

"Well, that's where we disagree," Daniels said. "Why don't we go to trial and sort it out?"

"Who are you again?" Miller asked. "I thought maybe the judge here brought his kid to work."

"Take it easy, Mr. Boddington," Harrison said. "Would you like to be on my bad side?"

Miller knew whom he could insult and whom he could not. He retreated.

"All right," Harrison said. "This is what will happen. You, Mr. Boddington, will appear next week with counsel. And that counsel will be someone who intends to represent you in this matter going forward. A new trial date will be set at that time. Is that understood?"

"Understood," Miller said, standing up. He looked at Daniels and then at Claire. "So we'll all get together next week. I'm looking forward to it." He smiled and walked out.

Outside, a few moments later, Claire crossed the expanse of lawn with Alex Daniels. Miller Boddington was fishing his cell phone from the fountain. He climbed out, his pants soaked to the knees.

"You intend to reimburse me for this?" he asked Claire.

She laughed and kept walking.

"What was that about?" Daniels asked.

"No idea," Claire said.

"Such a nice guy," Daniels said.

"Shit," Claire said. "Today was nothing. He was on his best behavior, with Harrison there."

"I don't want to see him at his worst."

"I've seen him at his worst. And I arrested him for it."

FOUR

When Jane came downstairs shortly after nine o'clock, Alan was at the kitchen counter, eating poached eggs on toast. The kitchen was a mess, evidence of his morning culinary activities. Half a loaf of bread, part of a pound of bacon, and a package of toaster waffles were scattered about. There was jam and maple syrup, coffee brewed, orange juice in a pitcher.

"Good morning," Jane said, pouring coffee for herself.

Alan nodded around a mouthful of eggs. Jane looked disdainfully at the carnage inflicted on her magazine-worthy kitchen; then took her coffee and the morning paper out onto the deck. They were calling for another hot day, but for now the air was still cool from the night. Set against the east and north walls of the house, the deck offered both morning sun and shade. Jane chose the sun.

She sat at one of the wrought-iron café tables, sipped her coffee, and looked inside at Alan. He was wearing nylon sweatpants and a Nike hoodie, and a yellow baseball cap with AC RECORDS in blue script across the front. She could tell he wasn't wearing his toupee underneath. He rarely bothered with it around the house anymore, although during the trial he'd worn it every day to the courthouse. The media covering the trial seemed obsessed with commenting on it. As she watched, he finished his eggs and sat back, as if pondering his next move, then slid two of the frozen waffles into the toaster. Ever since the acquittal he'd been on an eating binge that was monumental, even for him. In the weeks preceding the trial he had actually lost about forty pounds. Whether the drop in weight was a nod to vanity, knowing he would be in the public eye every day, or merely the result of the stress of being tried for murder, Jane couldn't say. There was a time when she would have asked him, but that time was long in the past. Whatever his reasons, he had done an about-face of late. At his heaviest, he had gone about three hundred pounds and was heading that way again. The medicine cabinet in his bathroom was filled with all manner of drugs that allowed him to carry on as he did. Lipitor and Diuril and the thyroid medicine. Dozens of other pills Jane couldn't identify and hadn't the inclination to try.

The phone rang as Alan was pouring syrup on his waffles. He answered and talked as he ate, finishing his plate and the conversation at roughly the same time. He sat stock-still for a moment as if contemplating something, either what he had heard on the phone or all that he had just ingested, then poured coffee in his cup and joined Jane on the deck outside. He sat across from her and looked off into the trees. There was a tiny spot of syrup at the corner of his mouth.

"That was Walter," he said. "They got the guy that killed Mickey Dupree."

"Oh?"

"It was the girl's husband. Cain."

"Well." Jane sipped her coffee. "I guess that makes sense, motive-wise. Apparently the husband found fault in the verdict?"

Alan continued to stare off into the trees that lined the curved walkway running through the property. She saw he was suddenly perspiring heavily, sweat running in thin rivulets down his temples.

"Do you think this is funny?" he asked.

"Not at all."

"Because it's not," he said, glaring at her. "If this guy was crazy enough to kill Mickey for getting me off, then don't you think I'm next on his list?"

"I would have thought you'd be first on his list."

"I'm glad you're enjoying this. I'm glad you're taking this . . . this near tragedy . . . and turning it into a scene from Nora Ephron."

"Near tragedy?" she repeated. "I doubt the Dupree family would consider it in those terms. Or are we just concerned with you here, as usual?"

He refused to respond to that. He drank his coffee and continued to watch into the woods, as if anticipating something out there. That was nothing new, though. He was always of the mind that something was out to get him, whether it was real or imagined.

"Listen, you said they arrested the guy, right?" she said after letting him dangle for a time.

"Yeah. Yesterday afternoon."

"Then you have nothing to be afraid of. It was premeditated. He'll get life."

"Apparently he's killed other people. Up in Canada."

"Really?" Jane picked up the newspaper and glanced at the front page. There was nothing about any arrest. The police probably never released the news in time for the early edition.

"Yeah. I think that's what Walter said. What happened to the immigration laws in this country, they let a guy like that in?" Alan drained his cup, set it on the table. He sat up straight. "But you're right. He can't get me now. I'm safe."

"Of course you are. What are you doing today?"

"I'm going to the studio." He looked at his watch. "The driver should be here."

"What are you doing there?"

"That French kid is driving up from the city. His label wants him to do an album of standards. Porter and Berlin, all that. They think they can break him out here that way."

"Well, it worked for Michael Bublé. Can the kid speak English?"

"Sort of."

"An American label is hiring you?" Jane asked.

"No. His French label. The French are more sophisticated than we are when it comes to dealing with these minor scandals. They are smart enough to look past superficial nonsense and focus on the intrinsic artistic merits."

Jane got to her feet. "Well, have fun with your new sophisticated friends. At least this one is a boy. Less chance of you getting yourself into another . . . *minor scandal*. I'm going running."

She took the wolfhounds and started along the trail that wound through the estate. The path was a good one, bulldozed through the hardwood forest and packed with gravel screening. Alan—who never walked more than a few feet, let alone ran—had wanted it big enough for four-wheeler traffic. He actually wanted to pave it, but Jane had put a halt to that idea. The job would have taken an entire summer, and she didn't intend to inhale that petroleum odor for months on end. Not only that, but a paved roadway running miles through the property would have detracted from the rustic nature of the grounds.

There were several routes of varying length she could take through the two-hundred-acre property. The longest one, which she had favored lately, ran roughly six miles. She intended to run the New York City Marathon—her first—that fall, and for now her goal was to run this particular route four times a day, a distance that would be close to marathon length.

She had started running in earnest just a year earlier, upon turning sixty. Up until then she had been a casual jogger—mostly on the treadmill so she could watch TV—but at a fundraiser in Woodstock a couple of years ago she met Edie Bryant, who jarred her into looking at her own languid lifestyle and to start considering her age.

"The ideal time to look sixty," Edie would tell Jane as the landmark approached, "is the day you turn seventy. Actually, eighty would be even better."

Edie was the US congresswoman for the area and had been so for nearly thirty years. She was seventy-three and, from across a room, looked fifty. She'd had the usual surgeries but hadn't gone overboard, settling in recent years on a combination of Botox and collagen, and diet and exercise to maintain her weight. Jane had been instrumental in raising money in Ulster County for Edie's last reelection campaign and, in turn, Edie had counseled Jane on a number of things, some health-related and some not so. She had advised her to leave Alan, for instance. Jane couldn't decide whether that particular piece of counsel fell under the guise of health-related or not.

Jane thought about Alan now as she ran up a slope at the rear of the property. The dogs had long since gone their own ways, sniffing through the underbrush, yelping when picking up the scent of one thing or another. From time to time they would come find her as she ran, as if making sure she was still with the program. Then they'd be off again.

It was probably a good thing Alan had a project to work on, although the plan to break the French kid in the American market seemed a little iffy. And Alan was an odd choice to helm any plan, especially in light of his recent notoriety. But aside from that, he hadn't had any real success—on an artistic or financial level—in nearly twenty years, a long time in popular music circles. During the trial, the newspapers often suggested that the business had passed him by, and the papers had been right. Lack of success, or even recognition, merely fed the insecurity of a man already so paranoid he had trouble trusting the mailman most days.

Jane had no idea what had happened in the studio the night Kirstie Stempler had been killed. She wasn't entirely sure that Alan knew himself. And even though it was true that Jane had abundant reasons to walk away from the marriage, she had no intention of doing so. She had put her time in. She loved her life, and she loved her home here in Ulster County. The only way she would ever end the marriage would be if Alan gave up this property to her. That would never happen. He would have no idea where to go.

FIVE

The ride into Kingston was quiet. The two men in the front didn't appear to have much in common. The younger one attempted, several times, to initiate conversation—mentioning the local softball league where he played, an upcoming fishing trip, a book he'd read about James Earl Ray—but the older cop, the thick one named Joe Brady, apparently had little interest in any of the topics.

Virgil knew who Joe Brady was. He was one of the detectives who'd testified at Alan Comstock's murder trial, and Virgil had watched as Mickey Dupree had chewed Brady into little pieces before spitting him out on the courtroom floor in front of the jury. Now Joe Brady had arrived at the farm to inform Virgil that he was under arrest for killing Dupree. Virgil wasn't sure if that was irony, but he was pretty sure it was something.

Neither man said anything to Virgil, which suited him perfectly. Generally speaking, he had nothing against cops but couldn't recall ever meeting one he liked. That was hardly surprising, since most of his previous encounters with police had ended with Virgil wearing handcuffs. Like now.

He sat in the backseat and watched the farmland pass by. The hay he'd cut earlier that afternoon would be ready to bale in a couple of days. He hated asking anyone for favors but if he couldn't persuade the cops to release him he would have to get someone to bale it up and put it in the mow for him. The youngest Tisdale kid had recently come back from the coalfields in Wyoming to take over his family farm down the road from Virgil's place, near Saugerties. He could probably use the extra money, if Virgil was to hire him. The Tisdale kid was a hard worker, Virgil had noticed, even if he did appear to be a bit of a dimwit. Of course, Virgil was hardly in a position to pass judgment on that front; he was the one locked in the backseat of a police cruiser.

Other than the hay, he was pretty much caught up. His wheat had come off two weeks earlier, and the cattle would be okay in the back pasture. There was a spring-fed pond there that never went dry. Mary would see to the horses. Most of them were as much hers as they were his anyway. He wasn't sure what to think of Mary, the way she looked at him when he was being handcuffed. And he was pretty sure Mary didn't know what to think of him, given the circumstances.

At the station they put him in an interrogation room and left him there for almost an hour, sitting at a wooden table. The room was windowless and hot. When the door finally opened, it was just the older cop, Brady. He walked in and plopped himself down in the chair opposite Virgil and didn't say anything. Instead he attempted to stare Virgil down, as if setting the tone for what would follow. Virgil looked at him for a bit but got bored and quit it. After a while he realized they were waiting for someone else to arrive.

That someone was a woman. At first glance, Virgil wondered what she was doing there. It was only after she removed her jacket and he saw the semiautomatic on her hip that he realized she was a cop. Virgil had seen cops before who happened to be beautiful women, but they had all been TV cops. Since it seemed unlikely they would call in a TV cop to interrogate him, Virgil had to assume this one was genuine. She was about forty, he guessed, and she had dark brown hair that was somewhat unruly, as if she'd just come in out of the wind. She removed her sunglasses, pushing them up into her hair, taming it just a little. Her eyes were also brown and she wore very little makeup. Beneath the jacket she was wearing a white cotton blouse and a navy-blue skirt that stopped a couple of inches above her knees. She had good legs.

She seemed slightly preoccupied when she entered, giving Virgil and Brady a quick nod each before removing her jacket. Then she seemed to gather herself, pushing from her mind whatever she'd been thinking about in order to focus on the task at hand.

She told Virgil her name was Claire Marchand and when she asked him if he wanted a coffee, he said yes. Brady, after a moment, took this as a cue and went somewhere to get it. Marchand told Virgil he could smoke if he wanted so he lit up. Before locking him in the room, they had taken his wallet and his belt and the laces from his work boots but allowed him to keep his cigarettes and lighter. They were being nice, at least for now, but that was usually how it worked. Marchand gave him a dirty paper cup for an ashtray and sat down in a chair against the wall. As she removed a notebook from her pocket she crossed her legs, and Virgil raised their grade from good to terrific. He knew there were far more pressing matters at hand, but—short of plucking out his eyes—it was impossible not to take notice of certain things.

"You want a lawyer?" she asked.

His eyes went from her legs to her face, a fair trade-off. In fact, there was nothing about her that wasn't extremely pleasant to look at. He reminded himself that he'd never met a cop he'd had any use for. This one would be no different. "Not right now," he told her.

"The guys read you your rights, though."

"Yeah."

"We have a few questions," she said. "You're going to appear before the judge in the morning. Just to read the charges, in and out."

Virgil smoked and they waited for Brady to come back. When he did, he put the coffee in front of Virgil and then sat down again. He had his laptop with him now; he must have forgotten it before. Marchand got to her feet. Virgil took a sip from the paper cup. It wasn't the worst coffee in the world, but it was pretty bad.

"You live on a farm located at 724 Windecker Road?" Marchand asked. It seemed she was in charge, although he would have guessed she was younger than Brady. He could only assume that she had been a detective longer.

"Yeah."

"How long you been there?"

Virgil had to think. "Six years. Maybe seven."

"We know you're Canadian. How did you end up in the Woodstock area?"

Virgil balked for a moment, wondering what interest his history would hold for her, what relevance it had for the matter at hand. He decided to play along, at least for the time being. "I stopped to visit an old friend, Tom Stempler. It was his farm. I used to play a little ball, minor league, and Tom was my manager for a while. I was hoping I might get back into it, thinking Tom might give me a recommendation. I knew he still did a little scouting."

"Did he give you a recommendation?" Marchand asked.

"No. What I didn't know was that Tom had Lou Gehrig's, just diagnosed. And it was just him there, trying to run the farm on his own. I ended up sticking around, helping out. It was fall, lots to do on a farm. You know. Well, maybe you don't. Anyway, by the time we had things squared away for winter, ball season was over for the year. So I stayed on."

"Because of the daughter?"

"What?"

"You stayed behind because you became . . . interested in Stempler's daughter. Kirstie."

"No. She wasn't around then. She might have been in Nashville at that time, I'm not sure. I didn't meet her until maybe a year later."

Brady leaned forward. "So why did you stick around?"

"I told you," Virgil said. "I found out Tom Stempler had ALS. I helped with the farm."

"Aren't you the good Samaritan?"

"That a question or just a snotty remark?"

"All right, all right," Marchand said, shooting Brady a look before turning to Virgil. "So you became something of a hired hand. Is that accurate?"

"Hired hand," Virgil repeated. "Yeah. That's what I put on my résumé."

"We'll need a copy of that résumé," Joe said at once.

Marchand spoke without taking her eyes off Virgil. "I think Mr. Cain is having a little fun with us, Joe. I have a feeling Mr. Cain doesn't have a résumé." She didn't seem pissed off; she even smiled before continuing. "You and Kirstie Stempler did eventually become involved. When were you married?"

Virgil put his cigarette out. "Couple of years ago, I guess."

"You don't remember when?"

"Yeah. It was . . . March, I think. Two years ago in March."

"And when did Tom Stempler die?"

"About a year before that. He held on a long time. He was a tough sonofabitch."

Marchand hesitated before she went on. "Tell us about Kirstie and Alan Comstock. How did that situation come about?"

Virgil shook his head. "Don't you read the newspapers?"

"I'd like to hear your version of it," Marchand said.

"Kirstie wanted to be a singer. Comstock told her he could make it happen."

"Did you discourage her from that?"

"No. Why would I discourage somebody from doing something they wanted to do?"

"How did you feel when she was killed?" Brady interjected.

"How the fuck do you think I felt?"

He saw Marchand give Brady another look. There was something between them that didn't feel right. Maybe Brady was chafing at the fact that he had made the arrest and now she was the one in charge. Or maybe it went deeper than that. But there was distance between them, Virgil was certain of that.

"Have you ever been to the city of Middletown?" Marchand asked.

"I've driven through there."

"You were there on Tuesday. You used your credit card to buy gas at the Quik Stop at"—Marchand scanned a page in her notebook—"seven thirty-six in the evening."

"I bought gas there. Yeah."

"Why were you in Middletown?"

"I was heading to Goshen to look at a seed bull."

"To buy?"

"Yeah."

"Who owned the bull?"

"A guy named Wayne Maklovich."

Marchand eyed Brady until he took the hint and opened his laptop and began to type. He stalled after a few seconds and had Virgil spell the name for him.

"He can verify you were there?" Marchand asked.

"No," Virgil said. "He was supposed to be there but nobody was home."

"So you left?"

"Not right away. I walked around and had a look at the bull anyway. He was in a field behind the barn with a bunch of yearling steers."

"What time was this?"

"When I was there? Nearly dark. Maybe eight thirty?"

"And you never spoke to Maklovich?"

"He wasn't there."

"Afterward, I mean. Did you call him about the bull?"

"No. I wasn't interested in the bull."

"Why not?" Brady asked. "Isn't one bull the same as the next?"

"They're like snowflakes," Virgil told him. "Or cops. Every one's different."

Marchand smiled again and this time she tried to hide it by scratching the side of her nose. Brady, returning to his computer, scowled but said nothing.

"Can anybody vouch for you being in the Goshen area at that time?" Marchand asked.

"I never talked to anybody. I would say no."

Marchand came over and sat down now. She leaned close. In spite of his predicament, Virgil couldn't help but notice how nice she smelled. He told himself to get a grip.

"Here's the thing, Virgil," she said. "From the city of Middletown it's roughly a twenty-minute drive to the Burr Oak Golf and Country Club. Somebody killed Mickey Dupree on the golf course. Somebody who took the time to learn Mickey's schedule. At eight thirty he was seen teeing off on the sixth hole. At nine o'clock he was found dead in a bunker on the seventh. At this point I'm going to give you some really, *really* good advice, Virgil. The next words out of your mouth should be that you want to talk to a lawyer."

"I didn't kill the guy," Virgil said. "And the only reason I'm sitting here is because I made a dumb remark in a bar. You figure on building a murder case around that?"

"Jesus," Marchand said. "You seem like a smart guy. Why don't you act like it?"

"You seem like a smart woman," Virgil said. "And look at the mess we're in."

She shook her head but before she could say anything else, a young cop in uniform stuck his head in the door and told Marchand she had a phone call.

She got to her feet, her eyes still on Virgil. "I was just about done here anyway."

She walked out. Brady leaned back in his chair for a moment, watching Virgil as he tapped his forefinger against his chin. That he was happy to be back in charge was written all over his face. It was becoming more evident by the moment that he was not an intelligent man. Virgil couldn't see that working in his favor.

"You just happened to be in the area," Brady said after a time. "At the right time, the right day. And your past record speaks for itself. A propensity for violence. A hatred of lawyers. A habit of taking the law into your own hands. We have a pretty strong circumstantial case already—and we're just beginning."

"You're only missing one thing," Virgil told him.

"What?"

"The guy who did it."

Claire's office was in an open area in the front of the station, basically just a desk with a shoulder-high glass partition around it. After talking to Cain, she finished her log for the day, took the steps to the lower level, and walked out to the parking lot where her Honda CR-V was parked. Sal Delano was putting a gym bag in the back of his Camaro.

"What happened out there today?" Claire asked.

Sal hadn't heard her approach and when he looked up, he glanced around, as if uncertain who she was talking to. "What do you mean?" he asked.

"You know what I mean."

Sal exhaled, then shrugged. "Buck fever? You know how he is. One minute I'm just talking to the guy and the next, Joe's reading him his rights. I'm the rookie out there. What am I supposed to do? Besides, once you tell a guy he's under arrest for murder, it's kinda hard to back off and tell him he's not."

"We don't even have the autopsy report yet. Or any physical evidence. All we've got is a dead lawyer."

"I know. They towed Cain's pickup in a while ago. They're going over it now. And I guess you know there's a team out at his house." He paused. "You heading out there?"

"I can't until morning. I have to drive up to Albany to give a deposition. The boys can give the place the once-over."

"Maybe they'll find a set of golf clubs missing a five iron."

"Yeah," Claire said. "I wouldn't hold my breath. Did you ask Joe why he was so quick on the trigger?"

"Yeah. He said he had to make a snap decision. He figured Cain was a flight risk."

"Based on what?"

"That he's not a citizen."

"Where the hell was he going to flee to, Canada? He goes to Canada, we go up there and bring him back."

"Hey, you don't need to tell me."

Claire turned and looked toward the station. "Well, it is what it is. Joe's in there checking out the story about the bull up at Goshen. Not that it works as an alibi anyway." She turned back. "Funny, Joe being so gung ho about going after the guy who iced Mickey Dupree. You'd think he would be down at the bar, buying rounds."

"I thought about that too." Sal closed the trunk. "But then I thought that Joe gets gung ho about jaywalkers."

Claire nodded absently.

"What's the matter?" Sal asked. "You don't think Cain is the guy?"

"Oh, he probably is. Everything fits. The DA's not going to have any problems establishing motive. I just wish we'd have moved a little slower on it. Guy's clammed up now, won't even talk to a lawyer. With a little finesse, we might have gotten a confession out of him. Save the taxpayers a bunch of money."

"You worried about the taxpayers, Claire?"

"That's me. I'm all about community. Not that the community deserves it. So I'm going to drive to Albany and do my sworn duty and then I'm going home. The medical establishment has advocated that red wine and chocolate are good for your health. I believe I'll partake of both."

"In moderation?"

"I have to put up with Joe Brady on a daily basis," Claire said. "Fuck moderation."

Sal smiled. "Chocolate and wine. That's what you do with your evenings, now that you're single?"

"I do what I want. Now that I'm single."

She soon realized she had jinxed herself with that last remark. She wanted to change her clothes before heading to Albany so she drove to her house on Pearl Street, on the south side of the city. She still wasn't used to it being *her* house. She'd taken possession eight months earlier but hadn't moved in until two months after that, when the renovations had been completed. The house was a story-and-a-half red brick, built in 1932, owned by the same couple for several decades. When Claire bought it the downstairs had consisted of several smaller cramped rooms, and the second floor was more of the same, with four tiny bedrooms. Claire had dropped a lot more money into the renovation than she had intended—a practice she'd been told was typical—but was extremely happy with the result. The downstairs was now entirely open, except for a back entryway and the half bath, and upstairs were two large bedrooms with a bathroom en suite off the master. A smaller room was designed to be an office but had, also typically, morphed into a giant closet.

Claire was still enthralled with the house—and of living alone in general—and noticed that she grew happier every time she approached the place, especially after a long day at work. Today, however, that house love was tempered more than a little by the fact that Todd was parked in her driveway when she drove up.

Claire had to park out front so as not to block him in, which would only encourage him to stay longer. He was looking at himself in the mirror above the visor and didn't notice her until she got out of the car and closed the door. He flipped the visor up—Claire wondered just how long he'd been admiring his own image—and got out to meet her. He was dressed, as usual, like a catalog model. But he looked tired.

"Hey," he said.

"You're in my spot."

"Oh. Sorry about that."

"What's up?"

"Oh, nothing."

"Then why are you here, Todd?"

"Oh," he said, as if just realizing he should have a reason. "Do you remember the name of the guy we hired to do the landscaping on the Taylor Road place?"

"Canfield Landscaping. They're in the book."

"Canfield. That's it."

"You came here to ask me that?" Claire asked. "That's one of those questions you can ask over the phone, Todd."

"Well, I was driving by. I left work early. Business is slow. You know how things are right now."

"Not really. We're always pretty busy down at the shop."

He smiled. "Yeah. I guess you guys are recession proof."

Claire nodded and looked at him a moment, knowing she shouldn't ask. "Everything okay?"

"Sure. Everything's good." He exhaled and turned to admire the house for a moment. "I don't know. Sometimes I miss, you know, just talking at the end of the day."

"Funny, I don't remember that we ever did much of that," Claire said.

"Go ahead and joke."

"Who's joking?" Claire asked. After a moment, she relented and smiled. "You realize you have a new wife, right? She can talk, can't she?"

"Of course she can. She happens to be a very intelligent woman."

"I never suggested otherwise. That time I actually was joking."

"I guess I can't get anything right."

"Maybe you got that right," Claire suggested.

"Fine," he said, having had enough, and turned toward his car. "I just wanted to ask the name of that landscape company. I won't bother you again."

But you will, Claire thought. "See you, Todd."

She watched as he backed out of the driveway and drove off.

50

He'd been stopping by too frequently lately and, when he wasn't coming by the house, calling her with inane questions about nothing in particular. More troubling still was the fact that he seemed obsessed with reminiscing about the good old days of their marriage, days that existed for only a very brief period twenty years ago. Which resulted in Claire worrying about his current marriage. She wanted him to be happy, but, more to the point, she wanted him to be happy as far away from her as possible.

SIX

Claire drove out to the Cain farm on Windecker Road early the next morning. When she found the place, she pulled in the driveway by the house and noticed a fairly new red Ford pickup parked by the barn. The truck somehow looked out of place so she drove over to park behind it.

There were several horses in a field in front of the barn, gathered round a water trough that was being filled at the moment by a plastic pipe that ran from a shed alongside the barn. Claire could hear the sound of a pump inside, running noisily.

The barn door was open so she walked in and saw, through an open door on the other side, a woman standing in a corral beside a gray horse. Claire approached just as the woman was injecting the horse with a syringe.

The woman was in her sixties, or possibly her seventies. Claire showed her badge and introduced herself, and the woman said her name was Mary Nelson and that she was a vet from Kingston. She told Claire she had rescued the gray horse the previous day and brought it here to recover.

"She ate the hay I left yesterday so I figured she could handle a shot of B12 and some worm medicine." She laughed, as though to herself. "Which I'm sure is more information than you need."

"Not at all," Claire said. "Virgil Cain rescues horses?"

"In a manner of speaking. It actually started with Kirstie. Virgil's wife. She owned two quarter horses—they're still here,

52

in fact, with that bunch in the pasture. She called me one day; she thought her gelding had the colic. I came out, we got to talking about horses. This was right around the time that a creep named Miller Boddington was in the news for mistreating his thoroughbreds. You know about that?"

Claire nodded. "Yeah. I know about that."

"Anyway," Mary went on, "I was telling Kirstie how many abused animals I run across, and how I'm always looking for homes for them. She volunteered right away. And that started it. Most of those horses in that pasture field out front came from bad situations."

"And Cain kept on, after she died."

"Rather reluctantly," Mary said, smiling. "I have to persuade him sometimes. Kirstie had a . . . softer heart, I suppose."

"Cain is hard-hearted?"

Mary shook her head at the assumption. "No, he's not. But he might give that impression."

"You were friends with Kirstie?"

"Not socially, if that's what you mean. I knew her father because I was his vet for a lot of years. He had beef cattle. Virgil raises them now. Or he did, anyway."

"So you know he was arrested?"

"I was here at the time."

"Oh," Claire said. She paused. "And were you surprised?"

The vet capped the needle of the syringe and put it in a plastic bag. She was not a tall woman and had to look up at Claire. "I'm going to assume that's a rhetorical question. If I said I wasn't surprised, what would your next question be?"

"Okay," Claire conceded. "You have a point. You were obviously surprised. Have you ever seen a violent side to Cain? Barroom brawl, anything like that?"

"I've never been to a bar with him."

"Did you ever hear him say anything about Mickey Dupree?"

"No."

"The guy's defending the man accused of killing his wife and he never talked about it?"

"Not to me, he didn't. I really don't know him very well. From what I do know, I don't think he's the confiding type."

"I kind of got that impression myself," Claire said. "Let's try this. From what little you do know of him, would you think he might be capable of murdering someone?"

"I wouldn't be bringing him horses if I thought he was capable of murdering someone. But maybe he fooled us all, right?"

"Maybe he did."

"I have to get to the clinic. Is there anything else?"

Claire said there wasn't and both women walked through the barn and out the other side. Mary went into the pump house and a moment later the chugging of the pump stopped and she came out, got into her truck, and drove off. She didn't say anything else to Claire.

Claire ducked under the yellow police tape surrounding the house and approached the door through the back porch. She made a call on her cell to get the combination to the police padlock, then opened the door and went inside. The house looked as she had imagined it would: not particularly neat but relatively clean, in a single guy sort of way. Newspapers and magazines lying around, with copies of *Sports Illustrated* and *The New Yorker*. She was surprised that Virgil Cain subscribed to the latter, but then admitted to herself that she had no reason to be. She knew virtually nothing about him.

There were dirty dishes in the sink. Off the kitchen was the living room, where the furniture was old and well worn, comfortable looking. There was a TV and a cheap stereo sitting on a rolltop desk, and beside them a stack of CDs—a lot of Merle

Haggard, some John Prine, Emmylou Harris, somebody called the Louvin Brothers.

Claire went through the antique desk's many drawers and compartments, although she knew it would have already been searched. She found photos and bills and some correspondence from an insurance company regarding the death of Kirstie Stempler. Apparently she had never taken the name "Cain." Most of the photos were of Kirstie, whom Claire recognized from the media coverage of the trial, and a man she assumed was Tom Stempler. Some were of Kirstie as a little girl, riding a pony, perched on a tractor with her father, playing a toy piano beside a Christmas tree strewn with tinsel and popcorn and lights. There was one snapshot of Kirstie and her father and a woman, obviously her mother; they stood on the front porch of the house, looking quite serious and dressed formally, as if heading off to church or perhaps a wedding or some other formal occasion. Kirstie was no more than five, Claire guessed. She wondered who took the snapshot.

There was a picture of Virgil Cain there, a Polaroid of him standing on a hay wagon, captured in the act of throwing a bale onto an elevator leading into the mow of a barn. He had his shirt off and was sweating, his arms streaked in dirt, laughing at something as he lifted the bale of hay.

Inside a small drawer of the rolltop she found a valid passport and an apparently brand-new Visa credit card in Cain's name. As Claire slid the drawer back into place she felt something shift inside it. She pulled it entirely out of the desk and turned it upside down. There was a false bottom to it. She slid the panel back and found ten fifty-dollar bills, folded and pinned with a paper clip.

She considered taking the items into evidence, but evidence for what? They had nothing to do with the case. Cain would be forced to surrender his passport if he managed to make bail, but Claire knew the chances of him making bail were nearly nonexistent. She put the items back where she had found them, secured the panel, and slid the drawer into the desk.

She went to the bottom of the stairs and stood there for a moment, asking herself what she was doing. Was she simply being nosy or was she looking for something that might contribute to the case against Virgil Cain? The line was fairly fudged, and since she couldn't decide which side of it she was on, then she probably was indeed snooping, even if that was, technically, part of her job description.

She went upstairs anyway.

Cain's clothes were strewn about the master bedroom, located toward the front of the house. A Toledo Mud Hens cap that looked as if it belonged in Cooperstown hung on a doorknob. A copy of a Robert Stone novel lay on the night table, bookmarked with a baseball card. Claire glanced at the card and did a double take at the photo on the front. It was Virgil Cain—a younger and leaner Virgil Cain—wearing the uniform of the Mud Hens. The stats indicated he had been a catcher.

The bedclothes were pulled carelessly back and the dresser drawers were open, the clothes tousled inside, and Claire realized that Joe and the boys would have given the place a going-over.

Two other rooms were obviously not used. Both had single beds and dressers of maple veneer and not much else. Aside from some wispy cobwebs in the ceiling corners and some dead flies on the windowsills, the rooms were pretty clean. But the fourth bedroom did seem to be in use. And by a woman. There were jeans and skirts and tops on the chair and dresser, even on the bed. There were dresses in the closet and lots of shoes. Three pairs of cowboy boots.

Claire had been under the impression that Cain lived alone but once again had no reason to assume that. For all she knew he could have been the leader of some hippie commune.

Although she was pretty sure he wasn't.

There was a Sony boom box on the dresser. On a whim, Claire hit the play button and heard a mournful intro followed by Neil Young's voice, singing about burning his credit card for fuel.

There were more CDs there: apparently everything Neil Young had ever recorded, along with some Joni Mitchell, Neko Case, and Leonard Cohen. Claire powered the CD player off, and when she turned toward the door, she noticed a twelve-string guitar in the corner—and then it came to her.

This was Kirstie's room.

But why would they have separate rooms? According to Cain, they'd been married only a year or so before she'd been killed. Of course it wasn't unheard of for married couples to keep separate sleeping quarters. She and Todd might just as well have the last few years of their marriage, but by then she and Todd might just as well have lived on different planets. This was different, though; these two were practically newlyweds. Other than for the purpose of investigation, she had never been particularly curious about the intimate details of anyone's married life, but there was something about this arrangement that didn't quite fit.

There was something about Virgil Cain that didn't quite fit either. He had been pretty collected in the interrogation room. At one point he had seemed more interested in Claire's legs than in the predicament he faced. Claire had interviewed cool customers in the past, pathological liars and deluded dreamers and more than a few dyed-in-the-wool morons. Cain didn't seem to fit into any of those categories. But maybe that meant he was just smoother than the others.

Time would tell. It always did.

When Jane got home from lunch at Le Select Café a little after two o'clock, Alan was already back from the studio. By the look of the kitchen, he'd enjoyed another monumental meal. The housekeeper worked every other day so Jane cleaned up the aftermath and then found him in the screening room, drinking gin and watching *Sunset Boulevard*. Neither activity was a good sign. Alan didn't do well under hard liquor and, as such, turned to it only when he was angry or depressed, otherwise sticking to wine or the occasional imported beer, and then only in the evenings. And he had certain movies that he watched over and over again, depending on his mood and the circumstances of his life at the moment. *Sunset Boulevard* was his touchstone when things, especially of a professional nature, weren't going well. It was obvious that he identified with Norma Desmond.

She stood in the doorway for a moment, watching the familiar drama on the wall. He glanced up at her; then he returned to the movie.

"How'd it go?"

He waved his hand above his head, as if batting away a volleyball. "I walked out."

"I had a feeling," Jane said.

Alan put the movie on pause. On the big screen, Gloria Swanson had been laughing and now her face froze in a grotesque grin. "And why is that?"

"Because you left here at eleven this morning and you're back at two. I don't think you can cut a record that quick."

"There was a time. I was in the room when Bobby Dylan recorded *Like a Rolling Stone* in one take. So don't tell me."

Jane knew that Alan was convinced he had been in the room when a lot of immortal songs had been recorded. Some of his stories were true, but Jane didn't know which ones anymore. And she was quite sure that Alan didn't know, either.

"So the French kid is the new Bob Dylan?"

"The French kid is a fucking brat. And his manager is an imbecile."

"That doesn't sound too encouraging."

Alan took a long drink, more of a gulp, of the gin and tonic. "I tried. I got there and they showed me this list of songs. 'Come Fly with Me,' 'You're Nobody Till Somebody Loves You,' 'All of Me' . . . and so on and so on. And we talked about the sound. Count Basie, Duke Ellington, that's what they wanted. Well, I know this stuff like I know my own fucking DNA. And so I start laying it out. Who we're going to need and for how long. And you know what they told me?"

"What did they tell you?"

"That there was no budget for a band."

"Then what did they want you to do?"

Alan's face twisted, not unlike Swanson's on the screen. "Digital synthesizers! They want Alan-fucking-Comstock to produce a big-band sound without a fucking band! I told that fucking frog cocksucker I would kick his ass all the way back to Paris. Who the fuck do they think they're dealing with? Do I look like some techno geek?"

"Clearly not," Jane told him. "Let it go. They obviously don't know what they're doing, and it's better you found that out going in than two weeks down the road." It was the standard speech she used whenever a project fell apart. She had been wearing it out in recent years.

"I'm going to sue them. You watch, they'll be badmouthing me all over this industry because of this. I'm calling Walter today to have him initiate a suit. They're not going to talk about me like that."

"They won't talk and who's going to listen anyway?" Jane said. "Nobody has ever heard of these people."

"Don't you see?" Alan said. "That's why they'll talk. They'll get media coverage by saying they fired the great Alan Comstock. I've won seventeen fucking Grammys. Trading on my name! That's how these people work." His mind was racing now and he seemed to forget that Jane was in the room. "They had this planned all along. They knew I would never agree to this. They knew exactly what they were gonna do. Make me out the villain, as usual. I'm calling Walter, right after the movie. I'm making a preemptive strike."

Having settled on a plan of action, he relaxed, if only a little, and sank back in his chair. He started the movie again. Jane left quietly and walked back to the kitchen. She took a banana from a bowl on the counter and looked out onto the property as she ate it. She decided to go for another run. Another six-plus miles. The marathon was only three months away.

Changing into her running clothes upstairs, she picked up the phone and called Walter's cell number. She didn't want to have to go through his secretary at the law office. She got his voice mail.

"Walter, it's Jane. Alan might be calling you. He lost another job and he's talking about suing the people. Some French management group. Could you just sit on it for a few days until it blows over? You know the drill. Thanks, Walter. You're the best."

She didn't take the dogs this time. They were both pushing ten years old—getting up there for wolfhounds—and she wouldn't allow them to make that run twice in a day. Of course they would try if she let them. Like a lot of people she knew, they never knew when to quit.

She was on her way back when she heard the shots. She was hardly surprised as it was part of the pattern. Gin, Gloria Swanson, and then guns. She was pissed off, though. He should have guessed that she had gone running. Would it kill him to err on the side of caution just once in his life? She swung toward the road and approached the house from the front.

He was on the deck, the bottle on the table beside him along with ice and tonic. Mounted on posts in the yard were several sheets of plywood painted with targets: one at twenty yards, one at thirty, and so on. Every couple of months he would have to replace the plywood, after reducing the sheets to splinters.

He had a long-barreled .22 revolver in his hand, and the 9mm Glock on the table. When Jane came closer she saw the nickel-plated Colt in his lap. It was a .32, with a short barrel and ivory grips. There was no mistaking it.

"You realize I was out there running," she said.

"As long as you weren't running between me and my target, you were safe."

"That plywood doesn't always stop the bullets," Jane said. "And you have half a bottle of gin in you, so you're not exactly Annie Oakley."

As if in reply, Alan emptied the .22 into the closest target. He smiled up at her as he reloaded from a box of shells on the table.

"I left Walter a message. Those French fuckers are going to get a surprise come tomorrow morning."

"On what grounds are you going to sue them, Alan?"

"Wrongful dismissal."

"You quit."

"That's what they'll try to say."

61

"That's what you told me."

"They set it up!" he snapped. "For Chrissake, they set it up so I would have no choice. Can't you see that? What the fuck is wrong with you?"

Jane couldn't see it, but she knew enough to let it go. There would be no lawsuit. By Monday, Alan would forget all about it. If he finished the bottle of gin, he might forget about it by morning. He held the loaded revolver toward her.

"You want to shoot?"

"No thanks."

"Come on. Have a go."

"You know I don't like to," she said. She indicated the .32 in his lap. "Where did that come from?"

"It's mine," he said.

"But the police had it."

"Yeah. And after I was acquitted, they gave it back."

"They just handed it over? It's a murder weapon."

"There was no murder," he reminded her. "Death by misadventure."

"Right. I just thought they might hang on to it."

"It's my fucking property. I bought it. I have a permit for it. So I told Mickey Dupree that I wanted it back." He put the loaded revolver on the table and had a drink of gin, spilling a little on his shirt. "Poor Mickey. There's a piece in the paper about the guy that killed him. Virgil Thomas Cain. They always give killers three names, don't they?"

"Not always," she said, and she went in the house.

SEVEN

After talking to Brady and the woman, Marchand, Virgil was driven to the Ulster County Jail outside of Kingston by two uniformed cops in a marked cruiser. The jail was a newer building of red brick and glass. It looked like an insurance office or a community college.

The cops took him inside, still cuffed, and presented him to a petite black woman with cropped hair and gold-framed glasses seated behind a counter. One of the uniforms gave her some paperwork.

"He's here for the night," the other uniform said. "Got a court appearance in the morning."

The woman glanced at the paperwork, then immediately gave Virgil another look. "Then back here?"

"Probably."

"Probably not," the woman said. "We have a population problem here. We can stick him in transition for the night, but we got no bed for him long-term."

"Well, whatever works for now," the uniform said.

"No sense me processing him if he's just gonna be here overnight," the woman said. She looked at Virgil. "What's in your pockets?"

Virgil brought out his cigarettes. The woman opened the package, saw the steel Zippo wedged inside. She glanced at the uniforms.

"How early in the morning?"

"Early."

She handed the cigarettes back to Virgil. "Keep these, sugar, but there's no smoking in the cell. You can smoke in the yard. I'm not doing possessions paperwork now and then ten hours from now for a pack of smokes and a Zippo looks like Humphrey Bogart once owned it. Okay?"

Virgil nodded. The woman had another look at the paperwork and then hit a button on the desk, and a minute later a guard came through the door behind her. One of the uniforms took the cuffs off Virgil and the guard led him into the jail.

They went down a long corridor and through a doorway, back outside into the fading daylight, into a yard maybe a hundred feet square. Inside, a couple dozen prisoners wearing stenciled overalls milled about, a few others sitting on the grass or on benches. The guard left Virgil there without a word and went into an office with large glass windows overlooking the yard. Virgil watched him talking to two other guards and then saw the first guard glance at a computer monitor. After reading what was there the guard turned and, like the woman at the desk out front, had a second look at Virgil.

Virgil sat on a bench, the setting sun on his face, and lit a cigarette. He realized he should have asked to make a phone call. He needed to make arrangements to get his hay off. Maybe, instead of hiring the Tisdale kid, he could call in some favors from his neighbors. Asking for help was not something he was any good at, but he couldn't afford to hire things out right now. The farm was his; it became Kirstie's after Tom Stempler had died, and then Virgil's after she was killed. But it came with a lot of debt. After her father died, Kirstie took out a mortgage on the place and spent the money recording an album in Nashville, an album that was never released. That was before she got involved with Alan Comstock, which didn't cost her anything.

Other than her life.

He thought back to the conversation with the two detectives at the station. They'd come off as smart cop, dumb cop, but he was pretty sure they weren't doing it on purpose. The woman was a looker, beautiful in a world-weary fashion, as if she'd seen enough of life that she'd decided to keep it at arm's length. She seemed genuinely concerned that Virgil get proper representation, but he reasoned she was interested in that just so the conviction down the road would be clean and tidy. She appeared to be very efficient and thorough—a bloodless characterization that Virgil wasn't sure fit her or not. He suspected that somewhere beneath the cool exterior might be some warm coals. All he knew for certain was that she had great legs.

He fell asleep on the bench. When he woke, the yard was cast in shadow. One of the guards was standing outside the office, talking with some of the prisoners. Virgil rubbed his eyes with his fingertips. He realized he hadn't eaten all day.

He heard shoes scuffing on the gravel path and looked up to see a gangly redhead approaching. The guy was young, maybe twenty-one or so, and his hair was shaved short on the sides, longer on top. He had a tattoo on his neck and several more up and down both arms. He was grinning like the village idiot.

"We was outside, I'd be buying you a drink, motherfucker," he was saying, sticking his hand out as he came.

Virgil regarded the proffered hand doubtfully but decided it was better to take it than not. He glanced toward the guardhouse, wondering how soon until lockup.

"Yeah, I know what you did, bro."

The redhead flopped down beside him on the bench, stretched his legs out. Virgil's head was fuzzy from the nap, and from the events of the past few hours.

"My mother was here, she'd kiss you on the mouth," the redhead said. He had foul breath, as if he hadn't brushed his teeth in weeks.

"I don't know who you think I am," Virgil said. "But I'm pretty sure I'm not."

"I know who you are, motherfucker. I know exactly who you are. Screw over there just told me. You the man popped a cap in lawyer Mickey's ass. Same day he threw me under the bus. What I call payback."

Virgil looked at the kid now. He had a crazy cast to his eyes and bad skin, blackheads and pimples on his chin and neck. He was a walking cliché, Opie Taylor channeling Snoop Dogg. "Dupree was your lawyer?" Virgil asked.

"Was. That's the key word. Thanks to you, I guess he ain't nobody's lawyer no more. You and me doin' the same dance here, homes. Murder in the first. Justifiable all the way round. Some guy bonin' my girl and thinks he gonna get away with that shit? Not on my watch."

"What's this about your mother?"

"Oh, my mother. She tore lawyer Mickey a new asshole same day Mickey bought it on the golf course. He turn his back on me and my mother ripped him. You don't fuck with my mama."

"What's your name?"

"You ain't figured it out yet? Shit. I'm almost famous, man. Call me Byron. Lord Byron, if you want."

"Byron what?"

"Byron Fairchild. You sayin' you never heard of me?"

"No. I guess that's why you're *almost* famous."

Virgil was rescued from Byron Fairchild when a guard's voice came over a speaker system and announced lockup. The guard from earlier led Virgil back inside and into an overnight holding cell. Virgil noticed with relief the other prisoners filing into another building. He'd had a disturbing premonition of sharing a cell with Lord Byron.

As it was, he had the cell to himself. He mentioned to the guard that he hadn't eaten and the guy told him it wasn't a cafeteria, but then he came back twenty minutes later with a couple of Snickers bars. Virgil ate them both and then lay down on the cot. He put himself to sleep by going over what he needed to do on the farm for the rest of the year to keep his head above water. He didn't allow himself to think about the situation at hand because he had no idea what to do about it.

The two cops that had come out to the farm, Brady and Delano, collected him in the morning and drove him to the courthouse in downtown Kingston. On the way, they stopped at McDonalds and bought him an Egg McMuffin and coffee. Delano removed the cuffs so Virgil could eat and left them off until they parked in the lot behind the courthouse.

They led Virgil inside through a back door, down a hallway lined with holding cells with iron doors, and into the courtroom, where they sat him in a prisoners' dock opposite a jury box. The room was old, the furnishings constructed mainly of oak. Virgil looked out at the gallery full of people poised with cameras and voice recorders and iPhones. He realized they were from the media and after a moment he further realized they were there for him.

Maybe for that reason, his case was called first. The judge was a woman of about sixty. She wore stylish half glasses, and a detached air. She did not look at Virgil until after the charge of first degree murder was read. Then she dropped her chin to look over her glasses at Virgil.

"Do you understand the charges, Mr. Cain?" Her voice was husky and lived-in, a voice that Virgil associated with late nights and honky-tonks and good whisky, although there was nothing else about the judge that suggested any of that.

"Yes," Virgil said. He wasn't sure if he was required to address her by some specific term—your honor, or whatever. But he couldn't imagine that failing to do so would land him in any more trouble than he was already in.

"Do you wish to enter a plea today?"

"Yes."

"How do you plead?" She was no longer looking at Virgil. It seemed she was looking past him, to the throng in the seats. Maybe she had just noticed them, although that seemed unlikely. By her expression it was hard to determine if she was delighted or dismayed to have them in her courtroom.

"Not guilty," Virgil said.

She shifted her gaze back to him. "Where is your lawyer?"

"I don't have one."

"And why not? I gather you were informed that you are entitled to representation. Is that correct?"

"That's correct."

"And surely you are aware of the gravity of these charges?"

"Yes, ma'am."

From her expression then, the slight arc of her eyebrows, Virgil was pretty certain that whatever he was supposed to call her, it wasn't ma'am. She held the look for a long moment, then consulted a ledger of sorts in front of her.

"You'll be back here on August fourteenth," she said. "Ten o'clock in the morning. And Mr. Cain, you will be accompanied by your lawyer at that time. If you are not accompanied by your lawyer at that time, this court will appoint you one.

Just to clarify, I am attempting to discourage any addle-brained notions you might be entertaining of defending yourself. Now, is that clear?"

"Yes, ma—" Virgil caught himself. "Yes."

She smiled then, and called the next case.

EIGHT

Claire drove out to Burr Oak Golf and Country Club later that morning. As a courtesy she called Joe Brady's cell to ask him to ride along, knowing full well he was busy escorting Cain to court for his arraignment and, as such, was unavailable. She didn't want him with her, today or any other day. In truth, she wished he wasn't involved in the case at all. It was her bad luck, and the bad luck of the department, that he had taken the call in the first place. When the tip came in from a civic-minded patron of Fat Phil's bar that Virgil Cain had threatened Mickey Dupree ten days before the murder, Claire had been driving back from Saratoga Springs, where she'd gone to visit a friend on her day off. Otherwise, she would have most definitely done an end run around Joe.

Claire had played golf once in her life. It was at the Ulster County Celebrity Classic, an event held annually to raise money for various area charities. The celebrities varied from year to year, but they were consistent in that they were usually people Claire had never heard of. The tournament was a best ball, or what was called a scramble, and she played with three other cops, all of whom were avid golfers. Each foursome was required to have at least one woman and so she was asked to play, even though she barely knew the difference between an iron and a wood. Nonetheless, she actually won a prize for longest putt made by a woman. Claire discovered that day that she could putt very well, a skill she attributed to her prowess on a pool table, honed back in her class-skipping high school days. But the term "by a woman" rankled her, smacking of both sexism and country club elitism. Not only that, but the game in general bored her to tears. She began to enjoy herself that particular day only after a few rounds from the beer cart, but, as her late great-uncle Willis used to say, "Hell, even killing rats can be fun, you got enough beer."

She arrived at Burr Oak shortly before noon, and a golfer in the parking lot directed her to the club pro, who was standing by the practice green helping an older man in green pants with his putting. The pro was midfifties, she guessed, with brittle blond hair and a deep tan. He wore a lot of gold—necklace, rings, bracelets on both wrists. Claire introduced herself and he smiled hopefully.

"You here to give me my golf course back?"

"I beg your pardon."

"Your guys still have the seventh green taped off," he said.

"Can't you just play the other holes?" she asked.

The old man in the green pants made a noise like he was blowing something out his nose. "I don't pay twenty grand a year to play seventeen holes." He said it without looking over, just kept hitting putts.

Claire watched him for a moment, then turned back to the pro. "Let's go out there and have a look. Where's the guy who found the body?"

He was a course worker named Jimmy, and he soon pulled up in a Gator to accompany Claire and the pro to the seventh hole. The green itself was surrounded by yellow tape, as was the bunker where Mickey Dupree had been found. The pro drove to the edge of the tape and stayed in the cart while Claire walked over to the sand trap. The slope down into it was steep, and the bottom of the trap was probably five feet below the level of the green. She could see Dupree's footsteps where he had descended, and she could see where he had stood before hitting his shot. The sand was flattened where the body fell. There was dried blood, but not a lot. Not as much as Claire would have thought.

"He was on his back?" she asked.

"Yeah," Jimmy said. "A little on his left side, but pretty much on his back."

Claire glanced over at him. He was a kid, early twenties, and was very earnest in his replies. "I know you've been over this a few times, but bear with me, okay?"

"Yeah. No problem."

She looked at the spot where the body had lain. There was no evidence that he had struggled in death, no sand disturbed where his arms or legs might have flailed, or where he may have tried to get up. Just a compressed area where the body had landed. Which meant that he was basically dead before he hit the ground. Or that the blow to the head had knocked him unconscious before he had been impaled.

"There was nothing else here," she said. "He was killed with just the shaft of the club. What about the end—what do you call it?"

"The head."

"What about that? You didn't see it anywhere?"

"No," Jimmy said.

"Your guys combed the bushes pretty good, looking for it," the pro said.

"What kind of club was it?"

"Ping," Jimmy said. "Five iron."

Claire kept looking at the spot where the body had lain. Something wasn't right. She turned. It was a good twenty feet to the bunker's edge. "Ping. Is that a good club?"

"Oh, yeah."

Behind the spot where Mickey Dupree had been found, the sand was disturbed where the ambulance crew had obviously pulled the body out of the sand trap and onto the grass a few feet away. The rest of the bunker had been raked here and there, presumably during play the day of the murder. As such, the grooming lacked uniformity, the sand being drawn this way or that. And then Claire realized.

"Was any of this raked *after* the body was found?"

"No," Jimmy said.

"Nobody touched it," the pro assured her.

"Then the killer must have flown in and out of here on gossamer wings," Claire said. "Because he didn't leave any footprints."

"You're right," the pro said. He thought a moment. "Well—obviously he raked them out himself."

"Obviously he did. But why?" Claire took a couple of steps in the fine sand and pointed at the marks she left. "Nothing distinct there at all. No tread, nothing. Look at Dupree's tracks. Nothing to show they were his. Now remember this guy was in a hurry. The course wasn't busy but it was hardly deserted. You were out here, Jimmy. Right?"

"Yeah."

She indicated the Gator. "Were you driving that?"

"Yeah, I was."

"He would have heard it. Quiet night, he would have heard it. But he still took the time to pick up a rake and obliterate his tracks."

The pro had an inspiration. "He was a golfer."

"He was?"

"It's second nature to a golfer to rake a trap," the pro said. "It's just standard etiquette."

Claire considered this for a moment. "I'm not sure about

73

that. I have to wonder if a golfer who follows a fellow golfer into a sand trap and kills him with a steel shaft to the heart hasn't just thrown etiquette out the window."

She smiled at the pro, who just shrugged, his contribution to the investigation over. Claire stepped out of the trap and looked around. Just past a copse of pine trees to the south was a wrought-iron fence, beyond which the property dropped into a ravine. She could see a narrow creek running along its course. On the far side of the ravine, maybe five hundred yards away, stood a wooden fence, stained or painted red.

"What's over there?" she asked.

"Coopers Falls Park," the pro told her.

Claire walked over to the trees and had a closer look at the ravine and the park on the other side. She had been to the park a couple of times but hadn't realized it practically backed up against the golf course. In the matted grass past the wrought-iron fence she could see innumerable golf balls, as well as sandwich wrappers and beer cans and other trash. She spotted a couple of golf club shafts there, and a putter that some unhappy duffer had bent into the shape of a horseshoe.

When they pulled up beside the clubhouse, the old man was still on the putting green. He looked over as Claire and the pro got out. Then he went back to his putting.

"Well," he said, again not favoring Claire with a glance. "Is she going to give us the course back?"

Claire regarded the old man, then said to the pro, "You can take the tape down. We're finished here."

"Good Christ," the old man said, rolling a putt six feet past the hole.

"Mr. Greenjeans here is chomping at the bit," Claire said. "Although if I couldn't putt any better than that, I'd take up knitting."

BRAD SMITH

The old man finally looked at her. "You think you could do any better?"

"Hell, yeah," Claire told him. "I won a trophy."

Mary was at the clinic when she got a phone call from Donald Lee at the SPCA, asking her to come by his office at lunchtime. There was somebody he wanted her to meet. It sounded very clandestine, although when she pressed him on it all he would say was that it concerned the horses they'd seized from the Hopman place.

She had scheduled three spays for the morning, and the last one took her until quarter past twelve so it was twenty to one when she walked into the SPCA compound on the north edge of town. Donald was in his office and with him was a teenager wearing baggy jeans and a T-shirt. His left forearm was in a cast and his face was bruised, his bottom lip cut. His name was Logan.

"What's going on?" she asked Donald.

"That gelding we had to put down turned out to be a thoroughbred. He was so emaciated you couldn't tell. But he was tattooed."

"And?"

"Horse belonged to Miller Boddington."

"Shit," Mary said. "How the hell did he end up there?"

"That's where this young man comes in," Donald said.

Logan looked at Mary, then shrugged like he was apologizing for something. "Hopman's been getting horses from Boddington for a couple years."

"How do you know this?"

"I been working for him. Until recent, anyway. He's been in a real bad mood lately and I had enough of it." He smiled ruefully. "I want to get smacked around, I can stay home with my old man. Least he tells me he loves me afterwards."

75

Mary indicated the broken arm. "Hopman do that?"

"Yeah."

The kid didn't elaborate and Mary wasn't of a mind to push him on it. "So what's the connection between him and Boddington?"

"Hopman's always looking for cheap horses," Logan said. "Or was, anyway."

"Tell her why," Donald said.

"Sends them to Europe for meat. People eat horses in Europe. Hopman had a guy over there, took all he could send him."

The kid wouldn't look at either Mary or Donald while he talked. His eyes moved back and forth across the tile floor, as if he were looking for something he'd lost. He had a bit of cringe in him, but it seemed it had come to him honestly. Mary glanced over at Donald.

"This doesn't make sense," she said. "A guy who's selling horses for meat wouldn't gain anything by starving them."

"He couldn't deliver that last bunch," Logan said. "So he just left them."

"Why couldn't he deliver them?"

"Way I heard it, he owes too much money to the shipping company. There was always people coming around there looking for money. I never saw anybody get paid, though."

"I've heard that about Mr. Hopman," Mary said. "He likes to get his hay for free."

She focused on the kid's cast again. "Why'd he do that?"

The kid shrugged, his eyes still sweeping across the tile.

"Hopman accused Logan of making the call to us about the animals," Donald said.

"Was Hopman right?" Mary asked the kid.

He looked at her finally, but didn't say anything. As if part of him was proud of what he'd done, but another part didn't want to acknowledge it.

"Good for you," Mary said. "Did you go to the police about him beating you?"

"No," the kid said quickly. "I'm not gonna do that."

"You have to do that."

"No. I'm just going to stay away from there. I'm gonna go live with my mom for a while. She wants me to go back to school."

"There's something else," Donald said. "Logan says the day we seized the horses, Hopman apparently found another shipping company that'll deal with him. Some Dutch liner. He was buying hay and grain to bring them back to weight. *And* he was buying more horses. That's why he was so pissed about us showing up."

"What's this about more horses?" Mary asked Logan.

"He said he had a bunch coming and they were ready to ship."

"I assume the court has told him he isn't allowed any animals while this case is pending," Mary said to Donald.

"He was told that," Donald said. "What's it worth? Guy like him."

"Christ," Mary said. She sat there thinking a moment. "Anybody talk to Boddington about this?"

"I called the police and told them about the gelding," Donald said. "Up to them to talk to him. But you know the routine there. First he pleads ignorance, and then he gets mad and starts to threaten everybody. He's certifiable. I actually think the cops are afraid of him."

"The cops aren't supposed to be afraid of people who are crazy."

"They're not afraid of him because he's crazy," Donald said.

"They're afraid of him because he's rich and crazy. With friends in high places. Geez, you were at the farm out on Harbor Road. You saw those horses. That was two years ago and they just get adjournment after adjournment. That was you or me, we'd be in jail."

Mary looked at her watch and then stood up. "I have to go squeeze a poodle's anal glands." She wagged her forefinger in Donald's direction. "We have to stay on top of Hopman. He's not going to quit."

"Easy to say."

"I'm going to be watching him." Mary turned to Logan. "Where does your mom live?"

"In town here."

"You like horses?"

"I love horses."

She thought for a moment, then took a business card from her purse. "Tell you what. You go back to school and then, if you're looking for a part-time job, come and see me. Mostly you'll be walking dogs and shoveling poop. But there'll be some horse stuff too."

The kid took the card and looked at it for a long moment, as if committing the information to memory. "Thanks."

"And stay away from Hopman," she said.

"That's good advice," Donald said. He turned to Mary. "For both of you."

Mary smiled. "Who asked you?"

NINE

After his appearance before the judge, Virgil was led by the duty officer to one of the cells he'd passed earlier. He remained locked inside for what seemed like two or three hours. He sat on a bench against the wall, next to the door, and from time to time he could hear people passing in the hallway outside. Once he heard a voice screaming obscenities at the judge as the voice's owner was led out of the courtroom and past the cell. After a while Virgil lay down on the hard bench and tried to sleep. He found he could doze for a few minutes at a time but that was it.

Finally the door opened and Delano was standing there. "Sorry for the wait," he said. "They were trying to figure where to send you."

"How about home?" Virgil suggested.

The cop smiled at that. "Not an option."

He put the cuffs on Virgil and the two of them went out the back door to the parking lot. The day was clear and warm, the sky faultless. Virgil thought about his hay, drying in the field.

"So where am I going?" he asked.

"Albany County Jail."

"Not where I was last night?"

"No."

Praise the Lord, Virgil thought, as Delano put him in the backseat of the cruiser. Joe Brady was already up front in the passenger seat, the laptop open in front of him. Delano started the engine and they drove off.

They headed north on 87, Delano driving and Brady busy on the laptop. He was like the teenagers Virgil saw around Woodstock, constantly typing into their cell phones. Virgil watched the countryside and thought about the events of the past couple of days and his appearance before the judge. As he saw the exit for Saugerties come into view, he leaned forward and spoke through the mesh divide.

"What happens on August fourteenth? Is that a bail hearing?"

Brady looked up, then over at Delano. "No. At that time your lawyer can ask for a bail hearing. He could have asked today but you didn't want a lawyer, remember?"

"And when would that be?" Virgil asked, letting the comment slide. "I have a farm to run."

"It would be pretty quick," Brady said. "I wouldn't worry too much about it, if I were you. You're not getting bail. Not on murder one. Unless you want to put up a million dollars. You got a million dollars?"

"No," Virgil said. "I don't have a million dollars."

He sat back, looked out the window at a service area in the distance. There was a Denny's and a Subway there. He leaned forward again.

"So where does your investigation go from here?" he asked.

Brady turned. "What do you mean?"

"I assume you have other suspects. A guy like Dupree would have made a few enemies."

Virgil saw Delano look with interest over at Brady.

"Any leads that filter in will be thoroughly checked out," Brady said, as if by rote. "You don't need to be concerned about that." And back to the laptop.

"Can you see why I might be concerned about that?" Virgil asked. He waited for Brady to reply but he didn't. "There's got to be somebody out there who knows who Dupree rubbed the wrong way."

"Buddy Townes might know," Delano said.

Brady shot him a dirty look. "Buddy Townes is a piss tank. He doesn't know squat."

Virgil watched as Delano shook his head slightly and turned his attention back to the road.

"So you're not going to be out there looking for suspects," Virgil said. "You know—on the off chance you might stumble across the guy who did it?"

Brady turned to Virgil once more. He was getting pissed now. "Far as I'm concerned, we have the right man in custody. And I think you know it." It seemed that Brady wanted to say more but he waited. The exit for 212 was coming up on the right and he instructed Delano to take it.

"I need a coffee," Brady said.

When they parked in the service center, Brady told Delano to go in while he stayed with the prisoner. Delano gave him a look suggesting he wasn't thrilled to be designated as an errand boy, but he kept quiet. Once Delano was out of the car, Brady turned back to Virgil.

"Do you want to talk about this, pal?" he asked. "We can go back to the precinct right now and sit down over coffee. Maybe it's time for you to make a statement. You'd be doing yourself a favor. I have a feeling I can get the DA to deal on this. The guy you killed wasn't exactly a well-liked individual. Truth is, he was an arrogant prick. Now if you were to come up with a story . . ." Brady hesitated, looking off into the distance as his mind worked. "Say, if you were to tell us what happened that evening. Maybe you confronted him on the golf course, and he attacked *you*. You had no choice but to fight back. Then maybe you're looking at second degree, or even manslaughter." Now

Brady looked back at Virgil. "Right now, it's murder one all the way."

"I don't think so," Virgil said.

"You don't think so?" Brady repeated, mocking him. "You like how this is going so far? That it?"

"I already have a story," Virgil said.

"Stick with it," Brady said. "You're so worried about that farm. You go down on murder one and they're going to lock you up for twenty-five years. You think that farm is gonna be there when you get out?"

"Probably not."

"So where does that leave you? Fresh out of prison without a pot to piss in."

"Maybe I'll put on about a hundred pounds and get half my brain removed," Virgil said. "Become a detective."

"Keep it up, asshole," Brady said. "See where it gets you."

That pretty much ended their little talk. They sat in silence until Delano came back with the coffee, and they headed out again, taking the ramp back onto 87. In a few minutes they were past Saugerties and back in the country. A few miles along they passed a large dairy farm to the west, where a man in a four-wheel-drive John Deere tractor was pulling into the adjacent field, a large round baler in tow. The hay had been cut in wide windrows. Virgil could almost smell it from inside the air-conditioned cruiser.

"You hear a weather report today?" he asked, looking at Delano.

"Supposed to be like this the next few days," Delano told him.

"You got to be in some sort of denial, all you're worried about is that crummy little farm," Brady said. "If I were you, I'd be worried about other things. Like who you're going to get to defend you."

Delano exhaled audibly as he pulled into the left lane to pass a bread truck. It occurred to Virgil that the two cops weren't on the same wavelength. Sort of like Brady and the woman. What was her name? Marchand. Virgil couldn't remember her first name, although her legs he remembered quite well. When the car swung back to the right lane, Delano glanced back at Virgil.

"There'll be a court-appointed lawyer at the jail. He can help you find somebody."

"Maybe you should get Mickey Dupree to defend you," Brady said and laughed. "Oh, I forgot. He's not available."

"There are some good lawyers out there," Delano said.

"Do yourself a favor," Brady said. "Take the court-appointed lawyer. Do it on the state's dime. You're looking at a conviction either way. You don't look like you got a lot of money to begin with. Why give it all away for nothing?"

Virgil was about to tell Brady to go fuck himself when a dispatcher came on over the radio. She announced that an armed standoff was in progress outside a biker compound near Clarksville. All area officers were to respond. Brady called in and identified himself and Delano.

"We're nearby, on 87 north," he said. "But we have a prisoner with us, heading for Albany County."

The dispatcher told him to stand by. Delano punched in the town of Clarksville on the GPS while they waited. After four or five minutes she came back on.

"They could use you on the scene. There's at least one officer down. Be advised to take your prisoner to the town of Kesselberg. The local detachment has a lockup there. They're expecting you."

Ten minutes later they pulled up in front of an aging brick courthouse on a tree-lined street a couple of blocks off the main drag of Kesselberg. A rotund sheriff was waiting for them on the sidewalk as they stopped.

"Jesus," Brady said. "You see Floyd the Barber around?"

"Let's move," Delano said.

"You go," Brady said. "I'll stay by the radio."

Delano and the portly sheriff escorted Virgil into the courthouse and up a flight of stairs, through a waiting room of sorts and into a hallway. Windows to the left overlooked an outdoor exercise yard, overgrown and unkempt. In fact, the whole place had a feeling of abandonment to it. At the end of the hallway were four rooms with steel doors.

"These are your cells?" Delano asked doubtfully.

"Holding units for prisoners for court," the sheriff explained. "Back when we had court here."

The units were all empty. They put Virgil in the nearest one. The cell, if that's what it was, was very clean and appeared to have been recently painted; the smell of fresh latex filled the room and Virgil spotted a piece of masking tape on the door casing and a few drops of paint on the scarred pine floor. Alongside an Arborite-topped table with a few magazines on it sat two wooden slat-back chairs, and behind it, a large, steel mesh–covered window, probably five feet high. The mesh also looked newly painted, green in contrast to the white walls.

Delano didn't seem too thrilled at the prospect of leaving his prisoner there, but he was obviously anxious to respond to the call. He removed Virgil's cuffs and he and the sheriff left, closing the door behind them. Virgil could hear the heavy lock fall into place.

He sat down at the table and had a look at the magazines. All were *Field & Stream* and the most recent issue was from 1997. He leafed through them absently and then stood up and walked to the window. The room faced east and he could see the Hudson River, maybe half a mile away. The town itself extended only a couple of blocks past the courthouse. Beyond that was a cornfield and a stand of hardwoods. Then the river. Immediately outside the window was another building, single story but attached to the courthouse. It looked to be a garage or storage facility.

As he looked down, an elderly man pushing a wheelbarrow came around the corner of the building and stopped by the flower bed along the wall. He got down on his knees and began pulling weeds from the bed and tossing them in the wheelbarrow.

Virgil watched the old man for a while and then walked over and sat down again. For the past two days he felt as if he'd been performing in a play he hadn't been allowed to read first. Everybody but him knew their lines. And he'd been waiting, scene after scene, for some indication that he was going to be let in on the joke. So far that hadn't happened.

Now he had to consider that it might not happen. If he thought that Joe Brady was going to start looking elsewhere for the person who killed Mickey Dupree, the joke really was on him. It was Virgil's bad luck that Brady was the cop who showed up at the farm that day. Not only was he convinced that Virgil was guilty, the man was obviously not all that bright to begin with—something Virgil had already known, having seen his act on the stand during Comstock's trial. Virgil might have been better off with Marchand, but that was only speculation, and likely irrelevant; she hadn't been in court today and Virgil wondered if her involvement with the case had ended.

The last time he'd been locked up, it had been in a tiny cell in a new concrete-and-chrome facility in Quebec. This time it was in a twelve-by-twelve room with fresh paint and worn wooden floors and a view of the historic Hudson. But there was no difference between the two, once the door lock fell into place.

After serving the two years back home, Virgil vowed that he would never again fuck up badly enough to go back. It had never occurred to him that it might happen as the result of somebody else fucking up. It wasn't something a man might consider. It wasn't something a man should have to consider.

How the hell did he end up here? People talk all the time about how things never turn out the way they plan. Well, Virgil couldn't recall ever planning anything. Things just happened. Or something happened, and then something else happened.

One thing leads to another.

It seemed like a good idea, driving down to see Tom Stempler after being released from jail. They'd kept in touch over the years, and Tom had written to Virgil regularly when Virgil was in stir, giving him advice much as he had back when he'd been a manager and Virgil had been behind the plate. Once he even drove up to visit Virgil in the medium-security unit a few miles outside of Three Rivers. Virgil knew, of course, that Tom was retired from baseball, but he also knew that Tom kept close contact with a number of teams, and even scouted a little when the farm work allowed him. What Virgil didn't know was that Tom had ALS.

So one thing led to another. Virgil was at the Stempler farm for only a day when he realized he would be sticking around to help the old man, who was stubbornly working the farm on his own while his strength was flowing out of him like a swiftly running stream. He was a stoic bastard, never asking for help or acknowledging it when Virgil provided it. Virgil never did bring up the subject of him getting back into baseball. He meant to, but he never did.

And one thing led to another again.

Kirstie came home the following spring. Virgil and Tom had finished the harvest and the fall plowing and made it through the winter, when, for the most part, running the farm was just a matter of looking after the stock and making odd repairs to the implements and the outbuildings. Tom had gone through some experimental treatments in Albany that had little effect on the ALS, although there were times when he seemed to be holding his own against the disease. That was as optimistic an outlook as anybody could have with ALS, and even that was temporary.

Kirstie had come home to look after her father. Although he had known Tom for several years, Virgil had never met Kirstie and was concerned at first that she might resent the presence of a stranger, or be suspicious of his motives, but she was neither. She'd had a souring experience in Nashville, after a fledgling producer persuaded her to make a demo of pop songs passing for country. There were a lot of pop songs passing for country these days, but this bunch was terrible, even by those low standards, and she couldn't find anyone to release the CD. Radio play was out of the question.

Kirstie didn't talk much about the record. She took on the role of the farm wife, doing the cooking and cleaning, and attempting to manage the faltering finances of the place. Her spare time was shared either with her guitar or her horses; it wasn't long after she returned that she began to board rescued animals as well.

She and Virgil had gotten along fine from the start. She seemed to sense in him a kindred spirit, not along artistic lines, but in a general sense of what she referred to as "detachment from the conventional." Virgil had been accused of worse. Once, after they started sleeping together, she told Virgil that he was "half a bubble off plumb," but that it was okay because she was too.

She never gave up on her music, though, and it was through

a friend, a mandolin player who had once backed Levon Helm at his barn down the road a piece, that she met Alan Comstock.

And one thing led to another.

Comstock agreed to produce an album of cover songs. And he agreed to do so for no money up front—his production fee being contingent on the success of the release. Kirstie was over the moon at the prospect, disregarding the fact that Comstock had produced virtually nothing for the past twenty years. It was true that in music circles he was a legend, and not just in his own mind.

Virgil met Comstock just once, when he dropped Kirstie off at the studio when her car wasn't running, and he came away convinced that the man was a lunatic—a fidgety, twitching neurotic who refused to shake Virgil's hand or even look him in the eye. As if there was something in his own gaze that might be revealed. But Virgil didn't need a closer look. He had been around enough crazy people in his life to know the real thing when he saw it.

What he didn't see was the part he would come to regret.

He knew that Comstock was infatuated with Kirstie and of course she knew it too. But she was convinced she could keep him at bay. "Takes two to tango," she had told Virgil. All she was focused on was finishing the album, which probably meant she ignored the signs that things were out of control. That Comstock was out of control. Guns and alcohol and drugs were a bad recipe, and Comstock was a walking mix of all three. Toss in a dash of the spurned and delusional would-be lover and somebody was sure to end up dead. How the shooting actually happened was something Virgil would never know. On a certain level, it didn't matter. Only the result mattered and it was something he couldn't change. It was simply a case of one thing leading to another.

And sonofabitch, look where he was now.

He could hire a lawyer and go along for the ride, put his faith in the system, in the belief that innocent people don't get convicted. It wasn't much of a plan. First of all, he had no money for a lawyer. And second, innocent people get convicted all the time. The ones who do usually have no money for a lawyer.

In the end, it all came down to money. That had been the case back home in Quebec too. Virgil had laid a shit-kicking on a crooked lawyer named Frank Finley, beat him up badly enough to put him in the hospital, because the Quebec courts were not going to punish the man, due in part to Finley's being rich enough to cover his swindling ass, at least where the law was concerned.

Now, like Yogi said, it was déjà vu all over again. The money always won. Comstock had walked because he was wealthy enough to pay Mickey Dupree to represent him. Unfortunately, that made it appear that Virgil had a motive for killing Dupree; in fact, he had frequently entertained thoughts of doing bodily harm to the lawyer. During the trial Dupree had, day after day, engaged in a character assassination of Kirstie, suggesting she was a drug addict, a liar, a mental case. Kirstie had been none of those things. Kirstie had been a dreamer but that was hardly a crime. Mickey Dupree was an arrogant creep who couldn't have cared less about the memory of a nice girl with the capacity to dream. He probably didn't care about Alan Comstock either, except that Comstock could meet his price. So again it was the money. Virgil was the only one involved who didn't have any, and he was the only one sitting in a jail cell.

The motive was there, as was his past, and the prosecution would tie the two nicely together and present them to a jury. It was becoming clear to Virgil that what he needed wasn't a good defense. What he needed was somebody who would try to find out who killed Mickey Dupree.

He pulled his cigarettes from his shirt pocket and lit one, tossing the Zippo on the table. As he smoked he watched the sky outside. Still cloudless. Perfect haying weather. Funny how everything revolved around the weather when you were a farmer. You thought about it even when you weren't thinking about it. Even when you had things of a more urgent nature to consider.

Looking out the window, his eyes shifted to the steel mesh that covered it. It was fastened to the frame with lag bolts, and the bolts appeared to be brand-new, of some brass alloy. Virgil realized that the mesh would have been removed for the recent repainting. Eight bolts held the screen in place, and the bolt heads, he guessed, were roughly three-eighths of an inch. He picked up the Zippo, flipped the top open, and studied it for a moment. He walked over to the window for a closer inspection. Then, with a twist, he broke the top off the lighter and pulled the guts from inside, placing both in his pocket. He pushed the lighter casing over the head of the lag bolt and found it fit snugly, like a socket. He applied pressure on the bolt.

And it turned.

Outside the window, the sun burned brightly on the tall corn, and the hardwood forest, and the rolling Hudson beyond.

TEN

Suzanne Boddington called to invite Jane to lunch. Jane declined, citing recent events, but then immediately thought better of it and called back to accept. She could use a dose of Suzanne. She drove the twenty minutes to the Boddington Stables and parked in the lot beneath the towering structure that was the main house. The place was built entirely of western cedar and local fieldstone and had actually been designed by Frank Lloyd Wright during his middle period, a bit of architectural trivia that Miller Boddington managed to insert into all conversations that involved the house, and quite a number that didn't. The place was all angles and no curves, and while it was not one of the master's better-known designs, it was still a unique building, a quirky, geometrical box dropped into the bucolic landscape a few miles west of the Hudson River, south of Albany.

When Jane walked up, Suzanne was on the terrace, a Bloody Mary in her hand, her long legs encased in Lee jeans, stretched out on the chair next to her. She squinted up at Jane, then picked up her sunglasses from the glass-topped table and put them on. Jane had no idea how old Suzanne was, and she was quite certain Suzanne wouldn't tell her if she asked. Or, if she did, Jane wouldn't know if she was hearing the truth. Still, Suzanne was one of the few people Jane had ever met who was truly at home in her own skin. She was a genuine voluptuary, maybe a few pounds overweight, a little rough around the edges, especially when she chose to be, but a purely sexual being. She had about her a no-bullshit quality that wasn't affected in the least. Today she was stretched out like a cat in the sun, wearing rope-soled sandals and a black V-neck that showed her impressive cleavage.

"Drink?" she asked as Jane sat down, indicating the half-full pitcher.

"Little early for me."

"Christ, it's one o'clock."

Jane looked at the mixture in the glass pitcher. "Maybe a glass of wine."

Henri, Suzanne's latest live-in chef, appeared thirty seconds later with a bottle of Chablis, so quickly that Jane assumed he must have been hovering just inside the French doors. Henri was thin and efficient and somewhat inscrutable. On the days that Jane didn't wonder if he was gay, she was convinced he was sleeping with Suzanne.

It was warm on the terrace and the two women sat partially in the shade of an awning attached to the rough cedar siding of the house. They could have stayed inside in the air conditioning, but Suzanne preferred the outdoors. She wasn't afraid of the sun; she didn't subscribe to anyone's global warming theories, or, more to the point, didn't care about them. She once told Jane there were all kinds of things out there that would kill a person and that avoiding them might be as dangerous as not.

"You dodge one and you just might jump in the path of another," she'd said.

Jane had been apprehensive that Miller might be joining them but it wasn't the case.

"He's in California," Suzanne said.

"Horse business?"

"He's buying wineries," Suzanne replied as she poured another Bloody Mary.

They talked a bit about Mickey Dupree's murder, and then about a play they were going to see in the city later that week, and then Jane steered the conversation toward politics. Jane was hosting a fund-raiser for Congresswoman Edie Bryant at the end of the month. Suzanne wasn't particularly political but she had volunteered Henri to help with the meal, and Jane wanted to go over the menu. For five thousand dollars a plate, people expected something on the exotic side. She was thinking New Zealand lamb.

"Grass fed," she added.

Suzanne snorted. "Right. Because New Zealand grass is far superior to the stuff we grow here."

"Edie wants a band too," Jane said. "She wants to dance."

"Christ, she's the Energizer Bunny," Suzanne said. "She ever going to stop?"

"I think she's getting close," Jane said. "She's made a couple of comments lately."

"I'll believe it when I see it."

Jane started to say something else but then let it go, instead announcing that she was going to attempt the New York City Marathon that fall.

"Wow," Suzanne said. "Maybe I'll do it too." She took a drink and laughed. "In my Mercedes."

Jane had a sip of wine. "One of these days you're going to get the fitness bug. Everybody does."

Suzanne made a point of reaching for a cigarette. "Yeah, that'll happen," she said as she lit up.

Henri brought lunch, seared salmon fillets and roasted potatoes and a green salad. Jane had more wine with the meal but Suzanne stayed with the Bloody Marys. Apparently the pitcher was not going to go to waste. Suzanne had grown up dirt-poor in the Midwest and still carried the effects of that with her. She wore ten-year-old jeans and T-shirts she'd bought at rock concerts a couple of decades earlier. Jane suspected that it was this element of bohemian behavior that had attracted Miller to her in the first place. Of course, it would have taken more than that to hold his attention. Three other women had tried and failed before Suzanne came along. She doubted any of the three possessed a fraction of Suzanne's subtle diplomatic skills, or her innate gift for self-preservation. And she'd be very surprised if any of them could match Suzanne in pure animal sensuality.

"So it's wineries now?" Jane said as they finished eating. Without being asked, Henri had cleared the table and brought out coffee, pouring cups for both women. Suzanne stayed with the vodka and tomato juice.

"Yeah," Suzanne said. "The shiny object du jour." She had a drink and looked out over the property. A half-dozen broodmares grazed in the field on the hill. "I can say one thing for the wine business. Nobody's going to take you to court for mistreating a grape."

"I suspect not," Jane said, pouring a little cream in her coffee. "Wait a minute. Wasn't Mickey Dupree your lawyer on that thing?"

"Miller's lawyer. I haven't been charged with anything."

"Miller's lawyer. Either way, Mickey's off the case."

Suzanne smiled. "Mickey's off the case all right. Which means Miller has to find somebody else. Which means another delay. This thing has already dragged on for two years. Shit, the first district attorney got voted out, some kid is handling it now."

"Why is it taking so long?"

Suzanne laughed. "The fact that Miller doesn't want to go to trial? Mickey didn't either, I'm guessing. He was used to defending murderers, and I don't think he knew what to do with this thing. Other than send Miller a sizable fucking bill every month." Suzanne took a drink; the pitcher was nearly gone. "It's a funny thing—under the right circumstances you can elicit sympathy for almost anybody, even a killer. Maybe not O. J., but your garden-variety killer. Tell sad stories about his wretched life, his social background, his emotional state. Who done him wrong, all that shit. It can be done." She smiled at Jane. "But I defy you to find somebody sympathetic to a man who has mistreated a horse. Or a dog. Look at Michael Vick."

Jane drank her coffee, frowning.

"You doubt me?" Suzanne said. "Look at you—you're like Gandhi's kid sister. But what would you do if you caught somebody hurting your dogs?"

"I'd kill them," Jane said. "But I'd feel badly about it for months afterward."

Suzanne laughed again, her throat thick from the liquor. "Anyway, I don't know where it's going. All this happened at the other farm, you should know. I've never seen anything. And I wouldn't allow it. But it never ends. There was a guy here yesterday, some skinny geek from the SPCA, saying they found one of Miller's horses on a farm near Woodstock, starving. But that's not necessarily his doing. If a horse doesn't perform on the track, he gets rid of it. That's the way he is. Now that I think about it, that's probably why he got rid of the other wives."

"They couldn't run fast enough?"

"They didn't deliver down the stretch."

"Aha," Jane said smiling. "So how will it end?"

"Oh, eventually Miller will plead guilty to something. And they'll hit him with a fine big enough for the public to think justice has been served. And Miller will go on as he always has. Blind to any and all consequences."

Jane nodded. "He's going to have to find another lawyer."

"Like that will be a problem. Kingston's full of them. You can't walk down Wall Street without stepping on a couple dozen of the slippery bastards."

Jane regarded the broodmares on the hill. "But Miller never personally abused a horse. He wouldn't do that."

"Oh?"

"Are you saying he would?"

"I have no idea."

"Did you ever ask him?"

"Hell, no. I've been married to him for seventeen years. I quit asking questions I didn't want to know the answer to a long time ago. For instance, I know Miller owed Mickey Dupree a lot of money at the time of Mickey's death. Is the estate going to see a nickel of it? I would be very surprised. But it's not *my* business."

Now Jane looked again at the mares, grazing in the summer sun. They were sleek and healthy looking.

"Did you ask Alan what happened in the studio that night?" Suzanne asked.

The question caught Jane unawares. "No," she said after a moment.

"Well, there you go," Suzanne said.

Henri came out of the house to ask if they needed anything else. He was going to the market. He was very quiet today. There seemed to be something going on between him and Suzanne. Maybe he *was* sleeping with her, and if that was true, perhaps he chafed at being her servant to boot—even though it was his job. Jane waited until he went back inside.

"Speaking of Alan and that whole . . . situation," she began. "I need to ask you . . . well, this is going to sound strange. I want you to tell me, how are we perceived out there?"

Suzanne was lighting a cigarette, and she exhaled before answering. "You want to know what people think of you?"

"Well . . . yes."

"Why the hell would you want to know that?"

"Because Edie Bryant is stepping down next year and she wants me to go after her seat in Washington."

If Jane thought she would surprise Suzanne, she was mistaken. "What about this fund-raiser we're planning?"

"Well," Jane said slowly, "the money would go to whoever runs in Edie's place."

Suzanne smiled. "Well, not to blow smoke up your skirt, but people think you're great. You're civic-minded, you're suitably liberal, you respect the arts. You clean up nicely."

"What about Alan?"

"What about Alan?" Suzanne repeated slowly, considering it. "Well, I can tell you this much. It sure as hell didn't hurt that he was acquitted."

"I suppose not."

Suzanne was still smiling.

"What's funny?" Jane asked.

"I was just thinking. I was a little surprised when you told me you intended to run a marathon. Now it's beginning to make sense."

"Oh?"

"Sure," Suzanne said. "It's a cool image. A congresswoman from upstate who runs marathons. Works on a number of levels."

"One has nothing to do with the other," Jane said. "I'm not that calculating."

Suzanne laughed. "Hey, there's nothing wrong with calculating."

Jane smiled and poured more coffee for herself. "I wish you wouldn't go to California. I'll miss you."

"I'm not going anywhere."

"But what about the wineries? Won't Miller want to move out there?"

"Miller can do what he wants," Suzanne said emphatically. "This place is all I've ever wanted." She finished the last of her Bloody Mary and set the glass noisily on the table. "I'm not fucking going anywhere."

ELEVEN

Mrs. Tom Walker and her daughter, Pamela, lived next to the courthouse in Kesselberg. Pamela worked at the bank in town and Mrs. Walker passed most days at home, watching her stories or reading romance novels or talking on the telephone. The downstairs phone was by the bay window in the room that had been called the parlor, back when Mr. Walker had come calling. While she talked, she could watch the river in the distance, and the fields and the bush lot in between, and, of course, the courthouse. There had been a time when the courthouse had been an entertaining place—better than television even before television got so bad—with police coming and going, escorting criminals to and from the various trials being held. In those days Mrs. Walker would take careful note of the men wearing the handcuffs and then later would try to match the faces with the police report in the weekly paper.

But that was no more. They had stopped holding court in Kesselberg seven years earlier. Now the only people she ever saw in and around the building were Sheriff Bumpy Jones and the people who came to cut the grass and tend to the grounds.

Late Friday afternoon, she turned off the TV after watching ten minutes of a talk show hosted by a shrill black woman with orange hair, and she looked out the window to see a worker on the roof of the large garage attached to the courthouse. The garage had once been a carriage house, and Mrs. Walker could remember the large chestnut horses that were stabled there when she was a little girl.

The man on the roof wore jeans and a faded brown shirt. Mrs. Walker assumed he was doing some sort of repair. She couldn't see a ladder anywhere and decided it must have been on the other side of the building. But then the worker did a strange thing. He slipped over the edge of the roof, hung there by the rain gutter for a moment, and then dropped to the ground. When he stood up, he turned and it seemed that he looked directly at her. Mrs. Walker, not wishing to appear like a snoop, pulled back from the window a bit.

The man then walked casually over to a wheelbarrow that was sitting by the flower bed alongside the garage. He picked up a shovel and a hoe from the grass, put them in the wheelbarrow, and started off, heading in the direction of the river. Mrs. Walker watched him as he made his way down the sloping lawn. When he was gone she went into the kitchen and made herself some tea.

Virgil left the wheelbarrow at the edge of the cornfield, slipped between the rows of corn, and began to run. He had seen a woman watching him from the window of a house next to the courthouse and had no idea who else might have seen him jump down from the roof. He was hoping that the two cops would be gone for a couple of hours at least, and maybe longer than that, if he was lucky. But there was always the chance that the rotund little sheriff might decide to check on him.

He'd kept a casual pace pushing the wheelbarrow down the slope, but now the corn stalks were high enough to conceal him and so he ran. He realized pretty quickly that it had been years since he had last run anywhere. Back to his baseball days, in fact. Even then, he had always tried to get out of it.

"I'm a catcher, skip," he would say to Tom Stempler when he was his manager. "What do I need to run for?"

"Run," Tom would say.

Virgil was blowing hard when he reached the far end of the field. He stopped there for a minute, catching his breath and listening. The forest before him was not as dense as it had appeared from the courthouse window. There were houses on either side within a few hundred yards, and a couple of small cabins along the river. He decided he would walk through the thicket, taking advantage of whatever cover it offered. Before setting out, he snapped a dead branch from a lower limb of a red oak and made himself a walking stick. Then he started for the river, doing his best impression of a man out for an afternoon stroll.

Emerging from the woods, he came upon a gravel roadway that ran parallel to the riverbank. The two cabins he had seen earlier sat on the flats, between the road and the river, roughly five hundred feet apart. A Chevy Blazer was parked on the lawn beside the first cabin but the second appeared deserted. Virgil started down the road, heading for the second shack.

He assumed the cops would use dogs to track him so he needed to use the river to hide his trail. Past the second cabin he angled his way toward the riverbank, looking at the expanse, wondering if he could swim it. He was doubtful; just running through the cornfield had winded him, and stopping to catch one's breath in the middle of a field was a lot easier than doing it halfway across a river. Not to mention it would mean waiting until dark.

Then he saw the aluminum punt, pulled up onto the riverbank and tied off to a willow tree. Virgil walked toward it and stopped on the slope, watching the door of the cabin.

"Hello!" he called.

He waited a few minutes and then untied the boat, climbed inside, and began to row, watching the cabins behind him as he did. No one appeared. There were a number of other boats on the river, fishermen and water skiers and the odd kayak or canoe, so he wasn't drawing attention to himself.

Partway across the river he stopped rowing and allowed the punt to drift as he watched the far shore, looking for a likely place to land. A few hundred yards to the north a small creek spilled into the river, the mouth of the stream surrounded by cattails and marsh. There were no buildings nearby. To the right of the creek, where the riverbank was solid, there were houses and a few cottages. Looking to his left, he could see Albany in the distance, and a railroad bridge spanning the river. The Rip Van Winkle Bridge was farther south, he knew.

He pulled on the oars, swinging the bow around, and headed for the mouth of the creek. As he rowed he kept an eye over his left shoulder on the buildings to the south. Drawing nearer, he saw a number of people gathered in the yard of a green frame cottage, drinking beer and grilling food. A few men were pitching horseshoes in pits near the water's edge. Virgil slowed, watching them for a moment, and then changed course and headed for the party.

He rowed the punt up to the bank a few yards from the closest horseshoe pit, got out, and pulled it onto the grass. He tied it off to a log and then walked directly toward the players, who had stopped playing and were watching him with interest as he approached.

"How you doing?" he asked as he passed.

A couple of people nodded to him as he walked along the property line and past the cottage. A chocolate Labrador trotted up to him, and without stopping he leaned down to pat the dog on the head.

"Who the hell is that?" he heard someone say.

Virgil walked to the roadway out front, where he turned and headed north.

Once he was a few hundred yards along the road, he risked looking back through the trees, toward the cottage. The horseshoe game had resumed. Somebody was throwing a stick in the river for the Labrador to retrieve.

Ten minutes later he came to a stone bridge that spanned the narrow creek he'd seen earlier. He headed down the embankment to the right of the road and waded into the stream. It was shallow and clear, the bottom covered with smooth stones that made walking easy. His work boots filled immediately and grew heavy.

Looking ahead he saw that the creek meandered through scrubland, bordered on either side by small pines and cottonwood saplings. There were farm buildings in the distance but to Virgil it seemed as if he was reasonably well concealed. About a mile to the east the acreage gave way to forest. He decided to stay in the creek until he reached the trees.

Make the dogs earn their keep.

By the time he reached the tree line, the sun was dropping behind him and his legs ached from the heavy slogging. Looking at the sun, he guessed it would be a couple of hours or so until nightfall. He sat down and pulled his boots off and poured the creek water from them. He wrung out his socks and then stuffed some dried leaves in his boots and pulled them on again.

He started south. As he walked he became aware of how hungry he was. He'd eaten nothing since the McDonald's breakfast early that morning. Supper last night had been a couple of chocolate bars. There was nothing to eat in the forest; it was too early for hickory nuts or walnuts and he had no way to shell them anyway. He could have picked a few tiny ears of field corn earlier, but, busy as he was breaking out of jail, it hadn't occurred to him.

He stayed in the woods, although twice he had to come out into the open to cross a side road. Occasionally he came upon a house built in the forest and would be forced to swing one way or another to avoid getting too close. He was in no particular hurry. He guessed the Rip Van Winkle Bridge was three or four miles away. When he got there he would have to wait until darkness fell.

After about an hour he heard the sound of traffic and a few minutes later came upon a fairly busy two-lane highway. He hunkered down by the edge of the thicket to have a look. There were a number of houses along the road, and a gas station with an adjoining restaurant at an intersection to his right. He had no chance of crossing unnoticed. He wondered if his absence had been discovered back in Kesselberg. Maybe they weren't looking for him yet.

But maybe they were. And if they were, the news would be on the radio, the TV, everywhere. Killer on the loose.

He turned toward the restaurant's large rear parking lot, where a couple of tractor trailers and a half-dozen cars were parked. There was also a boom truck, with a logo on the door and lettering that read HENSBRIDGE CONSTRUCTION. Beneath the hydraulic boom were chained a number of lengths of concrete sewer pipe. Virgil looked back to his left. A quarter mile away several orange construction signs marked where the shoulder of the highway was being excavated in preparation for new drainage.

Virgil walked through the bushes and dropped down to the restaurant parking lot. In the back of the boom truck he saw picks and shovels and various other tools. He stood behind the vehicle and regarded the restaurant a moment. Presumably the workers were done for the day and had gone inside for dinner, or maybe a few drinks. There were no windows in the rear of the place but as he watched, a large black man walked out and deposited a pail of garbage in a Dumpster. Virgil ducked down and waited until the man went back inside, and then he reached into the truck bed and took a hard hat and an orange vest and headed back into the thicket.

He walked through the bushes until he drew even with the construction site up the road. He put on the vest and the hard hat and moved down to the highway, where he picked up an orange construction triangle and carried it across the road, waiting for several cars to pass first. There he gathered another triangle and walked along the shoulder to a spot where a ravine led back into the woods. He placed one triangle on the gravel shoulder and walked a few yards to position the other. He had a look at the two, as if evaluating his work, and then dropped down into the ravine and walked away.

Back in the woods he discarded the hat and vest. A couple of miles along he came to State Highway 23. He guessed he was maybe a mile or so east of the bridge. It would be an hour or more before nightfall, so he found a spot beneath some pine trees and sat down. He removed his sodden boots and socks again and placed them where the setting sun hit them, and then lay down on the pine straw to wait for darkness.

He fell asleep and when he woke it was full dark. He pulled on his boots and headed back west, hurrying now. He wanted to cross the river before the moon came out. He reached the bridge in half an hour and crossed at once, meeting no one on the walkway. When he arrived on the west side he strode quickly past the tollgate, skirting the town of Catskill, and kept to the shoulder of the highway until he was past the thruway. Then he climbed down from the embankment and headed south.

TWELVE

Claire leaned against the grille of the Intrepid and sipped the lukewarm coffee. Beside her Joe Brady was talking on his cell phone. Before her was a sloping lawn that led to a cornfield, the corn giving way to a forest, which ran to the edge of the Hudson River. Behind her was the Kesselberg courthouse. And there she was.

"Stuck in the middle with you," she told Brady as he hung up. "Isn't that a song?"

"A sad song."

Brady was all amped up, in manhunt mode, and as such he had no time for Claire's cryptic references. Even at his most attentive, Joe didn't pick up on much.

"The dogs are out," he said. "I sent a uniform to Cain's house for a shirt, or something of his for scent. We know exactly where he landed on the other side. We have a positive ID from half a dozen people. No rain overnight. They'll have no problem picking up his trail. We'll have this man in custody within hours."

Claire finished her coffee and looked for a place to toss the cup. "Taking him into custody hasn't been a problem," she said. "Keeping him in custody is what we need to work on." She reached in the Dodge's window and put the cup on the dash. "Let's have a look at the lockup."

She had met the pudgy sheriff when she arrived earlier. It had been a little before eight and he'd pulled up in his own car, his eyes blinking and his hair tousled as if he'd just gotten up. He was like a schoolkid who was very worried that the escape was going on his permanent record. He kept saying over and over that this had never happened before. Finally Claire had sent him off to look for an area map that she didn't need.

She and Brady went upstairs to the room that had been, all too briefly it seemed, Cain's cell. There wasn't much to see. Two chairs and a table, some fishing magazines. And a steel mesh screen leaning neatly against the wall. Eight lag bolts lined up on the windowsill.

"I have an excellent witness from the house next door," Brady said. "Mrs. Tom Walker. She saw Cain on the roof here, right outside the window. He dropped down to the grass and took a wheelbarrow and headed toward the river. I showed her his mug shot. She said it was Cain, no question."

"She tell you anything you didn't already know?" Claire said. "She didn't happen to mention where Cain was going . . . ?"

She felt him stiffen beside her but it had gotten to the point where she didn't give a shit. She walked to the window and picked up one of the lag bolts. "How did he manage this?"

"I have a theory on that," Joe said. "The room and the trim were just painted. Whoever put the screen back on must have left the wrench behind."

Claire looked around the room. "A wrench. Wouldn't you have seen it when you locked him up?"

"Oh, I was never up here," Joe said quickly. "I stayed by the radio. Sal brought him up."

"Where is Sal anyway?"

When Joe didn't reply, she turned to look at him. "I said where's Sal?"

"I had to drop him from this," Joe said. He indicated the window. "This is inexcusable."

So is throwing your partner under a bus, Claire thought. Delano seemed like a decent kid. And Claire wasn't buying the wrench theory anyway. She crossed to the table and noticed a small pile of ashes on one of the magazines.

"Cain was smoking in here."

"So?"

"He still had his cigarettes and his lighter then?"

"I guess. What about it?"

Claire looked at the open window again. She shrugged. "Let's go see what the dogs are doing."

Brady suggested they take one car but Claire wasn't going for that. She said she would follow him. They took the high-way bridge south of town to cross the Hudson and drove along the river road to a row of cottages along the bank, stopping in front of a small green bungalow. Claire parked the Dodge out front and got out. The canine unit and SWAT team had been there since dawn, awaiting instructions from Joe. Two hounds lazed in the shade of the lawn, tongues lolling in the heat, as their handler, Ron Patterson, stood speaking with a man and a woman. Brady introduced them as Frank and Lindsay Richards. They were renting the cottage for the month. They were in their thirties, she guessed, and they both appeared a little hung over. Why not? she thought. They were on vacation.

"Come around back," Brady said, taking charge. "I'll show you where he exited the river."

Claire had never heard of anybody exiting a river before.

They left Patterson with the dogs, and the four of them walked around the little cottage and down to the shore. There were horseshoe pits and a few beer empties lying around. Across the river was the town of Kesselberg. Claire could see the steeple of the Anglican Church. She could see the court-house too.

Brady, like a retriever on the point, was standing by a small aluminum boat that was pulled up onto the bank a few yards away.

"I'm guessing that's the boat," Claire said.

"This is the boat he stole," Brady said, evidently feeling a need to emphasize this subsequent crime. First capital murder. And now the unconscionable theft of a twelve-foot punt.

"Where will it end?" Claire said to Joe, then turned to the couple. "And you guys were in the yard?"

"There was a bunch of us here," the man said. "We had friends over. He walked right up to us and said hello and kept on going."

"He petted my sister's dog," the woman said.

Claire walked past the boat and looked upriver. There was a marshy area a few hundred yards away where the shore curved inward. There were no buildings at all along that stretch.

"Petted her dog, did he?" Claire said, turning. "Man can't be all bad."

"If you want to disregard the fact that he killed a man in cold blood," Brady said.

"No, I think we should keep that in mind," Claire said. She indicated the marshy area. "What's over there?" she asked.

"Bullhead Creek," the man said.

"And what's Bullhead Creek?"

"Um . . . just a creek. Runs back into the woods."

"And where did he go when he finished petting the dog?"

"He walked along here," the woman said, indicating the edge of the lawn. "And out to the road. And then he headed that way."

"Toward Bullhead Creek," Claire said.

"Well . . . yeah."

"Was he in a hurry?"

"Didn't seem to be. Not at all."

Claire nodded. "Where are your friends now?"

"They've gone into town for breakfast," the man said. "We're supposed to meet them."

Claire took another look at the boat and then started back up toward the cottage. As she did, a marked cruiser came down the gravel road, moving too fast.

"Good," Joe Brady said. "We can put those dogs to work."

When they reached the front yard, the uniform was out of the car. He had been to the Cain farm and retrieved a sweatshirt and a ball cap. Patterson was looking at the items before letting the dogs have a sniff. Claire stepped in for a closer look. It was a plain navy sweatshirt, stained a little with grease and dirt. The cap was clean, and it had a picture of Toby Keith on the front.

"That's not his," Claire said.

"How do you know that?" Brady asked.

"It doesn't fit."

"Oh, you know his hat size?" Brady asked.

"Philosophically, it doesn't fit. You're either Merle Haggard or Toby Keith. This guy Cain is Haggard all the way."

Brady looked at Patterson. "Shit. How's that for your forensic science?"

Claire picked up the cap and put it on Brady's head, where it perched like a cherry on a sundae. "Look at that. This belongs to a woman, probably his wife." She looked at Patterson. "The shirt will do?"

"If it's his, they'll track him," Patterson said. He looked at the morning sky. "He's got a pretty good start, though."

He took the shirt to the hounds and let them get the scent. He led them around the yard and within a minute they had the trail. Patterson and the team set out after them, the SWAT guys loaded for bear with shotguns and MP5s. Brady looked at Claire.

"I'm going to tag along for a bit. You coming?"

"No."

"Suit yourself."

The couple from the cottage had been hanging back, as if unsure what their role was now. After Brady set off on foot behind the trackers, the woman stepped forward. "Um . . . do you need us for anything? We were gonna go meet our friends."

"Go ahead," Claire said.

The woman hesitated. There was something else, it seemed, so Claire asked her what it was.

"Detective Brady never told us this guy killed someone," the man said. "And we don't want to make this about us. But are we in danger here? Should we be thinking about spending the night somewheres else?"

"He won't be back this way," Claire said. "Joe should have told you, though."

"Is this guy dangerous?"

"Not to you."

The couple seemed to take her at her word. Good thing, as what she said was pure speculation on her part, and a tad careless to boot. They went into the house for a few minutes and then came out, got into their car, and drove off. When they were gone, Claire walked back down to the river's edge. She stood looking over at Kesselberg and imagined herself on the opposite shore, facing the spot where she stood. If she were Virgil Cain, in a stolen rowboat, she would have headed for the marsh. No question. It had been a stupid move, coming here and exposing himself to all these people.

And Claire didn't think for a moment that Cain was stupid. She walked to the nearest horseshoe pit and picked up a shoe and tossed it. She missed the other pit altogether, so she threw each of the remaining shoes, finally ringing one off the post. She walked over and sat down on a creaky Adirondack chair. Taking her cell from her pocket, she called the station, got Marina on the line.

"What have you got on Virgil Cain?"

"What have I got?"

"Yeah. I assume Joe asked you to check him out."

"Joe didn't ask me anything," Marina said. "His whole attitude is we got the guy. Game over."

Claire sighed. "And all of a sudden it's game on."

"What do you mean?"

"The guy escaped custody. You didn't know?"

"I just walked in. I'm not even supposed to be here. I'm on midnights." Claire could hear Marina hitting some computer keys. "Holy shit."

"Yeah."

"So where is he?"

"No idea. Joe and the boys have canine on the trail. See what you can find, Marina. Apparently he did time in Quebec. I assume he was born there but I really have no reason to assume that. Or anything else. But do what you can. If I don't know where he is, I might as well try to find out where he's been."

"Jesus Christ," Marina said. "An escaped convict. That's kind of scary, isn't it?"

"Scary? I was thinking more along the lines of inexcusable."

"Well, yeah." Marina paused. "It's actually kind of romantic too, when you think about it. Sort of like Butch Cassidy or somebody like that. You remember Butch Cassidy, with Paul Newman?"

"Yeah, well, this guy isn't Paul Newman."

"Oh, I know," Marina said. "I was just saying."

"See what you can find," Claire said and hung up. Maybe Marina was right. Maybe on a certain level, theoretically speaking, it was kind of romantic. But Claire wasn't going to allow herself to think about that until she had the sonofabitch back in custody.

The sun was climbing in the sky and already the day was hot. She wondered how far Cain could have gotten. She walked back to her car and was about to leave when she saw Joe Brady coming down the gravel road. He had his jacket off and the sweat was rolling off him in rivulets. Claire waited for him by the car.

"You fall in the river?" she asked.

"Very funny."

"Well?"

Brady stopped. He was actually breathing heavily. From walking.

"The dogs lost the trail in a creek up there a ways," he said, jerking his thumb over his shoulder. "He's heading east. He waded in the creek."

"Bullhead Creek."

"I guess. They'll get him, though. He could've only stayed in the water for so long. Canine's got a dog on each bank. They'll pick up his scent, wherever he came out."

"It won't matter," Claire said.

"Why the hell not?"

"You're on the wrong side of the river."

"What?" Joe asked. "Why do you say that?"

"Think about it," Claire said. "He could have rowed his little boat right into the mouth of that creek. Instead he pulled up on these people's doorstep, said howdy-do, petted their dog, and posed for group pictures for all we know. He wanted us to know he was on this side of the river. Which means he doubled back."

"And went where?" Brady asked.

"I've been thinking about that. You got somebody watching his farm?"

"Well . . . no."

"Why not?"

"He's not gonna go there. He knows we'll be watching it."

"You just said you're not."

Joe stood there, sweating quietly for a moment. "All right. I still say he's heading east. You're giving him too much credit. He's not that smart."

"He's been smarter than us so far," Claire said and got into the car. "Send me a card when you reach the Atlantic."

She grabbed another coffee on the way and drove straight out to the farm on Windecker Road. She attempted to do the math as she drove, but there were too many variables. The only thing she knew for sure was that Cain had escaped at shortly after four o'clock the previous afternoon. The Walker woman had been certain about that. What Claire didn't know was how long it had taken him to find a boat and cross the river, which direction he had traveled once he had, and which route he would have taken to get back across. In fact, she didn't know for certain that he had crossed again. Maybe Joe was right and he was heading for Massachusetts.

But she doubted it.

Approaching the farm she noticed the Ford F-250, parked in the same spot by the barn. As she pulled in the drive Mary Nelson walked around the corner of the building, leading the skinny mare by a rope. Claire drove over and parked well back, not wanting to frighten the horse.

"Hello again," she said as she got out.

Mary nodded to her but never broke stride. When she

reached the pasture in front of the barn, she opened a gate and released the rail-thin horse into the field. The other horses there began moving at once in the direction of the new arrival.

Claire walked over. Mary glanced toward her.

"Give me a minute here. I want to see how these other knuckleheads respond to that mare. Here comes the stud now. If he's okay with her, she'll be all right."

Claire watched as the dark stallion trotted up to the skinny mare and made a circle around her. She appeared nervous, jerking her head and sidestepping when he came near. But after a few moments spent sniffing and nuzzling her, he wandered off. The mare's tension seemed to vanish and in a few moments she was picking at the grass.

"Does that mean the stud's okay with her?" Claire asked.

Mary now turned to Claire. "So far, so good."

"It's a man's world, isn't it?"

"Well, he sure as hell thinks so," Mary said. "I'm still a little doubtful about the whole concept. But I'm just a silly old woman."

"Yeah, right."

"Come on." Mary walked toward the pump house. Claire watched as she stepped inside and a moment later the noisy pump started up, and the plastic line spewed water into the trough. Mary came out and looked at the flow.

Both women turned at the sound of commotion in the field. The paint gelding had trotted over to check out the new arrival and now the stallion was running him off.

Mary smiled. "See? Sometimes testosterone is a good thing." She looked over at Claire. "So what's up?"

"Just having another look around," Claire said. "You took off before I could ask you the most obvious question yesterday. Do you think Virgil Cain killed Mickey Dupree?"

"Oh, I have no idea. You guys are the professionals. You must have some pretty compelling evidence if you arrested him. Have you ever arrested somebody for murder and it turned out he was innocent?"

"No, I haven't," Claire said. She decided not to point out that she didn't arrest Virgil Cain.

The water trough was nearly full and Mary went into the shed to shut off the pump. Claire watched the stream from the pipe slow down and then trickle out to nothing. When Mary came back, it was clear she had something on her mind. She took her time, watching the horses at their grazing.

"Although," she said after a bit, "given the circumstances, the trial and the acquittal, you might think that if Virgil was of the mind to kill somebody, he would kill Alan Comstock."

"Maybe he was just getting started."

"Maybe he was," Mary said. "But the day he was arrested, he'd just got done cutting that hay field over there. Which reminds me, I have to hire somebody to bale that up. But yes, he'd just finished cutting hay and he and I were sitting by the milk house there, drinking beer and arguing about whether or not he was going to take that mare off my hands. Now I personally have never seen anybody on a killing spree. Is that generally how they act?"

"It varies from killer to killer," Claire said smiling. "You're going to pay to have his hay brought in? I thought you were just an acquaintance."

"Most of those horses in that field were forced on him by me. One way or the other, they're going to have to eat this winter. Whether Virgil's in jail or not."

Claire nodded at the explanation.

"But while we're on the subject of putting people in jail," Mary went on, "there's a jackass named Hopman who lives not three miles from here who's responsible for that mare's condition. We found starving animals on his farm, we found dying animals on his farm, and all he got was a misdemeanor charge and now he's back on the property. And rumor has it he's going back in the horse business." She paused. "You know, while we're on the subject."

"I'll make a note of that," Claire said. "Not exactly my bailiwick."

"He had horses from Miller Boddington too," Mary said. "Is that your bailiwick?"

"As a matter of fact, it is. I arrested Boddington."

"And when's he going to trial?"

"Unfortunately, Mickey Dupree was Boddington's lawyer," Claire said. "So I would have to say, not any time soon."

"I knew he was Boddington's lawyer," Mary said. "Wouldn't that mean that horse lovers everywhere would have a motive for killing Dupree? But then you say you have compelling evidence that Virgil did it."

"When did I say that?"

Mary shrugged. "I guess maybe you didn't."

"You know he escaped custody, right?"

"I heard about it on the news."

"I have a theory on where he's heading," Claire said.

"Oh?"

"Yeah," she said. She waited a moment, trying to read the older woman. "Has he been here yet?"

Mary indicated a machine shed across the yard. The sliding door was open to reveal an empty bay inside. "Been and gone, is my guess," she said.

"What do you mean?"

"Kirstie's Jeep was parked in there yesterday. And today it's not. Unless your people had it towed in."

"That would be to presume too much of my people," Claire said. She stood looking at the empty building for a time. "Shit."

"You thought you were ahead of him?"

"I wasn't sure," Claire said. "I just figured things out this morning. But I don't know how he got here. If he walked all that way, well it's about thirty miles so it would have taken him all night. Of course, he could have called a friend to come and pick him up." She glanced at Mary. "He could have called you to come and pick him up."

"He wouldn't know how to reach me," Mary said. "Except at the clinic and I wasn't at the clinic last night. Besides, if he called me, I would probably turn him in."

"Would you?"

"I would be obligated to," Mary said. "Your department is saying that he killed a man. Isn't that how it is?"

"That's how it is."

Mary started toward her truck. "I have to get back to work."

Claire fished a card from her pocket and gave it to the vet. "You'll call me if you hear from him?"

Mary looked at the card and then nodded as she put it in her shirt pocket.

"You will call me?" Claire persisted.

"Like I said . . . probably," Mary said. She got into the truck and drove off.

Claire watched her leave and then headed toward the house. There was one thing she wanted to check on. She went under the yellow tape and inside, through the kitchen, and into the living room. The small drawer on the rolltop desk was open. The credit card was gone, and so was the passport. She didn't need to check the false bottom to know that the five hundred dollars was gone as well. But she did anyway.

She drove back to the department and sat at her desk and

made the calls she needed to make. First she got the border patrol on the line and informed them that the Virgil Cain they'd been on the alert for was now traveling with a passport. She called Visa and asked them to let her know if Cain used his card. The woman on the other end asked if she wanted the card canceled and Claire said no. She wanted Cain to use it; that way she could track him. The Ulster County sheriff's department had the details on the Jeep, since they had so recently had the vehicle in their impound; so she retrieved that and put it out as well. She considered not calling Joe Brady for a while. Presumably he and the dogs were still on the trail, stumbling around in the thick woods east of the Hudson. Maybe Joe would bump his head on a tree limb and smarten up a little. In the end, she did call him, out of respect for Patterson and the SWAT guys. The dogs too.

THIRTEEN

Jane heard the news at a luncheon in Woodstock with Edie Bryant and a group of women who wanted to bend the congresswoman's ear about the proposed gas drilling in the area. Edie had invited Jane along, suggesting that the exposure to the group would be good for her, on a subliminal level. It helped that everyone at the lunch was on common ground. Nobody wanted the drilling in their backyard.

The luncheon began at one o'clock, at a new restaurant in a converted lumber mill on the east edge of town. The women present were well heeled and possibly overinformed, and the discussion around the table was what Jane expected: an abundance of talk about the power of grassroots, amid a faint undertone of privileged outrage. Nothing was accomplished, of course, although the group did receive a guarantee from Edie Bryant that she was with them all the way.

It was over dessert, with the conversation rambling here and there, that Jane learned that Virgil Cain had broken out of jail. One of the women had a husband who was retired and spent a good portion of his day listening to a police scanner. It was nearly three o'clock when he called her cell phone to tell her about the escape.

"How does someone do that, in this day and age?" one woman asked.

"He won't be out there long," another said. "They'll get him."

"Well, I'll be keeping my doors locked until they do."

120

Jane begged off soon afterward. Edie had to leave as well and they walked out to the parking lot together.

"There you go," Edie said. "Pretty glamorous, right?"

"Can they stop the drilling?" Jane asked. She had tried to keep her mind on the purpose of the lunch, but she was thinking about the news. More specifically, she was wondering if Alan had heard.

"Probably not. As long as there are people out there who'll sell them or lease them their land, who are we to try to stop them? This is America, darling. You start telling people what they can and can't do with their own property and you'll become very unpopular very quickly."

"What about the groundwater issues?"

"That's really the only thing they have going for them," Edie said. "Clean water is always a hot button. But then the drillers make all kinds of guarantees that the water table won't be affected. Guarantees that are impossible to keep, mind you, but people who stand to make money only hear what they want to hear." She paused. "But there's one good thing about it all."

"What's that?"

"This thing won't come to a head for at least a year." Edie smiled. "I'll be retired by then. See you later, sweetie."

And with that she got into her Prius and drove off.

Jane headed home, driving quickly, still hoping that Alan had not heard about the escape. She got her answer before she even entered the house. The front door was locked and she had to use the code to get in. Alan was sitting at the dining room table, eating a Domino's pizza and wearing a six-gun and holster over his sweatpants. There was an assault rifle of some kind on the table beside the pizza box. Looking through the French doors to the kitchen, she saw a shotgun on the counter.

"Did you set the alarm?" he asked.

"No."

"Set it."

She went back to the keypad by the front door and did so; then she came over to sit down at the table. "They'll pick him up in no time. They probably already have."

"Not yet, they haven't. I called those assholes downtown and told them to let me know. Then I called dickwad at the *Gazette* and told him too. They haven't got him." He paused dramatically. "It might be up to me to get him, Jane. I'm prepared for that."

She exhaled heavily. He had shifted back into movie talk. Not a good sign. "What did the police say?"

Alan took a large bite of the pizza and talked with his mouth full. "They offered to send a patrolman here to babysit me."

"That's good."

"I told them to fuck off."

Jane shook her head and looked at the large pizza in the box, already three-quarters gone. "Why would you do that, Alan?"

He took a drink from a can of Diet Pepsi. "You don't know? This is the same police department that tried to convict me of murder. And now they're claiming they're gonna try and protect me? I don't think so. I'll get to the bottom of this. I think there's a very good chance they let him go on purpose."

"What?"

"Come on, Jane. When was the last time anybody escaped from prison around here?"

"It wasn't exactly prison, was it? I heard it was a lockup in some little town along the river."

"Exactly! Why the fuck would they be holding a cold-blooded killer in a tin can like that? That doesn't strike you as suspicious? No, the fix is in. They're gunning for me. Fucking cops. They *want* this nut job to do their dirty work for them. They couldn't get a conviction so this is plan B. He got Mickey and now he's coming after me." He drank more soda. "I've got Walter on it."

"Walter's a litigation lawyer."

"Don't matter. I want him to know what's going down here. In case the deal goes sour."

He retrieved the last slice of pizza from the box and got to his feet. Jane watched as he headed into the kitchen, a ridiculous figure in his sweats and his hoodie and his slippers, Colt .45 strapped around his ever-expanding middle. She gathered up the pizza box and the empty soda can and followed him. He picked up the shotgun from the counter and walked over to look out the glass doors to the deck, the gun propped on his hip. After a moment, he went outside, ignoring the fact he'd just implored Jane to set the alarm. She got to the keypad before the siren started.

She tossed the scraps from the pizza box into the garbage and folded the cardboard for the recycling box. Retrieving a bottle of water from the fridge, she stood inside the glass and watched Alan standing by the railing, the shotgun over his left shoulder, his right hand on his hip, near the revolver. When he turned to look at her, she went outside.

"Suzanne and I are going down to the city to see a show tonight," she said. "Why don't you come? We'll stay at the townhouse until they pick this guy up."

"Suzanne rubs me the wrong way. White trash gone nouveau riche. Spare me that fucking cliché."

"We can drive down separately. You don't have to go to the show. You won't even see her."

"I can stay here and not see her," Alan said. He walked along the railing and back, like a sentry on duty. "I want to be here when he shows. I'm no lawyer in a fucking sand trap. At the end of the day, the only person a man can depend on is himself.

The spirit of the frontier." He turned to her. "You ought to know that. A girl from Montana."

"Except I'm from Chicago," Jane reminded him.

"Are you now? You sure about that?" Alan turned back toward the trees, scanned the property. "For some reason, I thought you were a Montana girl."

Jane sat down. "Okay. We're getting off topic here. Come with me to the city. Do it for me if you won't do it for yourself."

"I'm not running. This is where I make my stand."

She knew there would be no convincing him. On the drive to town earlier she had decided that today was the day she would talk to him about her interest in pursuing Edie Bryant's seat in Washington. She knew now that today wasn't the day. Looking at him in his outlandish getup, she realized that the day might never come. It would be a lot easier to conceal his mental state if he wasn't so hell-bent on advertising it. She knew he had stopped taking the Amoxapine. She'd been counting the pills.

"If you won't come with me, I'm staying here," she said.

"No," he said. "I won't have you in harm's way. I have a job to do, and where I go, you can't follow."

She recognized the line, lifted from *Casablanca*. Bogie at the end, sending Ingrid Bergman away on the plane.

"Then I'm going to have Walter send somebody out. Private security. You can trust Walter, right?"

She could see that the suggestion was at least getting consideration. Walter was one of the few people—maybe the only person—that Alan still had faith in.

"It would seem the better part of valor," he said after a moment.

She had no idea what that was from, but she went inside and called Walter.

FOURTEEN

Claire had never been to Alan Comstock's estate. At the time of his arrest for the killing of Kirstie Stempler, Claire had been working a multiple homicide, an arson that wiped out a family of six in a farmhouse near Ravena. She had nothing to do with Comstock's indictment or his trial. Joe had been the lead on that one, much to his regret, she suspected. Not that he would ever admit it, of course. After the acquittal, Joe behaved as if he were the only one who'd done his job during the investigation, even after Mickey Dupree made mincemeat out of him on the stand.

And now, on this warm summer morning, Joe was holding forth in the kitchen of the Comstock home. Claire had received the call to come to the house when she was on the road to Albany, and she'd had to turn around.

"I told canine he would double back," Joe was saying to a member of the forensics unit, his back to Claire. "They wouldn't listen. Shit, when he crossed the river he left a trail a five-year-old could follow and he did it on purpose. I knew damn well what he had on his mind."

When Joe finally turned and saw Claire, he fell quiet. She looked past him to the situation outside and kept on walking. She glanced at her watch. It was nine thirty.

Alan Comstock was on the deck, wearing a robe and slippers and a ball cap with AC RECORDS across the front. There was a holstered revolver on his waist, and a shotgun and nickel-plated small-caliber Smith & Wesson lying on a glass-topped, wrought-iron table a few feet away. Comstock was on his left side, his arm twisted awkwardly beneath him. He had been shot several times, and he was quite dead.

Beside the two weapons on the table was a nearly empty fifth of gin, along with a bottle of tonic and an ice bucket half-full of water.

Julie Hansen from the Ulster County sheriff's department was taking pictures. Claire said hello and Julie handed her latex gloves, which she put on.

"Who made the call?"

"The maid," Julie said. "She got here around eight."

"Where's the wife?"

"Gone to New York for the night. She left the maid a note."

Claire kneeled beside the body for a moment. The eyes were open, and the ball cap was twisted to one side, the bill propped against the cedar decking.

"Rigor set in?"

"Yeah," Julie said. "Been a few hours. At least."

Claire gestured to the nickel-plated revolver. "You got this?" she asked, indicating the camera.

"Go ahead."

Claire took a pen from her pocket and used it to pick up the gun, a .32 caliber. The cylinder was empty but the spent casings remained.

"Now did the recently deceased empty this revolver in the act of defending himself, or is this the murder weapon?"

"Either or," Julie said. "We'll know when we get the slugs out of him."

"If it's the shooter's gun, you won't find any prints on it."

"Why not?"

"Just a hunch. He wouldn't leave a gun behind with his prints on it. But you might find some on the casings, though, if he got careless." Claire indicated the revolver, holstered around Alan Comstock's ample waist and the shotgun on the table. "All this will have to go for tests, obviously. I noticed an assault weapon in the dining room and a semiautomatic on the kitchen counter. I assume they are all property of the deceased but you know what assuming can do."

"Lot of guns," Julie said. "What the hell was he expecting?"

"This, I'm guessing," Claire said. "But probably with a different outcome."

Joe walked out of the house, saw the .32 suspended in Claire's hand. "Recognize that?" he asked.

"Should I?"

"That's the Smith & Wesson that Comstock shot the girl with. And it looks to me that Cain used it on Comstock. How's that for irony?"

"How would Cain get it?" Claire asked. "Wasn't it in evidence?"

"We had to give it back after the trial," Joe said. "Comstock showed up downtown with his buddy Mickey Dupree backing him up, and he was raving about the Second Amendment and the right to bear arms. Blah, blah, blah. We had to give it back to him." Joe smiled. "How'd that work out for him? Either of them, come to think of it."

Claire looked around. Behind the house was heavy forest, with trails running off in several directions. There was a large garage, or a building that looked like a garage, a few yards away. The sound of dogs barking came from inside.

"Were the dogs out when you guys responded?" she asked.

"No," Joe said. "Lucky for the mutts. Cain would have killed them too."

"So you've identified a suspect, have you?" Claire asked.

"Give me a break," Joe said.

Claire indicated the body. "So how did he manage it? You have Comstock here, packing more heat than a Ranger patrol, and you've got Cain, presumably unarmed. If that thirty-two is the murder weapon, then Cain had to take it off him and empty it into him without Comstock returning fire."

Joe nodded toward the gin bottle on the table. "I figure Comstock was drunk. And I'm betting toxicology will bear me out. Cain either got the drop on him, or there's the possibility that Comstock fell asleep. How's that for cold? Shoot a sleeping man to death."

"Let's not get too far ahead of ourselves," Claire said. "We don't even know the thirty-two did the deed. Maybe Comstock emptied it, defending himself."

Joe snorted. "Look at the weaponry around here. You telling me if someone came gunning for you, you'd use the pop gun?"

"Probably not," Claire had to admit. She hated it when Joe was right. Luckily, it was a rare occurrence. "But let's have the lab do its work before we jump to any conclusions. You got people talking to the neighbors?"

"Well," Joe said, "there's nobody real close."

"Let's talk to them anyway. We need to—"

Claire, turning toward the house, stopped in midsentence.

Jane Comstock had walked out onto the deck. Claire had never met the woman, but she recognized her, having seen her almost daily on the TV news during Comstock's trial, accompanying her husband to and from the courtroom. She stood staring at the body, her hand on the doorjamb for support. Her bottom lip was trembling just slightly; other than that, she appeared pretty well composed. After several moments, she exhaled sharply, almost involuntarily, and then turned and went into the house.

"Canvass the neighborhood," Claire said to Joe, and she went inside.

She found Jane Comstock sitting on a leather couch in a front room, a telephone receiver in her hand. Claire sat across from her and introduced herself. She was suddenly aware that she was still wearing the latex gloves. She took them off and tucked them in her coat pocket.

"I should call somebody, but I can't think," Jane said.

"Do you guys have kids?"

"We didn't, no," she said. "But you're right. I need to call Gracie. Of course."

"Who's Gracie?" Claire asked.

"Alan's daughter. She's in Arizona."

Jane punched in the number. Claire could hear ringing on the other end and then the sound of the voice mail greeting.

"Gracie, it's Jane. Call me right away. It's important." Jane hung up and looked apologetically at Claire. "I couldn't very well tell her machine that her father—"

"No, of course not."

"And I need to call Walter," Jane decided, her brain beginning to work. "He's our lawyer. Wait a minute—where's the bodyguard? What's he saying?"

"What bodyguard?"

"We hired someone yesterday. Well, Walter did. Something Black . . . Security. They sent a guy out. He was here yesterday when I left for the city. Derek, I think."

"Can you call Walter?" Claire said, getting up. "I'll be right back."

She walked outside to where Joe was now talking to a couple of uniforms.

"This guy is beginning to piss me off," Joe was saying. "This doesn't happen—not on my watch."

"We need to take a good look around the grounds," Claire said. "There was a bodyguard here with Comstock."

"Christ, he killed him too?" Joe said.

Claire ignored him, turned to the uniforms. "Let's have a look, okay?"

When she got back to the living room, Jane was hanging up the phone.

"Walter's going to call the company. It's Black Walnut Security."

"Okay," Claire said. She took a pad from her pocket. "What time did you leave yesterday?"

"Around five."

"Alone?"

"With a friend. Suzanne Boddington."

It seemed the name Boddington kept popping up. Yesterday Mary Nelson had mentioned it. "You hired the bodyguard just yesterday? Is that what you said?"

"Yes."

"Why?"

"Because we heard that this Cain had escaped. Alan was . . . Alan was losing it, to tell you the truth."

"Yeah, I noticed all the guns," Claire said. "Did he talk to the police?"

"They offered to send somebody but he wouldn't have it. He, um . . . he was not a fan of your department. That's Brady outside, right? He was not a fan of his."

"So you decided to hire somebody private."

"Yeah. It was Walter's idea. I wasn't going to leave if we hadn't. The guy was very professional. Checked out the grounds and all the entrances. He was armed with . . . whatever they carry."

"What did you do in the city?"

"Dinner and the theater."

"What did you see?" Claire wanted to keep her talking, thinking it would help her.

"The Tennessee Williams revival. What's it called? Shit, what's wrong with me?"

Somebody just killed your husband, Claire thought. That's what's wrong with you. "*The Rose Tattoo*?"

"Yes, that's it. Have you seen it?"

"No. The reviews were good."

The phone rang then and Jane answered. She listened for maybe thirty seconds, frowning. "I don't understand," she said. "Can you talk to the police, Walter?"

Claire took the phone. "Claire Marchand."

"This is Walter Monroe." One of those voices, Claire thought at once. Disdainful and dismissive. Not a criminal lawyer. Criminal lawyers were invariably accommodating and forthcoming, especially early in the game, hoping to get something in return. "Okay, I'm operating in the fog here," the voice went on. "First of all, is Alan Comstock dead?"

"Yes."

"Do you guys have this man Cain in custody or not?"

"Do we have him in custody? No."

"Then what in blazes is going on? I just got off the phone with Black Walnut. Their guy was out there last night. On the job. At around midnight Alan received a phone call. He got off the phone and told the bodyguard that the cops had just picked Cain up. And so Alan sent the guy home."

"Did he say who made the call?"

"Did Alan say who made the call? I have no idea. Keep in mind that I have been on this for less than ten minutes. I didn't talk to the man himself. This was in his report."

Claire was writing on the pad. "You got a number for Black Walnut?"

The lawyer gave her the information. "Just to be perfectly clear on this," he said, "you do not have Virgil Cain in custody at this time?"

"No."

"But you had him in custody."

"Yeah. We did."

"And if he were still in custody, then my friend Alan Comstock would still be alive this morning. Is that correct?"

"That would be speculation on my part, Mr. Monroe. You've heard of due process, right?"

"Yeah, and I've heard of police incompetency too. I want to talk to Jane again."

Claire handed the phone back to Jane and left her alone to talk. She went outside to deliver the news that the bodyguard had been accounted for. Comstock's body was bagged now, and they were loading it into the wagon. Joe was overseeing.

"Well, I'm going to go talk to the security guard," Claire said.

"Ask him if he spotted a green Jeep anywhere in the area when he was leaving," Joe told her.

"Should I ask him about other suspicious vehicles too—or just the Jeep?" Claire asked.

"Ask whatever you want," Joe said. "We both know it was Cain."

"No," Claire said. "We both don't."

Driving away from the house she saw a man a couple hundred yards away, cutting the grass alongside his paved drive with an electric trimmer. She stopped to talk to him briefly. He hadn't seen anything the night before.

Black Walnut Security was located on Washington Avenue in Kingston. Claire called on the way and when she arrived, the guard, whose name was Derek James, was waiting for her, alone in an office just inside the front door. When Claire walked in, he stood and politely introduced himself. He was a big man, black, with his hair razored short. He had a very soft voice and was holding a notebook.

"I never had a job like that before," he told Claire. "I get there, the man's all Rambo-ed up like he's in a movie. Shotguns and assault weapons, revolvers, semis. I'm like, 'What do you need me for?'"

"So what did you do while you were there?"

"Most of the time, just sat out on the deck. He was shooting targets, all these sheets of plywood set up behind the house. Wanted me to join in. I kept telling him, 'I fire my weapon, I have to fill out a report.' So then he says I can shoot his guns. I'm, like, 'I'll pass.' All the time, he's talking in clichés. 'Back to the wall.' 'Where the bullet meets the bone,' stuff like that."

"Was he drinking?"

"Oh yeah. Gin and tonics, lots of gin and tonics."

"Do you remember him having a thirty-two caliber Smith & Wesson? Nickel plated?"

"Yeah, he had one of them. I kept trying to get him to move inside, especially after it got dark. But he was all 'No, this is where I make my stand. Like the Alamo,' he said. I wanted to remind him how that turned out."

"But you didn't."

"No. The client is always right."

"Tell me about the phone call."

"There were two calls." At this point Derek looked at the notebook. "First one was from his wife. At ten thirty-five. I wrote it down. He went into the kitchen to answer and talked to her for maybe five minutes."

"How did you know it was his wife?"

"He told me when he came out. Said she just got out of a show down in the city and she was calling to check in."

"What about the second call?"

"It came at twelve fourteen. He went in and answered the phone and like a minute later he walks out and says I can go. They just picked Cain up."

"Who called to tell him?"

"He didn't say and I didn't ask. Never occurred to me, you know? I just assumed it was you guys."

"So you left?"

"The guy you're working for tells you to go, you go."

"Did you see any vehicles on the road on your way out?"

"Not a one. I remember thinking how nice and quiet it was out there in the country. Be nice to live out there."

Claire stood up. "I'll probably want to talk to you again. Can I get a copy of your report?"

"I don't think that's a problem," Derek said. "Hey, I feel like shit about this. I was supposed to protect the guy."

"You did your job."

"It doesn't feel like it. Not when you get this kind of news."

When Claire got back to the station it was midafternoon. She'd grabbed a sandwich and a coffee on her way and now sat at her desk, eating while she checked her messages and e-mails. There had been no reported sightings of Virgil Cain, or the Jeep.

She called the phone company and asked for Comstock's phone records, incoming and outgoing. They said she would have them in the morning.

She leaned back and looked at the map on the wall as she sipped her coffee. Whether or not Cain had been at the Comstock house wreaking havoc, he would have been on the road since daylight, at the latest. Eight, nine hours. Maybe more. He could be holed up in Boston. Or New York City. Shit, eight hours, he could be halfway to Florida.

Claire was pretty sure he wasn't in any of those places, though. Claire was pretty sure he was heading north.

Joe Brady came in late in the afternoon, striding through the doors like a general arriving at the scene of a battle. His shirt was stained with sweat and his tie was in his pocket. He carried his suit jacket under his arm. He saw Claire at her desk and walked over.

"What have we got?" he demanded.

"What have *we* got?" she asked. "We've got a major league cluster fuck. Who did you have watching his farm?"

"It wasn't a priority. He was on the other side of the river."

"*Was* on the other side of the river."

She could tell Joe was not impressed by her tone. Generals didn't get spoken to that way. He glanced around, to see who was within earshot. "I knew he was a flight risk. Right from the start, I knew it."

He was like a dog, begging for approval. "You were right about that, Joe," Claire told him.

"And how do we know he even went back to the farm?" he asked.

"He took the Jeep, Joe. For fuck's sake."

"How do we know that for sure?" he asked. "He said something the day we picked him up about some punks casing the place, after the vehicle. There was a woman there, he told her to hide the car in the barn. Maybe the punks stole it."

"If they did, they took his passport and Visa card."

"You saying that's not possible?"

"I'm saying it's not likely. I don't see two punks breaking into a house wrapped with police tape."

135

Joe walked to his desk and draped his jacket over the chair. He sat down and after a moment turned to Claire.

"All I'm saying is that nobody around the Comstock place saw a Jeep." He paused for effect. "But the woman next door heard gunshots."

"When?" Claire asked.

"She couldn't put a time on it. Late, though."

"I talked to a neighbor who heard gunshots too," Claire said.

"You did?" Joe perked up.

"He heard them last night," Claire said. "And he heard them yesterday afternoon. And the day before that. And the week before that. In fact, he couldn't say for sure when the last day was that he *didn't* hear gunshots. Comstock was a gun nut."

Joe got up and said he was going for a coffee. When he came back he went to his desk and drank it in silence. Sulking now.

Visa called half an hour later. Cain had used the card at a gas station in Saranac Lake at eight o'clock that morning. Thirty-four dollars' worth of gas and a sandwich to go. There had been no other purchases on the card since.

"Headed for the border," Joe said when Claire told him. "Like I said."

"He's not exactly trying to hide it," Claire said. "Using the card."

"I keep telling you he's not too bright," Joe said. "And he's got no cash. We have his wallet, remember?"

But he does have cash, Claire thought. Why wouldn't he use it instead of the card? She was deciding whether to burden Joe with the information about the five hundred when the phone rang.

It was the police upstate. They had just found the Jeep, parked in a grove of trees on the Mohawk Reserve on the south shore of the St. Lawrence River, across from the Ontario town of Cornwall. The officer reported that the keys were in the ignition, the tank half-full. The vehicle was less than a mile from the river.

"Well, he's in Canada now," Joe said. "Just like I said."

Claire was getting tired of hearing about how right Joe was, albeit always in hindsight. Funny how he was throwing a perfect game and yet their side was getting pounded. But something else was bothering her. It was how Cain was running. He could have paid cash for the gasoline. And he could have hidden the Jeep in the deep woods anywhere along the river. He was acting precisely the way he'd acted the day before when he had crossed the Hudson and then doubled back. He wanted them to know where he was, right up until he didn't want them to know.

"No way he could have used his passport to cross," she said. "I put out the alarm yesterday morning. So if he's in Canada, how did he get across?"

"My guess is he would've stole another boat," Joe said. "Crossed at night."

"He hasn't been there at night. He bought gas in Saranac Lake this morning."

"I say he's in Canada," Joe insisted. "It's time to get the Mounties involved."

Claire stretched and stood up. "Let's do that. But check with state police up there to see if anybody's reported a stolen boat."

"The Mounties will get him," Joe said. "He's one of theirs."

"Yeah," Claire said. "They probably have some special insight on how a Canadian thinks." She started for the door.

"Where are you going?"

"Home. Then I'm meeting someone for dinner."

"Gosh. You going on a date, Claire?"

"I don't date," she said, and she left.

FIFTEEN

Claire had a date with Peter Vandervilt. It was a second date; the first one was exactly a week ago. That night he had picked her up at home and taken her to a very good restaurant in Rhinebeck, across the river. They had shared a whole chicken stuffed with truffles and wild leeks. Peter was a Realtor who apparently made a lot of money, and he was one of those guys who liked to spend money, but to spend it—well, *properly*—as he phrased it. He had a Lexus, and a place in Saratoga, and a nice home in Kingston. There was an ex-wife and a couple of kids in the mix somewhere, but Claire wasn't quite certain where. She didn't ask about them.

The first date had gone all right, but there had been nothing particularly earthshaking about it. Not that Claire was looking for—or believed in—earthshaking anyway. She liked the food and the wine and being treated nicely. Peter talked a lot, about a lot of different things. He knew everything about cars, and finance, and a bunch of other stuff, like fly-fishing in Alaska. Claire knew nothing of any of those things but enjoyed his enthusiasm when he talked about them. He was very much alive, in a way that most fifty-year-olds she knew were not.

Peter was tall, at least six two, with very good hair and a nice body. He worked out, of course, and was into some martial arts discipline Claire had never heard of. When he dropped her off, he kissed her on the cheek and said he would call her. She'd had a nice time but, getting out of the car, really didn't feel one way or the other about seeing him again.

Then, when he didn't call after a few days, she began to wonder why. A couple days more, and she wanted him to call. She suspected that she wanted him to call just because he hadn't and that pissed her off. She had been single now for a year, and before that she had not been single for almost twenty years. Apparently she didn't know how the game was played anymore.

So when he called, it made her happy.

He was driving back from New York so she said she would meet him at the restaurant, a Japanese place downtown. Things went very much the way they had on the first date, although at some point it occurred to her that Peter was a guy who needed to be constantly enthralled by something. Tonight that thing was his new BlackBerry, which he'd bought that afternoon. Apparently he was one of the first hundred people in the world to own this new model, although Claire had to wonder if that ego-stroking assurance could in any way be verified.

"My guy says this thing will do everything except remove your appendix," Peter said.

By the time dessert arrived, Claire was focusing on the fact that Peter had not, over the course of roughly a date and a half, asked her a single question about herself. Not about her job, or her family, or anything.

He hadn't even asked where she was from.

She was still thinking about it, and wondering at what point she might become the thing that enthralled him, when she heard herself tell him that she'd had a long day attempting to track down a man who had escaped from custody, and that she thought she should head home. Peter didn't ask about the escapee but did suggest she could use a back rub, an art in which he apparently excelled. Claire begged off, citing fatigue.

She attempted to pay for dinner but he wouldn't hear of it. He actually seemed angry that she even made the suggestion. He paid, mentioning that he always tipped twenty percent, and then walked her to her car. This time he attempted to kiss her on the mouth. She turned her head at the last second and felt his thin lips brush hers lightly. He said he would call her.

When she got home, she wasn't in the least bit tired. She poured herself a glass of red wine and had a long bath, drinking the wine in the tub as she thought about what she had to do the following day. First off, she needed to go see Buddy Townes. After that she wasn't sure, but it might just depend on what Buddy had to say. She was hoping he knew something that the police didn't. Which wouldn't have to be much, at this point.

When she climbed into bed, it was just past eleven. She was trying to read Virginia Woolf again but it wasn't going well. Claire suspected that the difficulty had more to do with herself than with Ms. Woolf. She'd had no problem during high school. Woolf provided angst and soul-searching, and for Claire, a typically insecure teenager in a new school, in a new town, those things were just what the doctor ordered. It wasn't until she was older that she realized virtually everybody went through a period in their lives when they tried to decide just where they fit in to the grand scheme of things. Some people never did figure it out.

She fell asleep with *To the Lighthouse* on the pillow beside her. When the phone woke her, she knocked the book from the bed, blindly reaching for the receiver in the dark. She glanced at the clock; it was eight minutes after midnight.

"Yeah," she said.

"Are you alone?"

It was a stranger's voice. Or, at least, it wasn't a voice she could recall at once, although there was something vaguely familiar there, in the tone more than anything.

"Who is this?"

"Tell me if you're alone. I need to talk to you."

The voice was deep, and bordering on laconic. Almost too laid-back, given the hour and the odd request. And then Claire sat up straight, realizing who it was. She looked over at the call display on the phone cradle. Call blocked. She took a moment to reply, and when she did she attempted to match his nonchalant tone.

"Mr. Cain," she said. "I am alone. I was just sitting here, waiting for your call."

"A lot of fumbling with the receiver, for somebody expecting a call."

"I was excited to hear from you."

"You were sleeping."

"Actually, I was reading in bed. So where are you?"

"Well, I'm not in jail."

"Can you be a little more specific?"

"No."

"I didn't think so. What do you want to talk about, Virgil? Is it okay if I call you Virgil?"

"Yup."

"You can call me Claire."

"Oh boy."

There was some noise in the background, what sounded like a chair or a table, scraping across a floor. Faint voices. Claire strained to hear.

"What was it you wanted to say?" she asked.

"I saw your fat little buddy Brady on the eleven o'clock news. He was talking about me. He's kind of suggesting that I killed

Alan Comstock last night. Well, not really suggesting. Apparently I'm wanted for the murder of Alan Comstock?"

"You're wanted for questioning in the Comstock murder," Claire said. "But you do recall that you've also been charged with the murder of Mickey Dupree. And then there's the matter of you escaping custody."

"Well, one out of three ain't bad," Virgil said. "Do you play baseball?"

"What do you mean?"

"I mean—do you play the game of baseball? One out of three is a .333 average."

"I know that. What are you talking about?"

"I escaped custody, but I didn't kill either one of those guys."

"Oh, one out of three," Claire said, finally getting the reference. "Well, the only way this is going to turn out well for you, Virgil, is if you surrender yourself and let these matters go before the court. At this point nobody is saying you are guilty of anything. That has to be proven in a court of law."

"You telling me that your buddy Brady hasn't already made up his mind? He's a little on the judgmental side, isn't he?"

Claire wished he would stop referring to Joe Brady as her buddy. She was wondering how to trace the call and then it came to her. She got up and went to the bureau where her badge and her Beretta and her cell phone were. She opened the phone and scrolled down to Marina's cell number, trying to remember her schedule. She had said something about working the midnight shift.

"What's with that guy anyway?" Virgil asked. "Don't you guys have some sort of intelligence tests you have to take before you become a cop?"

"I don't know that you're in any position to be questioning anyone's intelligence," Claire said. "All you've been up to." She kept her tone light, trying to joke with him, needing to keep him talking. She typed the message on her phone.

u there? i'm on home phone need a trace 845-445-5567

"Where are you anyway? Montreal? Toronto maybe?"

"I can't remember."

Claire smiled. "You're not lost, are you?"

"What was it that Davy Crockett said? 'I've never been lost in my life, but I was confused once for three days.'"

"I have a feeling you're not even a little confused," Claire said. "But what do you intend to accomplish out there on the run?"

"What do I intend to accomplish? That's why we're having this little talk. Now anybody who can turn on a TV knows that I'm a mad-dog killer, out there shooting folks and stabbing people with golf clubs and all that. But what if you were to pretend for a few minutes that I didn't do these things? What would you do then?"

"Try to find the person that did." Claire walked to the window and looked out. There was a half moon, a cloudless sky.

"Let's stay with that a minute. How would you do that?"

"Pardon?"

"How would you approach this thing?" Virgil asked. "I mean, there's obviously some common ground between Dupree and Comstock. That is, if the same person killed them both. But maybe it wasn't the same person. You ever think of that?"

"I have," Claire said. "You may not believe it, but I have imagined all kinds of scenarios regarding the two murders. I've considered the possibility that maybe you killed Mickey Dupree and then somebody else shot Comstock, knowing you'd be blamed."

"Well, you're half right. The second half."

"I have a suggestion for you. Why don't you come in and take a polygraph?"

"Well," Virgil said, then he hesitated. "There's a part of that plan I don't like."

"Which part?"

"The coming in part."

"The Canadian police are on your trail. They'll track you down and extradite you."

"Maybe."

"No maybe about it," Claire said. "When was the last time you heard of somebody escaping custody and not getting caught?"

"Ronald Biggs."

"Ronald Biggs," she repeated. "When was that—fifty years ago? Modern police methods are a little more advanced these days. And you're not in Brazil. So what do you want me to do while I'm waiting for the Mounties to pick you up?"

"Tell me you'll try to find out who killed these guys. Do your job."

"I always do my job." Claire waited for him to argue the point and was oddly disappointed when he didn't. "Why are you calling me if you're convinced I'm incompetent? Why not call Joe Brady?"

"Joe Brady is a fucking half-wit."

"Now *that* is judgmental."

"Besides, you got better legs."

That stopped her cold. Turning from the window, she caught a glimpse of herself in the mirror and saw that she was smiling like an idiot. What the hell was that?

"You were kinda pissed at Brady," he continued. "When you were interrogating me. There was something going on there."

"No. There wasn't."

"Yeah. There was."

She hesitated, and when she did, she was sure she heard a

voice in the background. A shout of some kind, like someone saying hello. Keep it going, she thought. Don't spook him and have him hang up.

"I thought he jumped the gun a little bit," she said. "With the arrest."

"How do you think I felt? How long you been a cop?"

"Twenty-two years."

"Really? So you signed up when you were what—eighteen?"

"Close. You have a silver tongue, Mr. Cain."

"Where are you from anyway?"

Shit, she thought. Why would *he* be the one to ask that? The handsome real estate mogul with the new Lexus and the cool homes and the BlackBerry from the future doesn't ask, but the escaped killer does.

"Lowell, Maine. Why do you want to know that?"

"Hey, you know all about me. Can't I ask a question about you?"

"But I don't know all about you." Her cell beeped then and she clamped her hand over the receiver, wondering if he had heard. She picked it up, read the text.

on it—m

"What was that?" Virgil asked.

"Setting my alarm," she told him. "I have to get up in the morning and do some investigating, so you won't think badly of me." She realized that the phony explanation might sound as if she wanted to end the call, so she kept talking. "I was saying—I don't know anything about you. What was the deal in Quebec? The guy you beat up. Why'd you do it?"

She could hear him exhale heavily, as if in deliberation. "He swindled a friend of mine. Took advantage of her and cheated her out of her property."

"Girlfriend?"

"No."

"So why didn't he go to jail?"

"He's rich. Sometimes rich people get away with stuff."

"You referring to Alan Comstock now?"

"Nope. But it occurred to you quick enough."

"Do you think he killed your wife?"

"I don't know what happened that night," Virgil said. "And if he's dead, there's nobody alive who does know. So that's that."

Claire put her cell on vibrate. Carrying it in her free hand, she walked over and sat in the wingback chair by the window. "Can I ask you something?" she said. "How was your marriage anyway?"

"Why?"

"Because. I was in your house. It kinda looks like you guys had separate rooms."

He was quiet for a few moments and she thought she'd gone too far. "Why would that matter now?" he finally asked.

"Just wondering. I mean, if you guys weren't getting along, the argument could be made that you would be less likely to start killing people in a grief-stricken rage."

"Well, I'm not in a rage, and I haven't killed anybody. So I really don't have to make that argument."

"But you will have to eventually. Once they bring you back."

"I forgot, I got Joe Brady on my trail. I got a feeling that boy couldn't track an elephant through a foot of snow." He hesitated again. Claire listened to his breathing. He didn't seem to be hurried in the least. "Tell you what," he said, "I'll make you a deal. I'll give you some details on my marriage if you tell me you'll try to find out who killed Dupree and Comstock."

"I intend to do that either way. You don't seem to have a lot of faith in me, Virgil."

"Hey, I want to have faith in you," he assured her. "You

might be all I got." She could sense his hesitation. "As far as my marriage goes, I guess I can tell you the truth. Doesn't much matter now anyway. A few months after Tom Stempler died—that's Kirstie's father—the immigration people came snooping around. Somebody dropped a dime on me, being here without a work visa or anything. There was a developer trying to buy the place and I suspect it might have been him but I don't know that for certain. I was running the place pretty much on my own. Kirstie was living there, chasing her music. But she wouldn't sell the family farm. I applied for a green card and got turned down, so one day she just said, let's get married. So we did. End of problem."

"So you were married on paper only? So you could stay in the country?"

"That's it. You gonna add another charge to me?"

"Your plate's pretty full as it is."

"No shit."

"So," Claire said, wondering why she was pushing it. "It wasn't a real marriage, it was just a thing of convenience." She paused but couldn't help herself. "You guys weren't ever sleeping together or anything . . . um, like that?"

"You need a real marriage for that?" Virgil asked. "I don't want to shock you, but I have slept with women I wasn't even a little bit married to. Where is Lowell, Maine—somewhere in the 1800s?"

"All right. I deserved that."

"Wasn't Kerouac from Lowell?"

"He was. Do you read Kerouac?"

"I read *On the Road* when I was a kid. Like everybody else."

"My grandmother knew his mother a little. They went to mass together."

"You a Catholic?"

"Lapsed. What about you?"

"I'm nothing," Virgil said. "Other than somebody in a lot of shit. Tell me how you're going to go about this. Comstock had to have enemies and I would imagine there's a lot of people who held a grudge against Dupree."

"I'd say you're right. And I intend to start tracking them down. I'm a few steps behind on this because the guy we had in custody broke out of jail and threw a monkey wrench into everything."

Virgil ignored the shot. "You going to talk to Buddy Townes?"

Claire was quiet for a moment. "What do you know about Buddy?"

"I heard he might be a good guy to talk to. Who is he?"

Claire hesitated a moment longer. "Buddy Townes was Dupree's private investigator, his go-to guy. He's an ex-cop, lost his shield for drinking and doping, all that shit you see movie cops doing. Sometimes real cops do it too."

"You'll be talking to him?"

"I suspect I will."

"Good. What else?"

"Well, it would be very nice for you if we could turn up some physical evidence placing somebody else at either murder scene."

"You don't have any physical evidence putting me there."

"How do you know that?"

"Because I wasn't there. Remember?"

"I haven't decided one way or the other on that, Mr. Cain."

She heard a rapping sound, like knuckles on glass. "Somebody at your door?" she asked. She opened her cell and checked for a text. Come on, Marina.

"All right," he said. "I have to go."

Claire got up and walked over to sit on the edge of the bed. "Oh, come on. I'm not tired yet."

"You're back in bed, though. I just heard it."

"I am back in bed." She was afraid he would hang up. "Is this where you ask me what I'm wearing?"

"I know what you're wearing."

"Oh yeah?"

"Sure. Girl like you—T-shirt and panties. Probably some logo on the shirt—Yankees or Giants or something."

"Not even close," she told him. She looked at herself in the mirror, at her pink panties and her Mets T-shirt. Sonofabitch.

"I'll be in touch," Virgil said.

"Wait," she said. "What if—what if I find something? I'll need to get in touch with you."

"Nice try," he said, laughing, and he hung up.

She listened for a few seconds but he was gone. As soon as she hung up the phone, she felt her cell buzz. She looked at the screen.

got it

She called the station and Marina answered on the first ring.

"You'd better not tell me it came from Brazil," Claire said.

"Did you say Brazil?"

"Never mind. What have you got?"

"You know the Broadway Lights Diner?" Marina said.

"No. The only Broadway Diner I know is here in Kingston."

"That's it."

"What?"

"That's where the call came from. A pay phone at the diner."

"What the fuck? That place is a few blocks from my house."

"That's where the call came from."

Claire got up and walked to the window. The Broadway

Lights Diner was a retro roadhouse, all vinyl and chrome and Wurlitzer jukeboxes. She could almost *see* it from her window. A diner. That explained the background noises.

"You there?" Marina asked.

"Yeah."

"What's going on? Who was on the line?"

Claire thought about it for a moment. To tell Marina was to inform the department. Which meant Joe Brady. She was pretty sure the only way she would be able to keep talking with Virgil Cain would be to do it in confidence.

"Nobody," she said. "Some guy asking me what I was wearing."

"Ew—one of them."

"Yeah. One of them. Thanks, Marina."

She hung up the phone and pulled on jeans and a sweatshirt and headed downstairs. It was going to be an exercise in futility but she had to go anyway.

When she got to the diner, the place was surprisingly busy, the after-bar crowd stopping in for burgers and fries. Driving there, she recalled there were three old-style phone booths in a row at the back of the place, glassed-in, with dial phones. Local calls were free. The booths were all empty when she walked in.

She talked to the waitstaff and a few customers. Some of them remembered a man using the phone, some didn't. Some remembered what he looked like, others had no idea. No two people remembered the same. It didn't matter.

Claire knew exactly what he looked like.

She walked outside and stood on the sidewalk, imagining which way he would have gone. It was only a half-dozen blocks to the highway and then beyond that was the forest. If she had to guess, she would say that's where he went. Unless he'd gotten a vehicle someplace. She could call canine but it would be next to impossible to pick up his trail, with all the pedestrian traffic in the area. She headed home, resigned to the fact she would have to let him go for now.

But she was buoyed by the knowledge that, apparently, he wasn't going very far.

SIXTEEN

When Virgil left the diner, it was just filling up. College kids, most of them three sheets to the wind, rowdy and raucous, talking trash back and forth across the restaurant. Virgil slipped out a side door and headed west out of town. He crossed the thruway a few hundred yards before the tollgate and walked along Route 28, staying mostly on the shoulder and hunkering down in a ditch whenever cars passed.

A mile or so along he angled to the north, crossing a hay field in the moonlight. He was taking a shortcut version of the route he normally traveled when he drove back to the farm from Kingston. He wasn't particularly worried about pursuit; it was evident from his conversation with Claire Marchand that the cops were convinced he'd left the country.

Good thing, because she'd kept him talking longer than he intended. All he really wanted to know was whether there was somebody involved in the investigation who hadn't already convicted him. But then she'd started talking about other things, personal things, and pretty soon Virgil was thinking about her legs, and her full mouth, and those eyes, intelligent and quick but with something else there, something guarded and wary. He'd seen that quality in horses before, horses that had been treated badly. It took a while to get close to them. Sometimes it couldn't be done.

She'd wanted to know about his marriage. What did that have to do with the murders? Once or twice during the conversation it had occurred to him that she was trying to keep him on the line long enough to get a trace. But that wasn't possible. She would have had to set it up beforehand, or during the call, and how could she have?

At least he had her word that she would look at other suspects. Whatever her word was worth. Of course, what else would she tell him? But he had a sense that she was being straight with him. And, if nothing else, she'd verified that the man named Buddy Townes was somebody who might know something.

He reached the back road that ran behind the farm in a couple of hours. He climbed the boundary fence and moved into the back pasture, where his cattle were settled for the night, herded up between the pond and the woods. He walked alongside the fence line and took a quick head count. He'd never lost a steer in the past, but with the news of him being on the run it was possible somebody decided there was free beef for the taking. The herd was intact, though.

Keeping to the fencerow along the lane, he made his way up behind the barn, where he stopped to watch the house and the road out front for thirty minutes. When he had arrived at the same spot two nights earlier, he'd waited there for more than an hour, until he was reasonably certain nobody was watching the place. It had been easy to take the Jeep and drive away unnoticed. And if there was no surveillance before, there would be none now. Virgil Cain was in Canada.

He walked around the barn and stopped to look at the horses in the front pasture field. They were standing sleeping beneath the big maple tree along the lane. Virgil could see that the skinny mare was among the bunch, apparently having settled in.

Virgil approached the house cautiously. He had discovered

the police lock the last time, and so he went in through the basement window, as he had then. It was pitch-black in the house but he couldn't risk a light. He went upstairs and into the bathroom, stripped down, and took a long shower. Getting out, he decided not to shave. For one, it was a tricky business in the dark, and two, a beard might be a good idea, given his circumstances.

When he walked into his bedroom for some clean clothes, he remembered that the woman—Claire—had confessed to being there. He stood quietly for a moment, imagining he could smell her perfume. Did she even wear perfume, or something of the sort? At work? Probably not, but he thought he could detect something.

He knew he needed to get his mind off the sexy cop and on to keeping himself out of her reach. Because all she wanted to do was lock him up.

He got dressed and went downstairs. He was suddenly tired. The only sleep he'd had in the past thirty-six hours was the nap he'd taken in the cab of the tractor trailer he'd hitched a ride with, heading south from the border area after ditching the Jeep. He'd approached the driver at a truck stop parking lot and convinced him that his old pickup had given up the ghost and that he would lose his job at a chicken farm near Saugerties if he didn't make it back there by morning. The driver was not the suspicious type, and, besides, anyone out looking for Virgil would not have considered his heading back to the scene.

He decided not to risk sleeping in the house. He went into a cupboard beneath the basement stairs and found an old sleeping bag. He pulled on a jacket and went up to the kitchen, risking the refrigerator light long enough to grab four eggs and a half-pound of bacon. He took down a frying pan from a hook above the stove. After putting everything in a canvas bag he remembered matches. He no longer had his lighter, having tossed the broken pieces in the Hudson after slipping the jail in Kesselberg. It took him a while, operating in the dark, but he finally found a pack. On his way out, he took down a pair of binoculars from a hook by the back door and put them in the bag.

Walking past the south end of the barn, he smelled fresh hay. He went inside and saw two full wagons parked in the runway. He went up the ladder, and where the moonlight showed through the cracks between the barn boards he saw that the north mow was half-full of freshly baled timothy from the field he had cut three days earlier. Three days. It seemed to Virgil he had traveled a thousand miles in that time. He pulled a handful of hay from a bale and held it to his nose, smelled the sweet, pungent aroma.

"Mary Nelson," he said. "Aiding and abetting."

He went out through the barnyard and retraced his steps to the woods. It was probably four o'clock or so, he guessed, when he got there. Dawn wasn't far away. Virgil found a spot along the edge of the woods and spread out the sleeping bag on the ground. Hungry as he was, he wouldn't risk a fire until daylight. He was too tired to cook anyway. He stretched out inside the sleeping bag and was asleep in minutes.

Suzanne showed up around five o'clock in the afternoon and persuaded Jane to come home with her. Jane had spent the previous few hours wandering around, occasionally talking to the cops and to Walter, who arrived shortly after noon with a platter of sandwiches and coffee from a local deli. Jane was not in the mood to eat. She offered the sandwiches to the cops and the forensics people and they cleaned them up with little encouragement.

The CSI unit was there all afternoon. There was a considerable amount of blood on the deck. Jane wanted to hire someone right away to come in and clean up but was told she wouldn't be able to do so for a couple of days at least. The unit placed yellow tape around the deck. A woman named Julie informed her that they intended to dust the entire house for fingerprints, a massive task given the size of the place.

"What makes you think the guy was in the house?" Jane asked.

"We don't, necessarily," the woman replied. "But we can't not do it. I also need you to check for any missing items. Jewelry, cash, credit cards. Passports. Anything at all."

Walter stayed with her while she went from room to room.

"I'm supposed to look for things that are no longer here," she told him. "There's something contradictory about that."

The search turned up nothing and they ended up in the sitting room. Jane felt suddenly light-headed and she stretched out on the sofa. Walter stood by the window, looking down at the police van in the drive.

"Our esteemed police force has a lot to answer for," he said. "They had this guy and he made monkeys out of them."

"You really think it was him? The guy that killed Mickey Dupree?"

"Who else would it be? Who else had a grudge against Alan?"

"Come on, Walter. A lot of people. Two days ago he was in a screaming match with that French kid's manager."

"I doubt the man would shoot somebody for calling him a fucking frog. No, I'm afraid it was this Cain. The cops are going to have a tough time explaining this one away. The irony is, maybe for the first time in his life Alan actually does have a legitimate reason to sue somebody. And he's not here to do it."

He turned to look at Jane. She had her eyes closed and it

seemed she hadn't heard him. He walked over and sat down in a chair beside the sofa.

"You okay?"

She spoke without opening her eyes. "Yeah. The whole thing is so surreal. I was thinking earlier—you hear about stuff like this on the news and you wonder how people handle it. I don't think you do handle it, though. It just kind of picks you up and carries you along." She sat up then, eyes open. "I need to go for a run."

"Maybe you should wait," Walter suggested. "Let the cops do their thing. They'd want to send somebody with you and I don't think that's what you want."

She nodded, seeing he was right. "Do you think this guy is done now?" she asked. "I mean, is there anybody else he thinks is responsible?"

"I'm holding out the naive hope that the police will actually arrest him again in the pretty near future. And maybe even find a way to *keep* him in jail this time. That's not asking too much, is it?"

"I don't know, Walter," Jane said. "I don't seem to know anything today."

When Suzanne arrived, Walter took it as an opportunity to leave. Jane watched the two of them talking on the lawn out front and when Suzanne came inside to announce they were going to her house, Jane assumed that she and Walter had conceived of the plan on the spot.

"What are you going to do—spend the night here alone?" Suzanne asked when Jane attempted to beg off.

"I've done it plenty of times."

"Not under these circumstances, you haven't. You throw some things in a bag and I'll tell the cops you're out of here."

"I'm not sure you can tell them I'm just leaving."

"Fuck them. They caused this mess."

Jane left her car there and rode with Suzanne to Bodding-ton Stables. Miller was still in California and the chef Henri was gone for the day. They sat in the Spanish-style kitchen and watched the sun go down as they picked at some cheese and crackers that Suzanne found. After a while Suzanne opened a bottle of good brandy and poured snifters for them both.

Suzanne never asked anything about the actual killing. She was not a details person. She knew that Alan had been shot, and, to her, that was all she needed to know. Who cared where, when, how many times? It wasn't as if she could undo the deed.

"Did he want to be cremated?" she asked. That was more of a Suzanne question. She'd been watching Jane in the chair staring blankly out the window.

"He never talked about it. I doubt he thought he would ever die."

"Then it's your call."

Jane nodded. "You know, I never really thought about it until this minute, but the only reason Alan would want a big funeral would be the chance to rant about the people who didn't bother to show up. And ridicule the people who did."

"He's going to hate to miss it."

Jane found herself smiling at that. "But no," she said after a moment. "I think something quiet is the way to go. I could scatter his ashes on the property. It was the one thing he loved unconditionally."

She took a drink and rotated the glass in her hands, looking at the liquor inside. "He does have his legacy, Suzanne. No mat-ter what else they'll say about him, he was a giant in his day. I mean, he created some great music."

"No question. Shit, I grew up on that stuff. And it'll all get revisited now. I daresay the *New York Times* will find reason to invoke the phrase 'musical genius.' Maybe Elton John can rewrite 'Candle In The Wind' one more time."

"Spare me that," Jane said. She took a drink of brandy and looked out at the fading light. "I have this weird feeling of . . . guilt. There have been times, you know, in recent years, that I actually thought I would be better off without him."

"Times you wished he was dead?"

Jane shook her head, as if to clear it, and then had another drink. "Have you ever thought that way?"

"About Miller?" Suzanne asked. "Two or three times a day on the average."

Jane laughed. "When is he coming home?"

"Tomorrow. Or so he says. That's one advantage I always had over you. He's gone at least half the time. Alan never left the house, other than to go to the studio."

"And that was pretty seldom," Jane said.

"Does he have any family? Isn't there a daughter somewhere?"

"There's a daughter. She basically hates him, but she cashes his check every month. She lives in Arizona, all that new-age nonsense, you know? She's an artist who never sells anything, so she struggles to get by on fifteen grand a month."

"Poor baby." Suzanne leaned forward to pour more brandy for them both. She was a little tipsy, and it occurred to Jane that she was probably that way when she drove over to pick her up.

"Did Miller buy his winery?" Jane asked.

"Yeah. Maybe two. He's talking about getting out of the horse game altogether." She hesitated. "I have a feeling he's going to want to move to the coast."

"He'd sell this place?"

"He'd better not try," Suzanne said. "He can go back and forth. Or just go. He has to get out from under these charges first. He's talking to a lawyer from out there about them. Now that Mickey's out of the picture. Miller was actually pretty upset about Mickey. They were kinda close, you know."

"I didn't know."

"Mickey liked the horses. He stayed in Saratoga with Miller last August. He basically cleared his schedule so he could do it. He bet big and he bet stupid, so he usually lost big."

"Well, he could afford it."

"I don't know how flush he was. He pissed a lot of it away. He was charging Miller a ton of money to defend him, especially when he didn't seem to be doing much defending. He had a private investigator on the case."

"Buddy Townes?"

"Yeah. How did you know?"

"He was on Alan's case too. He was Dupree's guy."

"Well, I'm pretty sure that Miller and Dupree argued about the money. Miller has a habit of not paying bills if he thinks he's being taken advantage of."

"Alan used to say that's how the rich stay rich."

"Maybe that's the problem with all these men. Too much money." Suzanne laughed and drained her glass. "But we wouldn't have it any other way, would we?"

Jane sat staring out the window and made no reply.

"Not to be blunt but there is a positive to take from this," Suzanne said.

Jane looked over. "Glad you're not being blunt."

"Fuck it," Suzanne replied. "Subtlety makes me crazy. I'm talking about Edie Bryant's seat in Washington. Alan was going to be a huge hindrance. You know that or you wouldn't have brought it up that day."

"Christ," Jane said. "I can't even think about that tonight. My brain is not functioning on that level. Right now, I don't even care about it."

"I'll think about it for you," Suzanne told her. "A grieving widow might make an appealing candidate. Especially one who runs marathons and has cool friends like me."

"Maybe you should run," Jane said.

"Not me," Suzanne snorted. "I have too many skeletons hidden away. Not to mention the unhidden one, flying home from the coast."

"Can we talk about it later?"

Suzanne smiled. "We can do whatever we want."

SEVENTEEN

Claire didn't sleep particularly well. She had brief disturbing dreams, one after another, and each time she woke she had trouble getting back to sleep. She didn't dream about Virgil Cain but couldn't help thinking about him while she was awake. She kept hearing his voice on the phone, his sardonic tone, his wit. He was an unusual man, joking, flirting even, in the face of the charges against him. And who the hell breaks out of jail and doesn't flee? On one hand, it suggested that maybe he really was innocent in these matters. Of course, if he was guilty, it meant that he was completely unhinged.

And if he was deranged, with two killings under his belt, what did that say about Claire, and the fact that she was looking forward to talking to him again?

In the early light of day, she put that out of her mind, attributing it to any number of things. To the late hour, to her disappointing date with Peter who couldn't bother to ask where she was from. To whatever. She got out of bed at half past seven, showered, and had a bowl of granola, then drove to the station.

The autopsy had been performed on Alan Comstock the night before. The six slugs taken from his body were indeed .32 caliber. The boys in ballistics would be testing the nickel-plated Smith & Wesson later that day to see if the slugs came from the gun, but already the smart money was on a match. There were no fingerprints on the thirty-two. It had been wiped meticulously clean; not even a partial print could be found. There were prints on the shell casings in the cylinder, but they proved to be Comstock's, as Claire had suspected. At the time of his death Comstock's blood alcohol level was three times the legal limit for driving. Specific cause of death was still unknown, as at least three of the bullet wounds could have proven fatal, depending on which had arrived first.

"But I think at this point we can rule out natural causes," Claire told Joe Brady when he came in a little after ten o'clock.

"Anything from the Canadians?" Joe asked.

"Nothing that I've heard," Claire said. "I'm pretty sure they haven't got him yet."

"Why are you so sure?"

"Women's intuition."

Joe gave her one of his impatient looks and headed for his desk.

"What have we got on Dupree so far?" Claire asked him.

"What do you mean?"

"What did forensics turn up? Any prints on the club or the golf cart?"

"The club that killed him? Nothing. All kinds of prints on the cart."

"Any of them belong to Virgil Cain?"

"No. Why would he touch the cart?"

"I don't know. What about the rake?"

"Same thing. Lots of prints. Who knows how many times it got used that day?"

"But none from Cain?"

"Who knows? There were prints on top of prints. Nothing you could match to any one person. I'm assuming he wore gloves anyway."

"Why are you assuming that?"

"Because we can't find his prints anywhere, Claire."

"All right," Claire said. "So what *do* we have putting him in the vicinity?"

"He was in Middletown a half hour earlier. Which makes it easy for him to show up at the seventh hole at the same time Dupree did. Or he was waiting for him. He must have known his routine. Dupree played there every Tuesday, we know that."

"Okay," Claire said. "How does he get from a gas station in Middletown to a sand trap on an exclusive golf course without anybody seeing him? He was driving a twenty-year-old pickup truck and from what I saw of the guy, I'm pretty sure he wasn't wearing Sansabelt slacks and a golf shirt. He would not have fit in with that crowd. Have we got anybody who saw him or his truck at the golf course?"

"Not yet."

"How about this?" Claire asked. "Whoever killed Dupree went through the park next to the course. He could have crossed that ravine on foot and scaled the fence to the grounds."

"Maybe," Joe said.

Claire sat tapping her pen against her teeth. "He would have to pay to get into the park. If it was Cain, they'd have a record, and his license plate."

Joe hesitated a moment. He was becoming perturbed, his color getting redder. Claire suddenly realized that he'd already considered what she was suggesting. "They don't have him driving in. But they say there's always a few people they let in for a short time for nothing. Parents dropping food off to kids camping, or somebody delivering medicine, shit like that. Or there's always a chance he parked outside the park and scaled the fence to get in. What the fuck are you doing here, Claire?"

"What am I doing? Well, while the Mounties are tracking Cain, I would like to find something of a physical nature to put him at the scene where Mickey Dupree bought it. Right now, you've got a semi-threat he made in a bar. A jury might just expect more."

"Yeah, that's all we got," Joe said sarcastically. "Oh yeah— that and the fact that he shot Dupree's client to death a couple days later. The client that walked away from killing Cain's wife. There is that little tidbit."

"Did he kill Alan Comstock?" Claire asked. "We have evidence placing him there?"

"It's a little early for that, Claire. The blood's not even dry yet. They'll find something. A hair, a print, something. He made a point of killing the man with the same gun that killed his wife. Who else would do that?"

"Somebody who wanted to make it look like Cain?"

"And who would that be?" Joe asked.

I have no idea, Claire admitted to herself. And if it didn't make sense for anybody else to have done the killing, then there was a pretty good chance Cain did it. But then why was he hanging around? What was in it for him? Maybe the phone conversation last night was another red herring. He wanted to put the notion in her head that he didn't do it, so she would start looking elsewhere. But why double back from the border to call her? He could have crossed and called her from Canada. Why was he still in the area and pretending he wasn't?

"Any reports of a stolen boat along the St. Lawrence?" she asked.

"Nothing," Joe said. "Oh, I'm sure he got across. The water's warm enough, he could have floated a log across."

Right, Claire thought. Or maybe he built an ark. Her desk phone rang and she picked it up. "Marchand."

It was a woman from the phone company, saying she had Alan Comstock's phone log.

Claire grabbed a pad. "Okay."

"You were looking for yesterday only?"

"For now. After, say, eleven at night."

"Hold on a sec. Okay, there were two calls. One at ten thirty-four. Second was twelve thirteen. First call was from a cell phone, number 914-487-9663. Number registered to Jane Comstock, same address. The second call was from a cell too, 914-487-5433."

"Whose phone?"

"No registration. Pay as you go. I checked it out. It was purchased at the Walmart in Kingston two weeks ago. June twenty-sixth, activated that same day. It has been used just this once."

"So it's a burn phone," Claire said.

"That's what they call them. I have a serial number."

Claire took down the number and thanked the woman. When she hung up she looked over to see Joe watching and listening.

"When did he buy it?"

"June twenty-sixth."

"Comstock was acquitted on the twenty-fourth," Joe said. "And Cain threatened Dupree in the bar that same night. Two days later he buys a burn phone. I would call that premeditation."

"What was he premeditating, Joe?" Claire asked. "Did he know that two weeks later he would need to call Alan Comstock prior to shooting him?"

"He was hedging his bets," Joe said after thinking about it. "Better to have it than not."

"That'll sound good in court. Maybe you can suggest that Cain is clairvoyant."

"Chrissake."

Claire looked at the information on the pad a moment. "Why would he pop Dupree first?" she asked. "It was me, I'd go after Comstock."

166

"Six of one, half dozen of the other," Joe said. "He obviously was going to do both either way. Maybe he thought Dupree would be harder to get to if he killed Comstock first. Mickey Dupree was a slippery little fucker."

"He wasn't on your Christmas card list, was he, Joe?"

"I'm thinking he wasn't on many people's."

"And yet you're sure there's only one person who might have wanted him dead."

Joe got to his feet. "I don't know what your problem is with this, Claire. Find me another suspect and I'll take a look at him. As it is, we got one guy. And he had motive, opportunity, and he actually threatened the life of one of the victims. Throw in the fact that he has since fled to another country, and I think he's our man. Tell you what, though—I'll go out there and see if I can't find some photographs of Cain actually pumping slugs into Comstock's belly. Will that convince you?"

"Wouldn't hurt."

"Screw you, Claire." Joe fairly spit the words at her and left.

When he was gone, Claire poured herself a coffee and went over the autopsy report again. Toxicology would take a few weeks, but she couldn't see it being a factor anyway. From looking in Alan Comstock's medicine cabinet the previous morning, Claire knew it was quite likely that the man's bloodstream was a playground of pharmaceutical delights. But whatever had influenced his behavior—gin or uppers or painkillers—none of them would have any impact on the case. The half-dozen injections from the Smith & Wesson took the other drugs out of the equation.

Claire was supposed to meet Buddy Townes at Kingston Koffee at noon. The time had been his suggestion, and she knew he was setting her up for a free lunch. Buddy being Buddy. Claire was okay with that; given Buddy's reputation, she figured she was getting off easy by buying him some soup and a sandwich. If he had suggested they meet later in the day, she might have had to spring for a dozen drinks to boot. She was early so she decided to swing by the Walmart on her way.

The kid working electronics was gangly and acne-scarred, with a lock of black hair hanging over his eyes and a tattoo of a spider on his neck. He surprised Claire when he spoke with a lilting Irish brogue.

"I can tell you what phones we sold that day," he said. "But maybe not to whom."

"I have the serial number," Claire said and handed him her notepad.

He punched some information into a computer and indicated for Claire to walk around the counter to look at the screen.

"Five phones," he said. "Three credit cards, one on debit. And one with cash. This doesn't show the serial numbers."

"The cash transaction is my guy, I'm guessing," Claire said. "But can you print me out the info on the other four anyway?"

"Sure thing."

"How does it work with this other one? With no contract?"

"Simple. You buy a phone and a SIM card. You make a call to activate it and it's good for X number of minutes. Fifty, a hundred. Depends on which card you buy."

"You don't have to give a name to activate it?" Claire asked.

"Nothing."

"Who said anonymity was dead?"

The kid smiled at that while he waited for the printer to finish.

"Were you working that day?" Claire asked. "The twenty-sixth?"

"I was."

"Do you remember selling the phones?"

"Just the one."

"Oh?"

The kid grinned somewhat sheepishly and pointed to the computer screen. "The Motorola. It was a girl from the college. A dead ringer for Julianne Moore, she was, could've been her younger sister. Red hair, and these huge blue eyes. I offered to come over to help set up her phone."

"I bet you did. Do you remember who paid cash?"

"No. But I can tell you he didn't look like Julianne Moore."

In the mall parking lot, Claire found numbers for the four cell phone buyers on her laptop and managed, surprisingly, to reach all of them. Talking to each, she didn't get the feeling that any of the four had been on a killing spree in the last couple of days. That included Julianne Moore's kid sister.

Kingston Koffee was on the east side of town, on the banks of Rondout Creek. Buddy Townes's Cadillac was parked on an angle near the front entrance. It was an aged Sedan de Ville that Buddy had owned since before Claire had come to town eighteen years earlier. She was quite certain Buddy had not washed the vehicle in that time.

She could see him at a booth along the side windows, sitting alone. His thick mane of hair was nearly white now and coiffed in the manner of certain country singers of his vintage. He was less meticulous about the rest of his appearance. Claire had never seen him in anything but worn jeans and cowboy boots. In the winter he wore a leather bomber jacket, and in the summer faded dress shirts with pearl snap buttons.

Buddy was a victim of Buddy and nobody else. He'd actually been a pretty good cop, on certain levels at least. He was a smart guy who knew right from wrong but who never learned to work within the system. Procedure was too slow for him and after a while, he began fudging the lines. He once told Claire that maybe he'd watched *Dirty Harry* too many times. When he wasn't inventing evidence that might help a case, he was hiding evidence that wouldn't. Add to that a chronic drinking problem and a propensity for trying to fuck anything that moved, and he soon alienated everybody he worked with, even the people who liked him. He washed out of the force when he was forty-two. Now he worked when he wanted to as a private investigator, mainly for Mickey Dupree in recent years. To Claire's way of thinking, he was still a smart guy who knew right from wrong. But it didn't appear that he cared either way anymore. Maybe he'd decided that it didn't make a difference if he did.

EIGHTEEN

Virgil slept until nearly noon and then got up and built a fire along the edge of the woods and cooked the bacon and eggs. He'd forgotten to bring utensils, so he scrambled the eggs with a stick and ate everything with his fingers, straight out of the pan.

After rinsing the pan in the creek, he walked back to the front edge of the woods and watched the house and farm for a time through the binoculars. He was reasonably certain that the cops were no longer watching the place but couldn't be entirely sure. The forest he was crouched in was out of sight of the neighboring farms, so as long as nobody out for a hike stumbled upon him he could stay indefinitely. But staying here wasn't going to help him. He knew he had to go back into town. There was somebody he needed to talk to.

At around six o'clock he spotted Mary Nelson's Ford F-250 pulling in the drive at the farm. Virgil trained the glasses on her and watched as she got out of the truck and walked into the shed. Turning the pump on, he knew. When she came out, she stood by the pasture fence as the horses walked toward her. Funny how fate had turned. Mary had persuaded Virgil to take the horses on and now it fell to her to look after them.

Virgil smiled. "That'll teach you."

Looking at the sun, he decided he would start walking toward town. Sticking to the woods, it would be close to dark when he got there. He headed north at first, moving the half mile or so to the Irish Line, then followed it east, keeping to the woods. The air was warm, although the sky had clouded over, and Virgil suspected there would be rain before morning. Which meant he could have a wet walk back. A couple of miles along he came to a lane, which he knew to be part of Dirk Hopman's farm. He could see the barn and the house a half mile away. There appeared to be some horses in the corral behind the barn. Virgil stopped when he saw them. Mary had told Virgil that Hopman was forbidden to keep any animals on his property while his charges were pending. Maybe the charges had been dropped but Virgil thought that was unlikely. That would require the blessing of Mary and the SPCA—and that was beyond unlikely.

Virgil trained the binoculars on the corral. Several horses were bunched together in the tiny paddock, picking at some strands of hay on the ground. There was plenty of pasture on either side of the barn, but to put the horses in either field would be to expose them to anyone driving by. Behind the building they were hidden, at least from the road out front.

Virgil lowered the glasses. He couldn't think of any good reason why Hopman would be hiding horses on his property. Or why a man who had starved his last bunch of horses would bother to obtain more. Whatever the reasons, Virgil didn't know what he could do about it. He toyed for a while with the notion of coming back later, when it was full dark, and stealing the nags. He could stash them at his farm and get word to Mary. Of course, it was a foolhardy idea and one that he didn't entertain very long. He was already wanted for complicity in two murders. He didn't need to add horse thief to his résumé.

He was about to keep walking when he spotted a flash of red in the trees along the side road that ran between the Irish Line and his farm. Raising the binoculars again, he saw it was Mary

Nelson's pickup. And it was slowing down as it approached the Hopman farm.

And then it was pulling in the driveway.

"Shit," Virgil said out loud. Mary must have spotted the horses from the side road. She had promised that she'd be watching the place. He waited in the trees, wondering what to do. If nobody was home at Hopman's, Mary might take note of the animals and leave. But if Hopman was there, it could be a different story.

Virgil watched as the truck came down the drive and then disappeared from his line of vision, obscured by the barn. The wind was in his face and he heard the truck door slam shut. He waited another two minutes and then, when Mary never reappeared behind the barn, Virgil began to move.

Goddamn it, Mary.

He kept to a row of trees along the left side of the lane, making sure the barn concealed his approach. He could hear voices when he was a couple hundred yards away, animated and loud. There was a broken wooden fence running from the front corner of the barn to an overgrown orchard beside the farmhouse. He made for the fence, keeping close to the sidewall of the barn. Looking through a crack between the boards he saw Mary and Dirk Hopman, faced off in the yard.

"—shit you caused me," Hopman was saying.

Hopman was bigger than Virgil remembered. He was wearing dirty overalls with no shirt beneath, his shoulders and arms matted with hair. He had on a greasy trucker's hat.

"You're not to have horses here," Mary said. "Do you think you're bigger than the law?"

"I got no horses here. You think you *are* the fucking law?"

At that point, one of the horses behind the barn whinnied loudly. Mary gave Hopman a triumphant look and started for the barn. He pushed his way in front of her, towering over her. He had to be two hundred and fifty pounds. Don't touch her, Virgil thought. Please don't touch her. He wished Mary would get in her truck and leave.

"You need to mind your business, old lady," Hopman said. "They got hay and they got water."

"Who has hay and water?" Mary asked. "The horses you denied having a minute ago? Your word doesn't mean anything. You starved horses before and you'd do it again."

She tried to walk around him and this time Hopman moved within inches of her, actually bumping her with his large gut. Don't touch her, Virgil thought. Get in the truck and go, Mary. Get in the truck and go.

"You're gonna report me anyway," Hopman said. "You know what you cost me last time?"

"Go," Virgil said. He realized he whispered the word this time. His pulse was running now, his breath coming quick.

Mary hesitated, and it seemed she suddenly realized what she was up against. She looked up at Hopman for a moment longer and then turned and started for her truck. Virgil exhaled.

"Don't call this in," Hopman warned her.

Mary turned, indicated the barn. "Where are they going?"

"None of your business. Don't call this in. You'll be a sorry old woman. You think I'm joking?"

Mary walked to the truck, moving quickly now. But her silence seemed to convince Hopman of what she would do. He jumped toward her and grabbed her by the hair as she was opening the door. Pulling her back roughly with one hand, he gripped her throat with the other and slammed her against the truck. Mary's eyes grew wide as she choked, grabbing at the hand around her neck.

"Call it in and I'll kill you," he said harshly.

Virgil was over the fence and on the run. Hopman heard him at the last minute and managed to make a half turn. Virgil landed an overhand right on Hopman's temple, causing the big man to grunt in pain. Virgil grabbed the bill of the dirty cap with his left hand, pulled it over Hopman's eyes, and jerked him forward, then landed several right hooks to the man's jaw. When Hopman staggered, Virgil gripped the greasy overalls with both hands and swung him around in a wide semicircle, slamming the crown of his head into the truck fender. Hopman bounced off the sheet metal like a cartoon figure and hit the ground heavily. He lay on his back with his knees up and his mouth open. He didn't move.

Mary was holding her throat, trying to figure out what was happening. "Virgil!" she exclaimed. And then, puzzled, "Virgil? What in the hell are you doing here?"

"What the hell are *you* doing here?" he asked her.

"I was driving by," she began and then stopped. "It said on the news you were in Canada."

Hopman made a gurgling noise and moved his feet as if he were trying to walk, even though he was still flat out on the ground. Virgil indicated the truck.

"Let's go."

He got behind the wheel and Mary climbed in the passenger side. When they reached the road, Virgil hesitated for a moment and then headed back toward his place. It was only a few minutes away. And even if the cops happened to drive by, they were used to seeing the Ford F-250 there by now. He felt Mary's eyes on him as he drove, watching him as she gingerly rubbed her throat where Hopman had choked her.

He parked where Mary usually parked when tending to the horses and got out, ducking into the milk house and indicating for Mary to follow.

The sun was setting now, and in the little room the shadow from the windows threw crosshatches against the wall, illuminating the cobwebs there. Virgil's pulse was still running from the encounter with Hopman. He stood looking at Mary and after a moment smiled at her, then opened the old round-shouldered refrigerator and took out two bottles of beer.

"We might as well have a cold one while you're trying to figure out whether or not to turn me in," he told her.

Mary took the beer from him. A good sign. "I'm still trying to figure out just where in the hell you came from," she said.

"Swung down from the trees like Tarzan."

"Never mind your nonsense. Tell me. How did you know I was there?"

"I didn't. I was passing by."

Mary gave him a long, disbelieving look and then sat down on one of the wooden chairs. She took a drink of beer.

"How is it that Hopman's got more horses?" Virgil asked.

"Virgil," she said after a moment. It sounded like a warning.

"What?"

"I think you have bigger problems than Hopman. Like this murder charge they have you on?"

"Oh, that."

"Yes, that. And the breaking out of jail. And then the other murder charge. Shouldn't I be frightened out of my wits right now?"

"You don't seem to be."

"Maybe not from where you're standing. What are you doing, Virgil?"

Now Virgil pulled the other chair over and sat. "I didn't kill anybody. But the cops are convinced I did. Which means they aren't looking real hard for anybody else. So I need to find out who actually did it, and I couldn't do that while I was in jail."

176

He laid things out in a line, like it was the simplest thing in the world.

"So why are you hanging around Hopman's? Do you think he's involved?"

"I wasn't hanging around. I was walking to town." He paused. "Through the woods."

"Walking to town," Mary said. "It's twelve miles."

"I know how far it is."

She took another drink of the beer and again ran her fingers across her throat where Hopman had choked her. "I've been thinking about you a lot, Virgil. I must lead a sheltered life because you're the first person I've ever known who's been arrested for murder. I know that both Dupree and Comstock were rather disreputable characters. I'm vain enough to think that I look at things from a moral, rather than legal, standpoint. But you had reason to hate both of these men. And apparently you committed an act of violence in Canada that landed you in prison. So I have to consider that you're capable of doing what they're accusing you of."

Virgil considered this. "But if I was the killer, and I thought you might turn me in, wouldn't I just kill you?" he asked.

"No, you wouldn't."

"Why not?"

"Because I'm not a disreputable character. There's that moral consideration, remember? And besides, you like me."

"How do you know that?"

"You offer me beer even when you're angry with me. And you let me take advantage of you when it comes to dropping off abused horses." She had a drink, thinking. "Oh—and you told me about your dreams."

"Like hell I did. I don't have any dreams."

"About becoming a weatherman."

Virgil laughed and stood up. He looked out the window to the road. "Do you think Hopman got a look at me?"

"No. It happened so fast I didn't even realize it was you until after it was over. Don't worry about him. I'll take care of that."

Virgil kept looking out the window. "So what are you going to do, Mary?"

"I guess nothing, for the time being. Everybody thinks you're in Canada anyway. Don't they?"

"I'm hoping."

"There is something else," Mary said. "There's the possibility that some overzealous cop might shoot you. If that were to happen, then I'd be stuck looking after these horses forever. I have a few dollars in the bank, Virgil. If you want to give yourself up, I'll hire you a good lawyer."

"I appreciate that," Virgil said.

"But the answer is no."

"I guess it is."

"Lord, you're stubborn." She watched him looking out the window and waited for him to agree with her, or to argue the point, or something. When he didn't, she asked, "Has that served you well in the past?"

He smiled and turned toward her. "I need a vehicle, Mary."

"What?"

"Walking back and forth to town gets old pretty quick."

Mary exhaled heavily and got to her feet. "I still have my old Dodge in the parking lot at the clinic. I didn't trade it in when I bought the Ford. It has the business logo on the door, so it's pretty good cover for a desperado on the run. But then, you knew all that—that's why you brought it up."

Virgil smiled again.

Mary finished her beer and put the empty on top of the

fridge. "So all of a sudden I'm Faye Dunaway to your Warren Beatty."

Virgil frowned, following her outside. It came to him as he was getting in the passenger side. He laughed.

"I get it," he said. "Bonnie and Clyde."

NINETEEN

Mary's "old" Dodge was a 2007 Ram, which made it four-teen years newer than Virgil's truck, which he presumed was still in the possession of the Ulster police. The truck was a V6 with overdrive. Power windows and seats, a CD player. Virgil assured Mary that in the event he was arrested while driving the truck, he would say he stole it.

"If you don't, I will," she told him before driving away, leav-ing him standing in the clinic parking lot, the truck keys in his hand.

He had found Buddy Townes's home address in the phone book earlier. The place was on Sycamore Street, past the mari-time museum and the old rail yards, a little shoebox bunga-low perched on a sharp incline. Virgil parked along the street a hundred yards away and shut the ignition off. It was just past nine o'clock.

The house had no driveway. There were three vehicles parked along the curb out front. Any one, he reasoned, could belong to Townes. A brown van with the fender wells rusted out, a cream Toyota with a spoiler on the trunk lid, and a dirty Cadillac from the late '80s. Virgil was betting on the Caddy.

He wasn't sure what to do next. Buddy Townes could be in for the evening. There were lights on in the house, and he could see the occasional flickering from a TV screen. Virgil wasn't thrilled with the idea of walking up and ringing the bell. And so he waited.

A little before ten, the front door of the bungalow opened and a man walked out. He was tall, with a considerable paunch, and had a full head of white hair, carefully combed. Jeans and a leather jacket. He walked to the Cadillac, got in, and drove off.

Virgil followed in the pickup. The Caddy made its way downtown and parked on a side street around the corner from the courthouse, the same courthouse where Virgil had appeared before the judge a couple of days earlier. The man who was quite likely Buddy Townes got out and walked around to Front Street and went into the bar Fat Phil's.

Down the street from the bar was a mini mall with a market and a liquor store and several other smaller shops. Virgil pulled into the parking lot there, shut the truck off, and sat looking at the drinking establishment up the street. He had been in Fat Phil's several times over the years, usually for a beer or two when he was in town picking up groceries or something for the farm. The last time he had been there, he had mentioned within earshot of Mickey Dupree that somebody ought to blow Mickey Dupree's head off. People had evidently taken notice. So even if he wasn't exactly a regular at Fat Phil's, it didn't seem like a good idea to walk in there tonight.

So again he would wait.

About ten minutes later, headlights swung across his rearview mirror and he looked up to see a red Honda CR-V wheeling into the mall parking lot. The driver pulled up in front of the liquor store, cut the lights, and killed the ignition.

Claire Marchand got out.

Virgil grabbed his cap, pulling it low, and slumped down in the seat, watching her in the side mirror. She walked around the car and started for the store. She was wearing jeans and a cream-colored V-neck sweater, a navy ball cap on her head, her hair in a ponytail beneath the cap. She looked good in the jeans.

Virgil thought for a moment about starting the Dodge and driving away, but that might be more conspicuous than staying put, particularly if she was to walk out just as he was leaving. As it was, she was inside for only a couple of minutes. She came out carrying a paper bag and got into the Honda, backed out of the parking spot, and drove out the same entrance she'd used when she arrived.

Virgil straightened in the truck, exhaled. He glanced across the street to Fat Phil's and then got out of the truck and walked over to the liquor store and went inside. The guy behind the counter was watching the Mets and the Braves on a small screen on the counter. Virgil picked up a pint of bourbon and carried it to the front.

"I think I saw my friend Claire leaving when I pulled in," he said.

The man kept his eyes on the game. The Mets had the bases loaded. "Yeah, she was picking up some wine." He glanced at the pint. "Be eight and a quarter."

"She still drinking the French stuff?" Virgil asked, giving the man a ten.

"She bought that Argentine Malbec," the man said. With a sideways jerk of his thumb, he indicated a display without actually looking at it. "Christ! I can't believe this."

Virgil looked at the screen, where the batter had just hit a ground ball to the second baseman. Double play, inning over. He gathered his change and left.

Walking back to the truck, he passed a convenience store and considered going in to buy cigarettes. He hadn't had a smoke since his escape from the tin can in Kesselberg. He couldn't decide if this was a good time to quit smoking, or not. In the end he kept on walking, got in the truck, and cracked the seal on the whisky. He took a sip and waited for Buddy Townes to emerge.

It was ten minutes to midnight when he saw the crop of white hair in the entranceway of the bar, and then the man himself walked out the door. When he headed for the Cadillac parked around the corner, Virgil got out and followed.

The Caddy was running and Buddy Townes was lighting a cigarette when Virgil approached the passenger side and rapped on the window. Buddy gave him a look and then powered the window down. Earlier Virgil had tucked a fifty-dollar bill in his shirt pocket, and now he offered it through the window.

"You got ten minutes?" he asked.

Buddy looked at him for maybe five seconds before reaching over to take the money. He unlocked the door and shut the engine off as Virgil got in. Buddy was smiling, looking at the fifty in his hand. He put it in his pocket.

"Shit, all I got from the cops was a cheeseburger and fries," he said. He had a voice like a rasp running across a rusty hinge. He appeared to be slightly drunk.

"You know who I am?" Virgil asked.

"I got a pretty good idea. Take that Mud Hens cap off and shave that half-assed beard and you'd look a lot like the guy whose mug shot I've been seeing on my TV all week. I thought you were in Canada."

"I get that a lot."

Buddy took a long pull on the smoke. "You're not in Canada. You broke out of jail but you're not smart enough to take a powder. William H. Bonney did the same thing, you know that?"

"William H. Bonney was Billy the Kid."

"Yeah. He broke out of the Lincoln County jail and for some reason he just stayed in the area. He could've gone to California or Mexico, anywhere. Those days, they never would've found him. But he wouldn't leave. You know what they did to him, right?"

"Yeah, I do."

"Shit," Buddy said, looking at Virgil as he tried to figure the angles. Then he laughed. "You didn't do it. Did you?"

"No."

"And you want me to tell you that I might have a theory who did."

"Something like that."

Buddy took another pull on the cigarette, the end burning brightly in the dim light. "Well, I can tell you that until a few seconds ago, I had you pegged as the guy. It works from a motive standpoint. And then the great escape."

"So who else had motive?"

"I'd have to stand back and take another look at this thing," Buddy said. "See, all anybody's talking about is who had it in for these guys. Who would want them dead? And you're the perfect fit for that. On both counts. But now . . . well, there are always other possibilities to consider, when it comes to murder. First off, there's the nut job who's killing people for no reason. Or for reasons that only make sense in his distorted brain. He's the toughest guy to catch because there's no logic behind it. I don't see that being an option here. Secondly, there's the popular theory, that you—or somebody like you—killed both these guys out of a sense of revenge, or vigilante justice, or whatever you want to label it. Comstock killed your wife and got off because of Mickey Dupree. So you did them both. From a human nature standpoint, that's very feasible. Everybody has those feelings, whether they admit to them or not. But nobody's talking about the third possible motive. And that is, who would stand to *benefit* from the demise of either of these two guys? Or both? You see where I'm going?"

"Yeah."

"I'm not saying that's it. Could be a grudge thing after all.

Both these guys rubbed a lot of people the wrong way. Not just you. But you have to look at everything. When Mickey was killed, I went over it. Now I probably know more about the man than anybody alive, I been working for him off and on for almost twenty years. So who would benefit from his death? You can forget about anybody making any money off it. Mickey was broke, year in and year out. If he made a million dollars, he spent a million and a half. He owed money all over the place and he was a lousy gambler to boot. He never once paid me on time for anything, still owes me fifteen hundred I'm never gonna see. He had two ex-wives he paid alimony to. I can tell you they're in mourning because they're toast now. All he left is debt. He would have had life insurance but they're not getting a nickel of that. His kids will get it. I guess you could argue that they'd benefit but they're both in college and I'm pretty sure neither of them came up here and drove a golf club through their old man's heart." He paused, then raised an index finger for emphasis. "Although I can't figure why there was no struggle when that went down. I'd have fucking struggled, man."

"So you're saying it had to be something personal."

"With Mickey, it seems likely." Buddy finished the smoke and slipped the butt out the side window, which was lowered maybe an inch. "Now look at Comstock. And I did take a long look at him when he was on trial for killing your wife. Who's going to benefit from his murder? Man had no will, you know that? Worth what, a couple hundred million, and he wouldn't make a will. He's got a daughter in the southwest, she's flakier than a blue ribbon pie crust. He sends her money every month so she's able to stay that way, I guess. I don't see her being a suspect. The wife, well, the wife gets everything, but then the wife already had everything. The properties are all in her name, for instance."

Buddy paused, drumming his fingers on the steering wheel while he thought. The inside of the car was as dirty as the exterior; the vinyl dashboard was grimy and empty cigarette packs and crushed cardboard coffee cups were strewn everywhere.

"Pretty strange couple," Buddy said then. "He came from a rich, established family, old Philadelphia money, and became a hippie music producer. A rich hippie, but still. She's the flip side, starts out a hippie, Haight-Ashbury and all that scene—man, she had some connections would blow your mind—and she becomes a wealthy society dame. Patron of the arts, loyal Democrat, all that. So there's nothing there that I could see. Who else? Well, Comstock has had more feuds over the years than the Hatfields and the McCoys. Keith Richards threatened to kill him in 1979; Dolly Parton pulled a gun on him in the studio in '86, said she was going to make him into a gelding. Courtney Love threw a bowie knife at him. Where the fuck would she get a bowie knife? You can add in a half a dozen fathers who wanted to kill him for making moves on their aspiring singer/ songwriter daughters. That's why he was such a gun nut. I hear he was loaded for bear the night he was killed, not that it did him any good. Thing is, there's a lot of people who wouldn't mind seeing him dead, but I doubt any of them actually did it. It would be entertaining as hell to slap subpoenas on Dolly and Courtney but I don't think it would get you anywhere."

"I'm starting to believe that maybe I'm the guy after all," Virgil said.

Buddy laughed. "Well, I'm starting to believe that somebody set you up to look like the guy. Maybe he only wanted one of them dead but did them both to make it look like you. You gotta admit, you're tailor-made for this. What do you know about Joe Brady?"

"Other than he's not the president of the local Mensa chapter?"

Buddy nodded his head. "No shit. Well, Mickey Dupree made a habit of bitch slapping Joe in the courtroom over the years. And Joe hated Mickey for it. In fact, Mickey made his bones off Joe's incompetence. Mickey's first murder case—a cokehead named Ronnie Dillard who was as guilty as O. J.—ended up walking because Joe produced the wrong gun as the murder weapon. Dillard had a thirty-eight with the front sight filed off—these kids do that so the gun doesn't get caught when they're yanking it out of their sweatpants, fucking idiots—but when the prosecutor presented the gun as evidence, the front sight was there. Well, they don't grow back. Wrong gun, the ballistics didn't match. See you later. Mickey worked Joe over pretty good on the stand, made Joe look like a fucking moron, which isn't real hard to do. And he's done it a few times since, most recently during Comstock's trial. But you saw that."

"Yeah, I saw that," Virgil said. "I have a feeling Brady has his heart set on me for this thing. I doubt he's out looking for anybody else."

"Claire Marchand is."

"What?"

"That's who bought me the cheeseburger and fries today," Buddy said. "She was asking the same questions you're asking."

"Did she come to the conclusion that I'm the guy?"

"I wouldn't be surprised." Buddy took his cigarettes from his coat, shook one out, then offered the pack to Virgil. He declined. "Of course, I have one piece of information she doesn't. She doesn't know you're hanging around."

"Like Billy the Kid."

Buddy laughed again. He was having a good time. "Yeah, like Billy the Kid." He lit the cigarette. "But you must have made an impression on Claire in the interrogation room that day. She told me you were smart."

187

"She did?" It seemed she hadn't mentioned the phone call. Not to Buddy Townes anyway.

"Yeah." Buddy exhaled and squinted through the smoke at Virgil. "She's a piece of ass, isn't she?"

Virgil thought of her earlier that night, in the jeans and the V-neck. The way she moved across the parking lot. "I never really noticed."

"You're full of shit," Buddy said. "You might like to know that she's basically the polar opposite of Joe Brady. She had a tough go of it on the home front for a while but she's getting it together now."

"What kind of tough go?"

"Oh, she was married to this fucking twit. Your classic ten-cent millionaire. He owned a car dealership. He had a million-dollar house, he had a cottage, he had a boat, he had a new Escalade. He didn't have a fucking nickel. He had this image of himself as a wheel, and everybody knew he was a joke. I'm sure they lived off Claire's salary. It took her about fifteen years to figure things out. She divorced him last year. Probably paid for everything herself."

"What happened to the husband?"

"He's still around, still playing the game. Guys like that don't change. He sells flooring now. Bought another house, married some chick with fake tits from Montreal. The chick is from Montreal, I don't know where the tits are from. If she's not an ex-stripper, I'll eat that dashboard."

Virgil thought about Claire, the way she'd talked to him on the phone that night. She was flirting with him, no doubt, to keep him on the line. But still. He was glad to hear she was single, but he couldn't say why. There was nothing in it for him, with two murder charges and an escaped custody charge to consider.

"All right," he said, putting her out of his mind, at least for the moment. "Let's get back to Dupree. You said he owed a lot of money."

"He did."

"Isn't that a motive?"

"Not as a rule," Buddy said. "Look, somebody owes you money, you don't want him dead. If he's dead, he's probably not going to pay you back. The people Mickey owed, they all knew he made a lot of money, so chances were they'd get paid eventually. Now, if they had found Mickey in that sand trap alive but with two broken legs, I'd say it was absolutely debt related. But not this."

Virgil nodded. After a moment, he reached for the door handle. Buddy Townes had given him a lot of information but really hadn't told him what he wanted to hear. What had Virgil expected, that Townes knew who the guilty party was and would be willing to spill it for fifty bucks?

Buddy smiled. "Hey, I just thought of something. You got Joe Brady on your trail. Billy the Kid had William Brady. You figure that's an omen?"

"If I'd known you were going to enjoy this so much, I would've only given you twenty."

"I would've taken it."

Virgil looked around to see if anybody was in the vicinity. "One more thing," he said. "You going to make a phone call when I leave?"

"And turn you in?" Buddy smiled and pulled his left hand from his coat pocket. In the hand was a snub-nosed revolver, which he pointed straight at Virgil. "I was going to do that, I wouldn't turn you in. I'd take you in."

Virgil looked at the gun, maybe eighteen inches from his face. He could see the perfect circle of dull gray slugs in the cylinder. Buddy put it back in his pocket.

"I wish I knew what the reward money was on you," Buddy said. "Might change my mind." He exhaled slowly, almost a sigh. "I'm tired of this nickel-and-dime shit. All I want at this point in my life is a million dollars and a little shack in the Keys. And a boat so I can fish every day. Nothing big, maybe a thirty-footer. I was a half-assed cop and now I'm a half-assed investigator. But I got a feeling I could be a top-of-the-line retiree." He sat looking out the windshield, maybe imagining that shack, early mornings out in the Gulf. Cold beer in the cooler and that night's supper in the hold. Then he glanced over at Virgil. "Whatever you're worth, it's not a million."

"You're right about that," Virgil said. He was happy not to be looking at the muzzle of the gun anymore.

Buddy was looking at Virgil's right hand on the door handle. The knuckles were swollen and the skin on the index finger was peeled back.

"What did you do to your hand?" he asked.

"I fell down."

Buddy shook his head, not believing it for a second. "You watch reality TV?"

"I watch baseball," Virgil said. "And the news. The weather occasionally but it tends to piss me off."

"I hate reality TV," Buddy said. "Sometimes I think it's the worst fucking thing ever to happen to this country. Nothing worth watching on television anymore. So I'm bored most of the time and I hate being bored. But you, you're entertaining as hell. I don't know what the fuck you're up to or what you're going to do next, but I'm going to keep watching."

TWENTY

When Claire got to the station the next morning, Joe was there ahead of her. That in and of itself was unusual. But Joe was wearing his dark-brown suit, his Brooks Brothers, the suit he normally saved for court. Claire assumed he was on his way there this morning. But he wasn't.

"I'm heading up into Canada," he told her. "To talk to the Mounties."

He made the announcement as if he were Meriwether Lewis and Canada was the great unknown expanse west of the Mississippi.

"Do us proud," Claire told him.

"I need to know what they're doing up there," he said. "We would have had this man in custody by now."

Claire knew it was futile to point out that they did have this man in custody once. "I'm sure they're doing all they can," she said. "I have a feeling this Cain is a little on the unpredictable side."

"Why do you say that?"

Claire shrugged. "The fact that we don't have any idea where he is?"

"I know where he is," Joe said. "North of the St. Lawrence. And I'm heading there today to ask a few questions about that."

When Joe was gone Claire sat at her desk feeling slight remorse that she didn't tell him that Virgil Cain was not in

Canada. But then, Claire didn't know that to be a fact. Two nights earlier he had still been in the country. He could very well have crossed the border since then. So she couldn't, in good conscience, have discouraged Joe anyway. Let him travel north in his Brooks Brothers–suitable-for-meeting-Mounties duds, and see what he might learn.

She heard a call come in to dispatch and half listened as she went through her e-mail. The name Dirk Hopman was mentioned and she looked up. She didn't know why it held some significance but it did. The man was reporting an assault. The address was the Irish Line, a side road about halfway between Saugerties and Woodstock.

Which was, she knew, just around the corner from Virgil Cain's farm.

Claire went into her notes and found where she had written Hopman's name. Mary Nelson had mentioned it, and not in a flattering way. Claire put the notebook in her pocket and walked over to the front desk.

"Who took this Hopman thing?"

"Sal Delano. He just walked out the door."

Claire caught up with the cruiser a few miles down the road and followed it to Route 212, through the back country, and finally into the driveway of Hopman's farm. The place looked like something from a Dorothea Lange photograph, the rain gutters falling off the house, shingles missing, the lawn uncut. A large man wearing overalls was standing in the yard, his legs spread, watching them approach.

Sal had been watching Claire in the mirror for several miles. Now, when he parked, he got out and approached her.

"What's up?" he asked.

"Thought I'd tag along," she said. "I'm bored."

Sal raised his eyebrows and she knew that he'd expected a

little more information than that. If there weren't other matters at hand, it seemed that he might ask her to be more specific. Claire liked that about him.

"Okay," she said. "I'm being nosy. I've heard about this guy Hopman."

Together they walked over to the man in the overalls. Claire saw now that his face was bruised badly, his left eye swollen nearly shut. He was standing with his arms folded across his chest, looking pretty damn defiant for somebody who'd just taken a shit kicking. Or maybe he was embarrassed and the defiance was a pose.

"Dirk Hopman?" Sal asked.

"Yeah."

"What's the story here?"

"The story here is that I was attacked last night. Right here on my own property."

"By who?"

"I only got one name for you. Mary Nelson. A vet from town's been harassing me for weeks."

"Harassing you how?"

"Claiming I mistreated horses. She's full of shit. Had me arrested once and then showed up here last night accusing me again. I don't have a single horse on the place. I ain't even allowed to because of her and those SPCA people. But that don't stop her from showing up and shooting her mouth off."

"What about the assault? Is that what happened to your face?"

"What do you think?" Hopman asked. "I was trying to get her to leave. I asked her politely to get the hell offa my property. And I got jumped. One minute I'm talking to the old broad and the next I get hit from behind by some guy—" Hopman hesitated. "It was two guys, you wanna know the truth. And I don't even get a chance to defend myself. They don't have the balls to come at me straight on."

Sal glanced over at Claire. She was listening to Hopman but wasn't looking at him, as if he wasn't worthy even of that. She wore the expression of someone who was listening to a mildly amusing joke that was taking far too long to tell.

"Did you get a look at these guys?" Sal asked.

"No. I told you, they jumped me from behind."

"I don't understand," Sal said. "Did they arrive here with the Nelson woman?"

"Well," Hopman said slowly. "I don't know how they got here. They musta snuck up somehow because I didn't see them. Lookit, I gave you her name. Arrest her and get her to tell."

"We intend to talk to her," Sal said.

"Any minute now," Claire said, looking toward the road. Mary Nelson's F-250 was coming down the lane, followed by a van with the SPCA logo on the side. Behind the vehicles was an Ulster County trooper in a marked cruiser. Claire turned to Hopman and smiled.

"You ought to charge admission to this place."

It took a few minutes to get everything straightened out. It seemed that while Hopman was filing an assault complaint against Mary Nelson and her unknown accomplices, Mary and the man from the SPCA, whose name was Donald Lee, were filing against Hopman, claiming he had horses in his possession, contravening a court order that denied him that right.

"And that's pure bullshit," Hopman said. "There's no horses here."

Mary Nelson looked at Claire. "There are horses in a corral behind that barn." She paused. "Let me put it this way. There were horses there at seven o'clock last night."

Claire indicated for Mary to go have a look.

"I don't want her snooping around my property," Hopman snapped.

"Shut up," Claire told him.

Donald Lee went with Mary and the two of them walked around the barn. Sal was talking to the trooper by the cruiser. It seemed the trooper was going to leave Sal with both complaints, to save doubling up on the paperwork. Claire waited in silence but was pretty sure there were no horses on the property. When Mary came back, she confirmed that with a shake of her head and a knowing look. Claire turned to Hopman, who was smirking like a kid who'd gotten away with stealing apples from a grocer.

"What time was this alleged assault?" Claire asked.

"Like she said. Seven, eight o'clock last night."

"So you waited for twelve hours to file a complaint."

"Well, I was in a daze," Hopman said. "I was pretty beat up. Lookit my face. Lookit this eye."

"While you were in this twelve-hour daze," Claire asked, "you wouldn't by any chance have trucked a bunch of horses out of here . . . ?"

"No."

"You're sure about that?"

"Yeah, I'm sure about that."

Claire turned to Mary. "Mr. Hopman claims that a couple of your friends jumped him and beat the hell out of him. Is that true?"

"No, that is not true."

"What happened?" Claire asked.

"I've been watching this place"—Mary raised her voice, glaring at Hopman—"because Mr. Hopman has abused and starved animals in the past. Last night, I saw six or eight horses behind the barn. By law, Mr. Hopman is not to have horses on this property. So I stopped to ask why they were here. He threatened me, and then he choked me."

"And?" Claire asked.

"So I hit him."

"*You* hit him?" Claire laughed.

"You lying fucking bitch!" Hopman said.

"I told you to shut up," Claire said. She looked at Mary. "There was nobody here with you?"

"No."

Claire was enjoying this now. It appeared that Mary Nelson was a character, and probably a straight shooter. She wasn't, however, a particularly accomplished liar.

"I'll take your statement in the car," Claire told her. "Sal, you can get Mr. Hopman's story."

In the car Mary Nelson stuck with her tale, although she seemed a little uncomfortable telling it one on one. Claire didn't push her too hard. She already knew no charges would be filed. Hopman couldn't identify his mysterious assailants so there would be nobody to arrest on that count. And there were no horses on the property for the moment so Hopman would be excused from violating the court order. Of course, Hopman could always charge Mary Nelson with assault, but Claire doubted that the man wanted to appear in court to say he'd been beaten up by a septuagenarian half his size.

"You say that Hopman choked you?" she asked Mary.

"Yes."

"Do you want to file a complaint?" Claire asked. "Because I'll charge him with assault here and now. I'll even go so far as to say it would make my day."

"No. It's okay."

Claire flipped her notepad closed and put it on the seat

between them. "And you're certain there was nobody else here last night? Just you and Hopman?"

"That's all I remember."

Mary looked away as Claire smiled.

"I assume you were out this way because you're still looking in on Virgil Cain's farm."

"Yes."

"You haven't heard from him?"

"No. I heard on the news that he might be in Canada."

"Yeah," Claire said. "He might be."

She looked over at Sal and Hopman, standing by the front fender of the cruiser. From Hopman's animated expression she assumed that Sal had informed him there would be no charges pending on the assault. Hopman was yapping and his arms were flapping up and down as if he were trying to take flight.

"What does he do with these horses?" Claire asked.

"Sends them to Europe to be butchered."

"That's not illegal."

"Eating horses is not illegal," Mary said. "Starving them is."

"You can go," Claire said. "Do me a favor and keep the bare-knuckle brawling to a minimum, will you? It's not very lady-like."

Mary opened the door and then looked back and smiled at Claire. "He started it," she said.

Claire left Sal to sort things out and, since she was in the area, drove over to Virgil Cain's farm. She didn't expect to find any-thing. She certainly didn't expect to find Virgil Cain, although if she did find him, she suspected he would be sporting some bruised knuckles this morning. How he would have ended up at Hopman's, though, was a mystery. Another in a line that was growing every day. The guy was turning into an upstate Scarlet Pimpernel.

She pulled up to the pasture field and got out to look at the horses. She picked out the skinny mare, the horse that Mary Nelson said had come from Hopman's. She was already looking healthier, moving along the fencerow and pulling at the grass. Claire saw that the water trough was nearly empty. Apparently Mary had not been here yet, or had forgotten, with the excitement at Hopman's. Claire walked into the shed and had a look around. An electrical line ran between a switch and a wall-mounted pump with a large steel wheel on it. Claire hit the switch and the pump kicked noisily into action. A moment later she heard water gushing into the trough outside.

When the trough was full she walked to the house and went inside. Nothing had been disturbed since her last visit. Nothing she could see, anyway. She went upstairs and had a look in the master bedroom. It had been left a mess by the police and was still a mess. She went into the bathroom and glanced quickly around. She was about to leave when something occurred to her. She opened the shower curtain. There was a washcloth hanging over the shower spout. The cloth was damp. In fact, the cloth was damp enough that Claire was certain it had been used in the past few hours.

"You got a lot of nerve, Virgil Cain," she said.

She searched the house then, not really believing he was hiding there at that moment, but knowing she had to anyway. Besides, every time she had tried to predict what he might be doing, she had been wrong. Thinking about that, she hoped that Joe was having a fruitful conversation with the RCMP. While he was urging the Mounties to throw a dragnet over the Great White North, Cain had been at home taking a shower.

After she left the house, she walked out to the barn and

looked around there as well. She even climbed the ladder to the haymow. The fresh, sweet-smelling hay immediately brought back memories, many years submerged, of her summers as a kid, when her mother would take her to her uncle's farm in Vermont. There she and her sister would catch frogs and build rafts and attempt to ride a brown and white pony that Claire realized years after the fact must have suffered from some mental disorder not unlike disorders she'd encountered in people she'd arrested over the past couple decades. The pony would kick anyone behind it, and bite anybody in front. And buck people off and scrape riders along the rough wall of the barn. Back then they had referred to the animal as frisky.

Claire climbed down and walked through the rest of the barn and the other outbuildings, thinking as she searched that she should be more nervous than she was, given the charges against the guy she was after. She was calm, though, partly because she really didn't expect to find him there, but also because she didn't think he was a danger to her, which was incredibly naive, given her years on the job.

She walked back to her car and leaned with her forearms over the roof, watching the farm buildings and the fields beyond. She wondered how he was getting around. Because he was definitely getting around. She knew that, if not much else.

She also knew that he was coming back here, at least from time to time. And if he was coming back, it stood to reason that she should be able to catch him when he did.

TWENTY-ONE

Jane might have stayed another night at Suzanne's, but Miller Boddington came home Monday morning. With him was a man named Rafael; Jane wasn't certain if that was his first name or his last. He had shoulder-length gray hair and was, Miller announced, the lawyer who would soon see him cleared of the animal abuse charges.

The two men were having breakfast in the dining room when Jane and Suzanne returned from an early-morning excursion to the farmers market in Bearsville. That was when Jane received the single-name introduction.

"Rafael's an old hippie," Miller said. "Everybody out there is an old hippie. You guys probably know each other from back in the day."

"How would we know each other?" Jane asked.

"From your wild years out on the coast," Miller said. He smiled. "With Charlie and the gang."

Jane stared at him. "I don't know what you're talking about."

"Oh, I think you do."

Shortly after that, Jane decided she wanted to go home. Suzanne drove her. She had been uncharacteristically on edge all morning. The suggestion that they go to the farmers market took Jane completely unawares; she doubted Suzanne had ever made the trip before. It seemed like an excuse to get out of the house. Jane knew she'd received a phone call from Miller the night before, telling her he was on his way home. Jane didn't know what else he'd told her, but Suzanne was definitely upset about something. At the moment she was driving too fast, her fingers drumming on the steering wheel, her attention span virtually nonexistent.

"What's going on?" Jane asked finally.

"Fuck," Suzanne said. "Miller says he's going to put the place up for sale."

"And move to California?"

"Fucking California." Suzanne spit out the words as if the entire state was a leper colony, and then reached for a cigarette.

Jane waited until she had lit up. "Can't you swing both places? It's not a question of money."

"Money's got nothing to do with it."

"Then what is it?"

"He feels this horse business has sullied his reputation. He wants to start life anew on the coast." Suzanne took a deep drag off her cigarette. "Where he can go about re-sullying it."

"What are you going to do?"

"I'm not going anywhere," Suzanne said flatly, exhaling. She pulled again on the cigarette. "He's not selling the house. That's *my* house."

"You'd better talk to him," Jane said as they pulled up to her house. "Before it goes too far."

"Oh, I'll talk to him," Suzanne assured her. "If he's as smart as he pretends to be, he knows that the one person he doesn't fuck with is me."

Jane got out and watched the Mercedes disappear down the winding road. When she went inside, she realized that Miller had not mentioned Alan's death. The two men had never been close, but they had known each other for years. Miller had little interest in music, or in any aspect of the arts. Alan held Miller in contempt, referring to him usually as a "phony little fuck," although that designation pretty much included almost everyone he encountered in recent years. Still, Jane found it odd that Miller never commented on the fact she had lost her husband. It seemed, given his cryptic comment about Jane's past, that he had other things on his mind. She tried not to read too much into it. Miller, by nature, liked to dig at people, as if getting under someone's skin somehow made him superior to them. He was a little man with an overblown ego, and he was always, it seemed, looking for ways to make those around him feel small.

The police had finished their forensics work on Monday, and Walter had arranged for a cleaning company to make everything appear as if nothing had ever happened. Even if they couldn't scrub away the images in Jane's head, they did a very good job otherwise. They ended up replacing the cedar deck boards where Alan's body had bled out that night. The blood had saturated the wood.

The house smelled of bleach and Pine-Sol. Jane got a bottle of water from the fridge and stood by the French doors, looking out at the deck. The new boards stuck out like a succession of sore thumbs. They would fade with age, though. As would it all, given enough time.

The message light on the kitchen phone was blinking. She heard the dogs barking and so ignored the phone for the time being and went outside to let them out of the run. They were excited to see her, having been given minimal attention from the maid these past couple of days, Jane assumed. After they settled, she sat down on the top step of the deck and watched the two animals run around the yard. She should go for a run with them, she knew. The dogs could use the exercise and Jane could use the distraction.

She thought about her conversation with Suzanne in the car. It was probably going to be an interesting day at the Boddington house. Suzanne's blood was up, and she wasn't the type to let things slide. Despite her laid-back demeanor, she was actually very good at confrontation, but only when she felt cornered. Jane had known for a long time that Suzanne regarded her marriage to Miller as a trade-off. Jane also knew that there were things Suzanne would not trade.

After a while she went inside and checked her messages. There were fifty-seven in total, most from friends offering condolences, shoulders to cry on, food and wine, tea and sympathy. One from a local casket maker, offering a rock-bottom price. Several calls from various media outlets looking for comments or begging for interviews. How they got the number was a mystery; it was unlisted but that didn't seem to matter anymore. Jane had it changed three or four times during the trial but still they got through. There were two messages from Edie Bryant, one to say she was thinking of Jane, and the second asking Jane to call back. Jane wondered what that was about.

And there was a message, finally, from Gracie. She'd heard the news, of course; she would have had to be living in a cave not to have heard. As it turned out, she nearly had been. Or a tent, at least. Her message said she had been camping in New Mexico with Andre. It was the first Jane had heard of Andre. Gracie had asked Jane to call her back. She made a cup of espresso before dialing the number.

"Hey, it's Jane," she said when Gracie picked up.

"Oh, hi," Gracie's voice was hoarse, thick with sleep.

Jane looked at the clock and realized it was twenty after nine in Arizona. Much too early for Gracie to be up and about.

"I got your message," Jane said. "So you were camping. I wondered."

"Yeah. Andre is a rock climber. So we went to this place north of Santa Fe. Awesome spot. The light there is amazing."

"And Andre is . . . ?"

"He's my boyfriend." Gracie's tone suggested that Jane should know this, even though they hadn't spoken in over a year. "Andre is a world-class sculptor."

Gracie was inordinately enamored of terms like "world-class," just as she was always enamored of somebody or something new: graphic writers, independent filmmakers, visual artists, heirloom tomatoes, Oregon ice wine. She had turned forty earlier that year and was still skipping through life as if it were a schoolyard playground. Of course, the trust fund helped.

"So what's going on there?" she asked. "Have they caught the guy?"

"No."

Gracie was silent for a bit, as if expecting Jane to carry the conversation. "So he killed that lawyer and then he just showed up and . . . and he shot my father?"

"That's the way it looks."

"Freaky."

Yeah, freaky, Jane thought.

"It said on the news there wouldn't be a service. My father didn't want one?"

"No. He's been cremated. We'll have to decide what to do with the ashes at some point down the road."

Jane could hear Gracie moving around, and then she heard the flare of a match. Lighting a cigarette.

"Do you need me to come there, Jane?"

"Well . . . no. I guess not."

"Because, like, this thing with Andre is kinda new and for me to take off now . . . well . . . and I got my work too. I'm working on some new pieces. Still lifes. So if there's nothing I can do to help out right now, it's probably better that I stay here. Keep my nose to the grindstone, you know?"

"I understand completely. Were you working when I called?"

"Yeah," Gracie said quickly. "As far as the rest goes, um, I guess everything stays the same? You know, until it all gets sorted out?"

"Do you mean your monthly check?"

"Well . . . yeah."

"I'll make sure you get it," Jane said.

"Thanks, Jane. That's cool. Because I'm kind of in a groove right now. I want to get this done and start selling some pieces. You know, get it out there."

"Sure."

"And then . . . like, I can make it up there for the reading of the will and all that," Gracie said. "But you probably don't know when that will be yet?"

"Alan never had a will," Jane said.

"Really?" Jane heard her inhale sharply on the cigarette. "Then . . . how does that work?"

"Basically everything stays the same, like you said," Jane said.

"Oh." Gracie's voice dropped like she swallowed a piece of lead. "Well, I should get back to work."

You mean you should get off the phone with me and start calling lawyers, Jane thought.

"This is so sad," Gracie said and hung up.

Jane wasn't sure what she was referring to as being so sad, but she could make a pretty accurate guess. She walked outside to see what the dogs were up to as she dialed Edie Bryant's number.

"Hi, Edie, it's Jane."

"Oh, Jane, I'm so glad you called. I'm just in the car heading to the airport. How are you doing?"

"I'm okay. I've been at a friend's house for a couple days and I just got your message."

"It wasn't important. I just wanted to make sure you were okay."

"Day by day. You know."

"Such a terrible thing. I know it's a rotten cliché, but the only thing that can heal a tragedy is time. But there is something to be said about keeping yourself busy. So listen—you can absolutely say no to this, given the timing, but there's a fundraiser in Washington at the end of the month I'd love for you to attend. A lot of people you know, but more importantly quite a number you haven't met yet. It would be good for you."

"Oh, I don't know," Jane said. "I actually thought that maybe you would want to rethink this, after what has happened. Politicians and baggage, and all that."

"No, no. I'm not thinking anything of the kind. This isn't the time to talk about this, not after what you've been through. But we will talk. Not to be crass, but something like this can work in your favor. To show your strength, your resilience. You didn't do anything wrong here, Jane."

Jane watched the dogs chase a black squirrel through the trees. "Okay. We can at least talk about it later. And I'll think about the fund-raiser."

"Good. I have to run. But call me if there's anything at all. I mean that. We have to keep this conversation going."

Jane pressed the end button and set the phone on the railing of the deck. The dogs had treed the squirrel just off the edge of the path and were going crazy, circling the big maple, first one way and then the other. The squirrel kept on the move, jumping from branch to branch, one side of the tree to the other, trying to keep out of sight of its pursuers. A couple years earlier the dogs had trapped another squirrel in an identical situation. The squirrel eventually got dizzy from circling the tree and fell to the ground, virtually at the feet of the animals, who were so surprised by the turn of events that they stood there, looking at the squirrel as if it had arrived from another planet. The squirrel jumped up and escaped into the evergreens.

Jane had always thought there was a parable in there somewhere but had never decided what it was. She went inside and changed her clothes and took the dogs for a run.

Claire was sitting at her desk, playing a game in her head in which she was a hound and Virgil Cain was a fox, when she looked up to see Alex Daniels approaching. She couldn't remember the last time she had seen a district attorney at the station.

"Mr. Daniels," she said. "What, is it my birthday?"

Daniels sat across from her. "What are you working on?"

"Virgil Cain."

"The Canucks can't find that guy?"

"You know what my grandmother used to tell me when I couldn't find something?" Claire asked.

"What?"

"That I was looking in the wrong place."

"Did you tell the Mounties that?"

"They'll figure it out. What's up?"

"You ready for court in the morning?"

Claire leaned forward to pick up her desk calendar. "I don't have anything for tomorrow. Well, Miller Boddington, but you know that's going to be a push, with Mickey Dupree out of the picture. Boddington won't even be there; he'll send one of his minions. And if he's not showing up, neither am I."

"He's going to be there," Daniels said.

"Yeah?"

"Yeah. There's something going on." Daniels shook his head. "Apparently Boddington's brand-new lawyer intends to file a motion tomorrow, and he wants to make sure our side is present and accounted for."

"What kind of motion?"

"He's not saying. He's giving us notice that he's filing just to ensure that we're there, ready for whatever he's going to throw at us. He doesn't want to give us the opportunity to say we weren't prepared because we assumed we were looking at a remand as a result of the Dupree thing."

"But we have no idea what the motion's going to be," Claire said. "Change of venue?"

"I can't see it," Daniels said. "Why now?"

"Who's the new lawyer?"

"Guy named Rafael de Costa, from San Francisco."

"You check him out?"

"Googled him. He's basically a real estate lawyer. High-end real estate—Napa Valley, for the most part."

"Isn't Boddington rumored to be getting into the wine business?" Claire asked.

"It's not a rumor anymore," Daniels told her. "He bought two wineries last week, also according to Google. What they call boutique wineries. Very small. Paid five mil for one and three for the other."

"Chump change," Claire said. She sat thinking about it. "Why would he bring a real estate lawyer from California to a criminal trial in New York? That doesn't make any sense. Judge Harrison just might take this the wrong way. You know what he's like."

"He won't be there."

"Why not?"

"He's in the hospital. Emergency triple bypass."

Claire put the calendar back. She liked the old Scot. "Is he going to be okay?"

"It looks pretty good, from what I hear."

"So who's presiding?"

"Somebody from the city. Judge Santiago."

"You know him?"

"No."

"Better hope he's not a wine lover."

"I suppose," Daniels said. "I really don't think there's anything to this. But we have to be on our game. Which means you need to prepare to be called, in case this guy wants to challenge anything in evidence, or matters of procedure. Which also means you're going to have to cancel any social engagements you have planned for this evening. So you can cram."

"What's a social engagement?" Claire asked.

"There you go," Daniels said. "Now you have something to do."

"I had something to do."

"What?"

"Oh," Claire said, putting her calendar back. "I was thinking about staking out a farmhouse."

"Grow op?"

"Not exactly." She looked at him, telling him that's all she could offer for the moment.

"Take your files with you," he said. "For when you get bored."

"That won't work," Claire told him. "I'll give it a pass for a night. I don't think the situation is going to change all that much in twenty-four hours."

Daniels got to his feet. "See you in court."

TWENTY-TWO

Late in the morning, rain began coming down in torrents. It was midafternoon when Virgil drove the Dodge pickup out of the brush and onto the side road and then east to the thruway. From there he headed south. All he knew about the location of the golf course was that it was somewhere near the town of Middletown.

He buckled his seat belt and kept to the speed limit. He didn't litter or cut anybody off in traffic or flip anyone the bird. There was no reason for anybody to be suspicious of a pickup truck with a local veterinary clinic's logo on the door, and Virgil wanted to keep it that way.

In Middletown he bought gas at a self-serve station and when he went inside to pay he asked the woman behind the counter for directions to the golf course.

"Which one? There's two close by."

Virgil couldn't remember the name of the course. He thought it had a tree in it.

"There's Whisky Links," the woman said. "It's just down the road. My husband plays there. And there's Burr Oak, over toward the river."

"Burr Oak," Virgil said, remembering.

"That's where all the doctors play," the woman said and she gave him directions.

Virgil took the highway out of Middletown, heading back east, and then turned left at a secondary road the woman had described. Ten minutes later, he came upon Burr Oak Golf and Country Club. The place would have been impossible to miss. It rose up out of the forest on Virgil's left like an English estate, with wrought-iron fencing surrounding the property and stone pillars marking the entrances.

The course was immaculately landscaped and the grass looked as if it had been cut with a scalpel. The surrounding countryside was relatively flat, but the course had long ago been bulldozed into rounded hills and long-running slopes. There were stands of birch trees and Norwegian spruce strategically planted here and there, and a fast-running stream, swollen by the rain, cutting across the layout. The fairways were lush and seemingly without a single weed.

All in all, it looked to Virgil like a waste of good farmland.

He drove half a mile before coming to the main gate, where he pulled into the entranceway and stopped. Sitting back several hundred yards was a massive fieldstone clubhouse, flanked by a pro shop on one side and utility buildings on the other. Due to the weather there were only a dozen or so cars in the large parking lot—mostly Mercedes-Benzes, Porsches, Cadillacs, and the odd Lexus. No clunkers and not a single Dodge pickup with a vet clinic logo on the door.

Virgil sat there for a time, looking at the place through the intermittent passes of the windshield wipers. Then he backed out and continued down the road. A couple miles along he came to an intersection and turned left. Heading west now, with the golf course hidden somewhere beyond the forest to his left, he came to a stone bridge, which spanned a narrow creek. He saw a sign that read COOPERS FALLS PARK and the beginning of a fence that ran the perimeter of the park. The fencing was about six feet high and built of redwood, or at least of wood stained to look like redwood. Virgil wondered if the park actually butted up against the back of the golf course.

Soon he came to another side road, this one running only to the left and marked by a large sign advertising the park entrance, with an arrow. Virgil turned and drove for several minutes before reaching the front gate. He pulled over and stopped. The park itself appeared to be huge, and there were signs advertising cabins, campgrounds, fishing, miniature golf, and horseback riding. The entrance road was cut through forest, what appeared to be virgin hardwood, with paved trails winding through the bush. As Virgil watched, a middle-aged couple jogged into view along one of the paths, a small white dog on a leash at their heels. They were wearing rain gear, hoods and nylon pants, and jogged with their heads down, following the trail where it ran close to the fence along the road and then curved back into the park.

Virgil drove into the park entrance and when he pulled up to the gatehouse, a young woman came out carrying a clipboard. She wore khaki shorts and a yellow T-shirt and was pulling on a windbreaker as she stepped out to meet him.

"Hi," she said.

"I thought I would go for a hike."

"In the rain?"

"I'm a die-hard. My only day off."

The girl shrugged. "Day pass?"

"Yeah."

"Eight dollars."

Virgil gave her a ten, and she went inside to get his change. Coming back outside, she took a moment to write down the license plate number from the Dodge. Then she walked over and handed Virgil two singles and the pass. She looked into the cab.

"You got rain gear?"

Virgil smiled. "Like I said. Old school."

"Have a nice hike," she said. She smiled at him as if he were an old geezer in a diner with soup on his chin.

Virgil followed the paved road into the grounds until he came to a parking lot beside a large pavilion with an imitation log cabin exterior. The pavilion served as a hub from which the paved trails ran in virtually every direction. Virgil parked in the lot and took the first path, heading toward the south—and the golf course.

He walked through the thick bush for maybe a mile, the trail twisting east and then back to the south. There were cabins nestled in the woods here and there, as well as areas designated for tents only. He saw several vehicles but few people, as everyone was presumably staying in out of the rain. Presently he came upon an opening in the trees and wood fencing that marked the boundary of the park. He found a stump to stand on and looked over the top rail. There was a ravine in front of him, and on the far side, about a quarter mile away, was the wrought-iron fence that bordered the back of the golf course.

Virgil glanced around him, but there was nobody in sight. He pulled himself up and over the fence, dropping onto the wet grass on the far side before starting down into the ravine. The creek he'd crossed earlier in the truck ran through the gully, and he waded across the shallow expanse, soaking himself to his knees. He climbed the far side of the ravine and approached the golf course. There were a number of golf balls in the long grass on the slope, as well as some beer cans, wine cooler bottles, and other trash. He stopped at the fence and found himself standing a short distance from a large, two-tiered green. The flag had a number five on it.

He heard the sound of an approaching cart and of men talking. He stepped back from the fence and crouched down by a scrub oak and waited. Apparently he wasn't the only one out in the rain. After a few moments he heard a ball hit the ground and looked to see it rolling onto the green. Another ball arrived shortly, this one missing the green and stopping in the longer grass alongside. Two men arrived in the cart and hurried up onto the green and putted out, running with their heads pulled down into their windbreakers like they were turtles, as if that would keep them dry. Then they were back in the cart and gone.

Virgil watched them drive off, apparently heading for the sixth hole. Joe Brady had said that Mickey Dupree had been killed in a sand trap on number seven. The golfers drove a short distance, then got out and teed off. The fairway they hit onto ran away from the boundary fence, down a hollow, and around to the right. Virgil wondered then if the next hole would angle back toward him. He looked far to his right and saw another green in the distance, partially hidden by a stand of pine trees. He started toward it and when he got close he could see through the pine needles the number on the flag. Seven. The green was no more than a hundred yards from the fence, with the evergreens serving as a buffer between the two.

A little farther along he was surprised to see a gate in the wrought-iron fence. The opening was six feet, wide enough for a cart to pass through. A worn path ran through the pine trees to the gate, and outside the fence, on the edge of the ravine, were large mounds of grass clippings, apparently dumped there by the course workers. There was a latch on the gate but no lock.

Virgil stayed out of sight until the two golfers played both the sixth and seventh holes. It was raining harder now, and he was soaked to the skin, his feet sloshing in his work boots.

When they were gone, he went through the gate and walked over to the green. There were two sand traps alongside, one in the front right, and the other at the rear. Virgil didn't know which trap the lawyer had died in, and he couldn't say what good the information might do him, even if he did.

In fact, he hadn't the slightest notion what he expected to find today. When he'd left the farm a couple of hours earlier, it had seemed like a good idea, visiting the scene of the crime. It was what someone in a detective novel would do. Now, standing there, with his boots full, his shirt soaked, and his hair dripping wet beneath his Mud Hens cap, he wondered what the gumshoe in the novel would do next. What would Sam Spade see that Virgil didn't? From the proximity of hole number seven to the fence line, and the cover the pine trees provided, it made sense to assume that the killer had entered the golf course from the direction of the park, but Virgil had to reason that the cops had already come to that conclusion. Forget Sam Spade, even Joe Brady would be able to figure that one out.

Virgil walked around the green and then stopped by the front bunker. He imagined Mickey Dupree lying there. A golf club shaft through the heart, Brady had said. Dupree had been a big man, six feet tall or more, and quite heavy. It wouldn't be an easy thing to do, to walk up to a man that size and drive a steel rod into his heart. Unless it was from behind. But Brady would have specified if it had been from behind. It's the type of thing he would have harped on: the equivalent of shooting a man in the back, a cowardly act.

Virgil heard the sound of another approaching motor, this one louder than the golf cart. He stood and walked into the pines and waited until he saw a Gator driving up the fairway, a man behind the wheel wearing a pith helmet and work coveralls. Virgil decided he had seen enough, and before the man got too close, he turned and went out through the gate and down into the gully.

When he got back to the truck he removed his boots and his wet socks and drove off in his bare feet. He went back to the highway and was headed for the thruway when he realized he didn't know where he was heading. He didn't want to risk going back to the farm so soon after the scrap at Hopman's place. He didn't think Hopman had recognized him but couldn't be sure. The man wasn't bright, but it didn't take a genius to put two and two together. Virgil could spend the night in the woods behind the farm again, but he wasn't looking forward to that, not in the pouring rain. He'd be forced to sleep in the truck and that held little appeal.

He stayed on the highway and drove west until he came to a town, a crossroads really, that had a motel and a corner store. He bought himself a six-pack of Budweiser in the corner store and took a room for the night at the motel. The registration form at the front desk required that he list his occupation. Despite the logo on the truck, Virgil knew he didn't look much like a veterinary doctor in his drenched state. So he put down "farrier."

It was close enough, he figured.

TWENTY-THREE

Claire sat in the front row and watched as Miller Boddington made his way into the courtroom through the side entrance. With him was his new lawyer, the man named Rafael, a West Coast bohemian of about sixty-five with shoulder-length gray hair, the mane expensively cut and quite lovely, if you liked that sort of thing. Claire didn't. Long hair on adult males was for people in heavy metal rock bands, or who thought they were Jesus. She might be willing to make an exception for Jesus himself, if he were to show up. Everybody else should get a haircut.

But it was Boddington himself who held her eye. He was wearing a white linen suit and a matching fedora. The last time she had seen him in this courtroom, he'd been wearing blue jeans and Tony Lama boots. But back then he had been a horseman, and now he was a newly minted vintner. A little man in constant flux. Claire wondered how a guy the size of an average thirteen-year-old managed to find such haberdashery.

Judge Santiago turned out to be a woman, which Claire hoped was a positive development. During preliminary discussions regarding jury selection for the upcoming trial, it had been determined that women were more intolerant of animal cruelty than were men.

Claire had spent the previous evening at home, going over her notes. She'd had difficulty concentrating, as her mind kept returning to Virgil Cain's farm. She hoped she wasn't missing out on a chance to catch him. Given the incident the night before at Hopman's—if he actually was the assailant, and she'd wager a month's pay that he was—she was confident he wasn't straying all that far afield. But then her mind would play the devil's advocate, and she would worry that the fight at Hopman's might have convinced him it was finally time to hit the road. She'd gone to bed with the notion but was too wound up to sleep. When she finally nodded off, it seemed her alarm was ringing within minutes. Time to go to court.

When Alex Daniels walked in, he stopped for a moment by Claire's side.

"You ready?" he asked.

"Sure," Claire said. "Be nice if I knew what for."

"You and me both."

Boddington's case was first up on the docket and after Judge Santiago was announced and seated, the real estate lawyer Rafael from San Francisco stood and humbly introduced himself. He went on to ask in advance the court's forgiveness for any naïveté he might display during the proceedings, as he was somewhat out of his element—although, he hastened to add, he was indeed licensed to practice in the state of New York—and had been in possession of the facts of the case for only a few short days. Lawyers were always referring to short days, Claire thought, watching him. Unless they were referring to time spent on a case. Those were invariably long days, and nights as well, especially when converted into billable hours. Rafael concluded his little soliloquy by thanking Judge Santiago, apparently for allowing him to babble.

And then he filed a motion that all charges against Miller Boddington be withdrawn.

"Your honor," he said, "I have spent many long hours examining these papers, and it has become abundantly clear to me that this is the most blatant violation of the Sixth Amendment I have ever seen."

Claire wondered just how often Rafael ran afoul of the Sixth when doing property searches out in wine country. Daniels, at the prosecution table, turned to glance at her, his eyebrows raised.

"Twenty-five months!" Rafael thundered then, his voice soaring like that of a TV preacher. "And in that time we haven't even made it through the discovery phase. What in the world is going on here? This thing has cost my client an enormous amount of money and, more to the point, it has cost his personal reputation more than we could ever calculate. He has wanted from day one—"

"Your honor," Daniels interrupted, getting to his feet. "I see now why my friend made a point of establishing his unfamiliarity with the facts. That turns out to be an understatement. Yes, this case has been on the books for twenty-five months, but the blame for that snail-like pace can be laid entirely at the feet of the accused. If your honor would take a look at the court's history of this matter, she will see that on virtually every occasion, the continuances granted were at the request of Mr. Boddington's lawyer."

"Yes!" Rafael said emphatically. Holding his forefinger in the air, as if testing the wind, he walked toward the bench. "However, these continuances were not in compliance with Mr. Boddington's wishes. They were forced upon him, in each and every instance, by his legal representation at the time."

Daniels came forward now as well. "If my friend is in agreement that the delays were all perpetrated by Mr. Boddington's counsel, I have a question, your honor." He smiled. "What does that have to do with us?"

"I must raise a point," Rafael said before Santiago could

reply. He addressed Daniels now. "Have you served as prosecutor on this matter from the start, sir?"

"No, I haven't."

"I thought not. So is there a chance that you are not as familiar with the facts of the case as you lead us to believe?"

"I've been on it for ten months," Daniels said. "You've been involved for ten minutes. Do you wish to pursue that argument?" He paused. "As I said, what does this have to do with us?"

Santiago seemed inclined to agree. She looked at Rafael. "Mr. Rafael?"

"It has everything to do with you, Mr. Daniels," Rafael said. Careful not to go after Santiago, Claire noted. "This court has acted as an enabler for Michael Dupree. Now we are all aware of the tragedy that has since befallen Mr. Dupree, but that cannot stand in the way of what has happened here. Let not one tragedy give birth to another. The Sixth Amendment clearly states under length of delay—that a delay of a year or more—"

"I think we are all aware of the guarantees of the amendment," Santiago said.

"Of course," Rafael said, bowing slightly. The guy was an act. "Not to waste the court's time then. But I suggest that my client has been prepared to answer to these charges from day one. And yet his representation, for reasons which I fear will remain unknown to us, was loath to do so. My client is a layman, a winemaker by trade, and he is unfamiliar with this business of courtroom procedure. He trusted his counsel to do the right thing, but, more to the point, he trusted this court to do the right thing. Why did this court not hold Michael Dupree to task? Why did this court deny my client his right to a speedy trial?"

Santiago turned to Daniels. "I wasn't here, Mr. Daniels. So I'm going to ask you to field that one."

"Mr. Boddington's lawyer asked for and received nine continuances over the twenty-five-month period," Daniels said. "His reasons were varied, but they had one thing in common: in each instance the presiding judge asked Mr. Boddington if he was in agreement with his lawyer's request. And each time Mr. Boddington said yes. And I submit that even a . . . layman winemaker . . . knows the difference between yes and no."

Santiago took a moment and then actually released a sigh of resignation. Watching her, Claire suspected that she'd had no notion of what she was getting into, filling in for Harrison for the day. She was probably thinking it would be a nice road trip upstate, a few minor rulings, perhaps a quiet dinner along the river, and then back to the city.

"All right," she decided. "This is what we're going to do. We're going to go over these continuances, one by one. I suggest you two sit down and get comfortable."

Claire stayed for fifteen minutes or so. Her presence wasn't required; the details for the remands were painstakingly transcribed in the court records. After listening for a while, she went looking for a cup of coffee.

Instead she found Joe Brady, hurrying up the stairs to the second-floor lobby. He had just arrived from Canada, he told her, and came straight to the courthouse.

"You bring me any maple syrup?" Claire asked.

"Huh?"

"What are you doing here?" she asked. She saw now that he hadn't shaved. She could smell his body odor as well.

"I have a trial starting," he said. "The dentist with the DUI. I didn't even have time to stop at the house."

"You've got more time than you think," Claire said. "Miller Boddington's in there with a spanking-new lawyer and they're trying to have everything tossed."

"What?"

"That's what I said." Claire started for the stairs. There was a coffee shop on the main floor.

Joe followed. "Don't you want to hear what I found out up north?"

"Oh yeah," Claire said without stopping. "Did you bring Cain back?"

"No. But they're getting close."

Claire smiled. Joe tagged along but didn't say anything else until Claire got her coffee and they were seated at a table.

"You were saying they're getting close," she said.

"They figure he's in Quebec, somewhere around Three Rivers. He has history there. In fact, that's where he did time for attempted murder."

"I thought it was aggravated assault."

"The original charge was attempted murder."

"But the conviction wasn't," Claire said. "Did you find out what was behind that?"

"Well . . . no."

"Why not?" Claire asked. "Aren't you kind of curious why he beat that guy up? I mean, there must have been a reason."

Joe snorted in dismissal. "I'm not concerned with what he did in another country years ago. I'm concerned with what he did here. And you should be too."

"I am very concerned," Claire said. "My sleep is suffering."

"Anyway," Joe said, "these guys always return to their old stomping grounds. They have the provincial police on it, and the Mounties too. He'll turn up, or someone will roll over on him."

"Somebody always does," Claire said. She sipped her coffee and looked around the little shop. Joe's aroma was getting to her.

He exhaled heavily, trying to get her attention. "You don't seem real interested in this."

"No?" she asked. "I guess my mind's on Boddington and his new lawyer. I think he might be wearing hair extensions."

"Boddington?"

"The lawyer." Claire had another drink. "Hey, I hope the Mounties get Cain. If they catch him, we don't have to."

"This guy killed two people, Claire. In cold blood, in our backyard."

"Somebody killed two people. Let's give the guy his day in court."

"Don't start that shit."

"Two people that you hated, Joe." Claire decided that if she had to sit there with him, she wasn't going to pretend to enjoy it.

"I don't hate anybody."

"No?" Claire asked. "You didn't hate Mickey Dupree? I sat in that courtroom upstairs and listened to him call you an imbecile. On the stand. In front of a judge and a jury and the whole wide world of the media."

"I didn't like the man," Joe said. "But that doesn't mean I'm glad that he's dead. And I'll tell you something else—I think Alan Comstock killed that girl. But I didn't want him dead either. I believe in the system. Even when it fails, I still believe in it."

"Then how come you've already convicted Cain?"

"I haven't," Joe said and got to his feet. "But the courts will. Who else had reason to do this, Claire? Who else wanted both those guys dead? Answer that for me."

"I don't know, Joe."

"I'm going to get some breakfast. I've been driving all night. You've gotten awful negative over the last couple years, Claire. I don't know what's wrong with you."

She watched him walk away. *What's wrong with me isn't the issue here, Joe.*

When she went back into the courtroom they were still slogging through the court's history with Miller Boddington. The man himself was seated at the defendant's table, his legs crossed, the new fedora on his knee. He was looking very confident, Claire thought, but then she had never seen him looking otherwise. He had a detachment about him, something he had perfected long ago, Claire suspected, a defense mechanism that allowed him to give the impression that he knew a lot more than he did. But to Claire he was a skinny little prick of five foot four who had never accomplished anything of merit in his life, save being born to an absentee father who had left him roughly half a billion dollars when he died. The old man had been in the banking business in Texas, pre-Enron, and had he not died in a plane crash off the coast of Belize, he probably would have been indicted with the rest of that bunch when everything turned to shit in the '90s. If he had, then maybe the courts and the investors would have taken him down and there would have been no fortune for Miller to inherit. Without the money, it was likely that Miller wouldn't be wearing that smug look today.

When the record was finally read in full, it was a quarter past noon. Rafael then performed another star turn as the indignant constitutionalist, and Alex Daniels responded by detailing how his office had been attempting to get Mickey Dupree to commit to a trial date for two years. Judge Santiago adjourned for lunch, saying she would make a ruling later that day.

At four o'clock that afternoon, she dismissed all the charges against Miller Boddington.

Claire was back in the courtroom at the time and didn't even wait for the judge to finish talking. She went back to the station and started going through her messages. Alex Daniels walked in ten minutes later.

"What the hell just happened?" he asked, sitting down.

Claire looked at him. "You here again? People are going to start to talk."

"What happened?"

"We just got snookered by the dashing Rafael de Costa," Claire said. "That's what happened. By the way, I did some digging on that guy. His real name is Ralphie Cox. He's from Cleveland."

"You're kidding."

"Yes, I'm kidding."

"Well, I'm going to indict Boddington again," Daniels said.

"That might not be easy," Claire told him.

"Why not? It's not double jeopardy. We never made it to trial."

"Yeah, but we had trouble the first time around," Claire said. "You weren't here yet. There was a whole to-do about whether or not he was in control of what happened to the horses, or if it fell to his underlings. Boddington tried to say he was totally hands-off, that he had no idea how the animals were being treated. And then he threw his foreman to the wolves, saying it was all his fault. We had to argue that everything was in his name, so he was responsible. So there's that. And now the case is tainted with what went down today. Thanks to Rafael and his Sixth fucking Amendment."

"You think he got to her?"

"The judge?" Claire asked.

"Yeah."

"No. What he got was shit lucky. He came in swinging for the fences and he happened to connect. Harrison wouldn't have dismissed."

"That's because Harrison was the judge who granted the continuances," Daniels said.

"That's right. But somehow Boddington knew we had a fill-in and he took a shot. Like when you had a substitute teacher in school—you always had to see what you could get away with. He probably had a ten percent chance of dismissal and he won. Santiago should have held it over until next month and let Harrison rule. But how old is the woman, thirty-five? She's a rookie judge and she must have figured, you know, she needed to make her mark. First day here and all. And twenty-five months is twenty-five months."

"You're a lot calmer about this than I expected," Daniels said.

"I'm a lot calmer than you," Claire said, smiling.

"But it was your case."

"Yeah. But I knew all along that I wasn't going to get any great satisfaction out of it. What were they going to do, put Boddington in jail? Not fucking likely, Alex. With a guy like that, sometimes all you can hope for is that his reputation takes a big hit, and he stops doing whatever he was doing. He's looked pretty bad in the media over this. Everybody loves horses, even people who have never been within a mile of one."

"You think Boddington cares about that part of it?"

"About his image?" Claire asked. "Did you see the outfit on the guy today? That's all he cares about. How he looks."

Daniels got to his feet. "Speaking of image, this thing today doesn't do much for my office. What the hell do I do about that?"

"In the short term? Not much." Claire smiled. "Bear in mind the words of a great American philosopher. 'Keep your eyes on the road and your hands upon the wheel.'"

"Who said that, Dale Earnhardt?"

"Jim Morrison."

Daniels was too young and too buttoned-down to be hip to

The Doors. "Right. I'll let you get back to work. You got your stakeout tonight?"

"I'm still thinking about it."

"You want to tell me what it is?"

"I'm still thinking about that too."

Claire packed up and left a few minutes after Daniels. When she got home, she plugged her cell phone in to charge and slid a frozen mini pizza in the oven. She showered and changed into jeans and an old Everlast T-shirt. She put a couple of water bottles and a banana in a knapsack, along with her Beretta, her badge, and her cuffs.

She opened a beer and sat in the living room and ate the pizza. She had been trying to decide for two days the best way to approach the farmhouse. If she showed up when it was still daylight, she risked being seen, either by Cain if he was in the area, or by somebody else. Like Mary Nelson, for instance. And she was pretty sure where Mary Nelson's loyalties lay, especially after the incident at Hopman's. Damsels in distress tend to stand by their rescuers. Claire knew that she herself would, if anybody ever rescued her. Of course, no one ever had. Not even close.

She had been back and forth in her mind on whether she should take someone with her. But she couldn't do that without alerting the department as to what she was up to. That much surveillance could blow the whole deal. She was fairly certain of one thing: if Cain knew they were aware he was still in the area, he'd be gone. And he was smart enough, Claire was convinced, that he wouldn't head north into Canada. In fact, he was smart enough that they might never find him. Which meant that the prevailing opinion that he was guilty would not change. The department would consider the case solved, with the suspect still at large.

She knew she had to go alone. Even one uniform would be one too many. She was, she knew, feeling a little possessive about Virgil Cain, and that part bothered her. But part of that was his doing. He hadn't chosen to call Joe Brady at home. She told herself he'd called her not because she had good legs but because he'd considered her to be smart as well. Maybe she was going this alone because she was determined to prove she was smarter than him. Nothing that had happened so far would suggest that was true.

She finished the pizza and leaned back and drank the beer, trying to decide whether to go or to stay. It would help if she knew what time he would be showing up. It would help if she knew if he would be showing up at all.

She was still deliberating when there was a knock on the door. She opened it and Todd slouched in, wearing his hangdog look as if it were a novelty mask.

"Hey," he said.

"What are you doing here?" she demanded.

He either missed her tone or chose to ignore it. He walked over and flopped on the couch. Stretching out his legs, he put his feet on the coffee table. "Oh, what a day."

Claire stood looking at him. He was wearing his usual outfit. Dockers and a knit shirt with the name of his flooring company on it. Top-Siders with no socks.

"Should I get you a highball and your slippers, honey?" she asked.

"Pardon?"

"What the fuck are you doing here?" Claire practically shouted it.

"I don't know," he mumbled and took his feet off the table. "Just thought I'd stop and say hi."

"Hi," Claire said with mock gaiety. "Now hit the road. I have to go to work."

He sat there glumly for a few more seconds and then got to his feet. He was like a mopey teenager. "I might have to sell the house," he told her. "If things don't pick up, I'm going to have to do something."

What does this have to do with me, Claire wanted to ask. Talking to him was like watching the same rerun, over and over. It was like that movie *Groundhog Day*. Claire was a real-life version of Bill Murray in the film. Too bad it wasn't a movie; at least then she could hit the mute button whenever Todd started talking.

"I don't know how things got so screwed up, Claire," he said. "I keep thinking that everything was good when we were together. Why couldn't I see that?"

"Did you hit your head?" she asked. "Things were a mess when we were together. You were always broke and I had to bail us out. Look at you now. Who the fuck told you to buy an eight-hundred-thousand-dollar house? *And* a cottage. And all the rest of your toys. Who's going to come to your rescue now? Miss Implants? I don't think so. You need to start living in the real world, Todd."

"See? You can talk sense to me."

"For the love of—" Claire said, offering her palms in surrender. "I have to go to work. You want to talk to somebody but you don't want to listen. You don't need a counselor, you need a dog. But knowing you, you'll pay ten grand for the mutt."

He started for the door and stopped. She thought for a moment that she had gotten through to him. At long last. Then he turned to her. "Do you want to have lunch tomorrow?"

"Go home, Todd."

TWENTY-FOUR

By morning Virgil's clothes weren't quite dry, and his boots weren't even close. The motel had no laundry facilities and even if it did, he had nothing to wear while he washed what was on his back anyway. He could find a department store and buy new clothes and shoes, but his money was dwindling. And a man wearing everything brand-new was conspicuous. He would have to go back to the house.

He waited until late afternoon and then drove to the woods at the back of the farm. He'd been hiding the truck on an old snowmobile trail deep in the woods, out of sight of anybody who happened down the side road. The lane was muddy from the rain the previous day, and pulling in, he immediately got stuck. It took him half an hour to free the truck, after piling pine branches under the back wheels.

Carrying the binoculars, he walked past the cattle herd to his lookout point in the cedars. There were no vehicles in the vicinity of the house or barns, but then he hadn't expected there to be. He watched the windows of the house for a time, and the road out front, but couldn't see anything out of the ordinary. It was dry under the evergreens. After a while he stretched out on the needles and waited for darkness.

At dusk, he got up and started along the lane, staying close to the fencerow. As he walked, he thought about the prospect of dry feet. He had bought a new pair of work boots six months earlier but hadn't worn them as he'd wanted to get as many miles as possible out of the pair he was wearing. But now he was looking forward to the new boots as well as dry socks. Funny how a man never gives any thought to dry feet until he doesn't have dry feet.

Arriving at the house, he went in through the basement window again. It took him a while, fumbling in the darkness, to find the new work boots, still in their box on a shelf above the furnace. Feeling his way up the stairs, he went to the second floor and into his room. He searched through the dresser for jeans and underwear and socks. Walking across the hallway into the bathroom, he ran the shower while he stripped down.

As he was stepping into the tub, he heard an approaching vehicle and glanced out the window to see car headlights illuminating the road out front, moving past the farm. When he saw lights on the roof of the car he did a double take, but then he realized it was a taxicab, not a police cruiser.

He had a long shower in the dark, washing his hair and scrubbing the scratchy beard. He wished he could shave but knew he shouldn't chance it. Turning the water off, he pulled the shower curtain back and, as he did, it occurred to him that he had never seen a taxi this far out of town before. He was still thinking about it when the bathroom light clicked on.

Claire Marchand was standing just inside the doorway, holding a towel in her left hand and a Beretta semiautomatic in her right. She offered Virgil the towel and pointed the muzzle of the gun at his chest.

"I don't want to shoot you, Virgil Cain," she said. "But I will."

Claire knew that the thing to do was just call it in. Have a couple uniforms come out and take him back to Kingston and lock him up. And maybe even make a concentrated effort to keep him locked up this time. But for reasons that she couldn't fully identify, even to herself, she didn't choose to do that. At least not right away. She remembered the last time they'd had him in custody, how he'd clammed up. Not willing to talk, not wanting a lawyer even. He had been a lot more communicative the night he had called her on the phone.

She let him dry off and get dressed, although she had to admit he looked pretty good not dressed. He looked like a guy who worked out, although she doubted he did. Maybe farmers didn't need to.

Once he was fully clothed, she tossed her handcuffs to him and instructed him to put them on. She stayed back, keeping the 9mm trained on him as he did so. She was aware that he was bigger and stronger than she was and that he had little compunction against the notion of flight. When he was cuffed, she took him by the collar and directed him downstairs, turning lights on as they went. She sat him down at the kitchen table and took the chair opposite. He spoke for the first time since stepping out of the shower.

"What the hell are you doing here?"

His tone was identical to the one she'd used on Todd a couple of hours earlier, and that alone was enough to set her back on her heels. She didn't reply for a few seconds. She was feeling strangely shy in his presence, and the feeling both puzzled and aggravated her. She looked at his hair, mussed and still wet from the shower, and at the rough growth of beard. He had a scar on his chin she hadn't noticed before. The whiskers didn't grow in the scar tissue, making it more prevalent. She wondered how he got it.

"I'm investigating an assault in the area," she told him.

"That a fact?" He sounded skeptical.

"Yes, it is. You know a guy named Dirk Hopman?"

"Yeah."

"I thought so. Friend of yours?"

"No."

"Well, you won't be too upset then to hear that somebody kicked the shit out of him a few nights ago."

"Now who would do a thing like that?"

"I have my suspicions."

"Guy like Hopman, he might've deserved it," Virgil said.

"That was my thinking too."

He twisted his wrists in the handcuffs. They were obviously uncomfortable. Claire saw now that the knuckles on his right hand were raw and bruised.

"Your hand is a mess," she said.

"I was fixing a fan belt on my truck."

"We have your truck."

"Oh yeah." He placed his hands atop the Arborite table, turning the knuckles away from her eyes. "So you don't care about Hopman, then why bother with him? I thought you said you'd try to find out who killed Dupree and Comstock."

"I'm working on it," Claire said. "But I've been tracking an escaped prisoner too. Not to boast, but I can do more than one thing at a time."

"If you found out who killed those guys, the escaped prisoner would turn himself in. Then you wouldn't have to be snooping around his farm, sneaking up in a taxicab."

"Okay, this third-person shit is beginning to bother me," Claire said. "By the way—aren't you supposed to be in Canada?"

"Supposed to be? Is anybody where they're supposed to be?"

"You're going to get philosophical on me?" Claire asked. He didn't reply and she didn't expect him to. "Well, you fooled some of the people. Joe Brady thinks you're in Canada."

"Joe Brady probably thinks the world is flat," Virgil said. "When you get done patting yourself on the back for finding me, maybe you could tell me what you found out. Since you're so good at doing more than one thing at a time."

"You have a lot of attitude for somebody wearing handcuffs," Claire told him. "You want to know about the murder investigation? I can tell you that I just captured the prime suspect."

"But you don't believe I did it."

"Says who?" Claire asked.

"Me. If you did, you'd have called for a paddy wagon by now. Instead, we're sitting around the kitchen table like it's downhome Saturday night. I expect you'll break out the checkerboard any moment now."

"How do you know I didn't call before I came into the bathroom?"

"I got a hunch. So why don't you tell me what you've found out? What did Buddy Townes have to say?"

"How do you know I talked to Buddy?"

"You told me you were going to talk to him. You don't remember our phone conversation?"

"I remember our phone conversation. Every word." This was going too fast. Claire got up and walked over and looked in the fridge. There were things in there that needed to be thrown away. "As I recall, you were calling from the local diner and letting on you were at the North Pole."

Turning, she saw that she surprised him with that. She smiled. "Buddy didn't tell me a lot," she said. She closed the door. "But then, like everybody else, he's of the opinion that you're the guy. Problem is, you're still the best fit for this thing, you know."

"He changed his mind, I think," Virgil said. "When I talked to him."

Claire walked back to the table. "You talked to Buddy? When?"

"Same day you did. Well, later that night. Outside of Fat Phil's. You were actually in the vicinity. I saw you going into the liquor store across the street." He returned the smile.

"You did not."

"I did. You bought two bottles of Argentinean red. You were wearing jeans and a V-neck and driving a Honda. You looked very nice. If I wasn't a desperate killer on the run, I might have followed you home."

"And I might have shot you."

"I guess," Virgil said. "We'll never know."

"That's right. You'll never know. What did Buddy tell you?"

"He said there's a lot of people who—what word did you use? Who *fit*. Buddy told me he could name a couple dozen people who had motive of one kind or another. Just a matter of finding the right one and then connecting them to the crime scenes. You got nothing that puts me at either place. By the way, I assume you know that whoever killed Dupree went through the park. You know, to get to the golf course."

"How would you—" Claire began, then she realized. "You do get around, don't you? When were you there?"

"Yesterday. In the pouring rain."

"Right. Because you knew nobody would be on the course in a rainstorm."

"Actually, it was a coincidence," Virgil told her. "But you agree with me?"

"Either that or he could have walked in from the highway, along the ravine," Claire said.

"That's a long, wet walk along that creek. I say he went through the park. Which means the gatehouse would have his license number. Did anybody check that out?"

"Detective Virgil Cain," Claire said, smiling. "Yeah, Joe Brady checked it out."

"Joe Brady," Virgil said doubtfully. "What else has he been doing?"

"Well, he was in Canada yesterday, asking the police up there why they haven't run you to ground yet. Apparently they're watching your old haunts, among other things."

"You let Joe drive all the way up there when you knew I was here?"

Virgil waited for Claire to say something and when she didn't, he smiled again.

"So Joe checked out the license plates," he said. "Tell me something, if a cop drove into the park, would the kid working there write down his license plate number? I'm thinking probably not."

"What are you saying?" Claire asked. "You think Joe killed Mickey Dupree?"

"I think Joe Brady is a little too convinced I'm the guy," Virgil said. "And I'd like to know why. Buddy Townes tells me that Dupree made a fool out of Brady in public, more than once. I'm guessing it wasn't hard to do. I saw it with my own eyes at Alan Comstock's trial. Doesn't that put Brady on the list of people who might want to bump Dupree off?"

"Joe Brady didn't kill Mickey Dupree."

"You saying that because you think I did? Then why haven't you called for a cruiser to come get me yet?"

"I intend to," Claire said.

"What's keeping you?"

"Well, it appears you've been doing some amateur police work. I thought I might pick your brain before I hand you over. I'm not worried about you escaping. That's not going to happen again."

He looked at the tabletop and said nothing.

236

"How'd you get that screen off anyway?" she asked. "In Kesselberg."

"Remember the lighter you let me keep? The Zippo?"

"Yeah."

"In a pinch, you can use it as a socket wrench." Virgil looked at her now.

"Well, well," Claire said. "You learn something new every day."

"If I tell you something else you don't know, will you let me go?"

"You could tell me the winning numbers for the New York State Lottery and I wouldn't let you go."

He shrugged, his expression indifferent. She might as well have been a waitress, informing him they were out of the sea bass. He raised the handcuffs and scratched the whiskers on his chin with the back of his hand. She realized that she no longer thought it was just a possibility that he could be innocent. But she wasn't supposed to be making that kind of judgment. She was supposed to arrest him and take him in and let the courts decide who was guilty and who was not.

"So what do you want to tell me?" she asked.

"We have a deal?"

"No," she said emphatically. "You think I'm going to lose my badge over you? I let you go and this time you really are going to disappear. My job is to bring you in. And that's what I'm going to do."

"But you know I won't disappear," Virgil said. "I would've already. The way I see it, I take off and I spend the rest of my life waiting for a knock on the door. Or a pretty girl standing outside the shower with a semiautomatic in her hand."

"You think flattering me is going to work?"

"I'm pulling out all the stops here," Virgil said. "But hey, you are a pretty girl with a semiautomatic."

She waited for him to smile. But this time he didn't.

"Give me three days," he said.

"What are you going to do with three days?"

"I want to talk to Buddy Townes again. For starters."

"Why?"

"I told you. Buddy said he could name a lot of people who might have motive. But he couldn't come up with the common denominator, you know, between Dupree and Comstock. Other than me. Well, I figured something out since then."

"What?"

"We have a deal?"

"Stop asking me that. Why would I let you go?"

"Because you haven't had any luck with this so far. If you're not going to do your job, maybe I can do it for you."

Claire pulled her cell phone from her pocket. "I've heard enough. Let's see if we can find a paddy wagon big enough for you and your ego."

She punched in a number and waited. Then she told whoever answered to send a cruiser to the farm. She gave them the address and hung up. Virgil was looking at her.

"Did I hurt your feelings or something?" he asked.

"Now you're flattering yourself."

"All I meant was that maybe I could approach it from a different angle. You've got to admit that I have more to lose than you do."

"That's why you need to hire a good lawyer. You're not the Lone Ranger. If you're innocent, you get off. That's how the system works."

Claire pulled a chair out and sat down, keeping her distance. They waited in silence for a time. There was an uncomfortable feeling in the air, as if they had just had their first fight and neither was willing to make a conciliatory move.

"Would you mind if I check that the horses have water?" Virgil asked finally.

"We'll wait here," Claire told him.

But then she remembered that the last time she had been there, the trough had been nearly empty. Well, that wasn't her concern. She wasn't an agent of the SPCA; she had bigger issues to deal with. She put it from her mind and forced herself to think about her day. Capturing Virgil Cain had been the only positive. In the negative column, there had been yet another annoying Todd visit, and the rookie judge's decision to kick Miller Boddington free. As soon as Boddington came to mind, she thought about all he'd done that he would never have to answer to. Abusing his own horses, depriving them of food. And water.

Jesus Christ, she thought, and stood up. "You try to run and I'll shoot you."

Virgil got to his feet. "You keep saying that."

"Only because I mean it."

He turned on a switch for a yard light, and they went outside and headed for the pump house. Claire had a small flashlight in her pocket and when they got there she shined it in the water trough. It was roughly a quarter full. They walked into the pump house, where Virgil turned on an overhead light and then hit the switch for the pump. It clanked noisily into action and ran for maybe a minute, and then sparks flew from the side of it and it stopped. Virgil turned the switch off at once and walked over to kneel beside the pump.

"What's wrong?" Claire asked.

"Probably a loose connection," he said. "Pump needs new bearings and it vibrates a lot. I have to tighten the wires every now and then. Can you hand me that screwdriver on the windowsill?"

Claire found the screwdriver and gave it to him. He removed the cover from the connection box and began to tighten the screws. It was a clumsy procedure due to the handcuffs, yet he never suggested she remove them. Claire felt odd, standing there with the Beretta in her hand, watching while he fixed his water pump.

"So you're an electrician too?" she asked.

"No."

"Then how do you know how to do that?" she asked. "Just a smart guy, I guess."

"Shit," he said, standing up. "I'm trying to make a living off a hundred acres. Nobody's going to call that smart. This isn't exactly prime farmland around here. If I get enough rain, but not too much, I can grow enough hay and grain to feed my stock. Make a few bucks on my soybeans, *maybe*. Send a couple dozen steers to market come fall. And if everything goes right, I might have just enough money to be dumb enough to try again next year. If that's smart, I'd hate to see stupid."

"Then why do you do it?"

"Well, I used to play ball but I got too old for that," Virgil said. "And I don't think I'm cut out for punching a time clock. I guess I could be a cop but apparently to do that you have to keep threatening to shoot people all day long, and I'm not interested in that either."

"You could always be a comedian."

"You think so?"

"Or you could just answer me. Why do you do it?"

Virgil walked over to the pump switch, hesitated there as he tried to come up with a reply. "I just stumbled into this, trying to help a friend, but the truth of the matter is, I like being a farmer. Pretty simple, eh? I don't know, maybe I was born in the wrong century. I'm not good with abstracts. When I'm working, I need to see that I've accomplished something. You got a field of hay, for instance. You cut it and bale it and then put it in the mow. There's no . . . theory to it." He shrugged. "I like how it makes me feel at the end of the day."

He hit the switch and the pump kicked into action again. This time it ran fine. Claire could hear the water gushing into the trough outside. Virgil walked to the window, his face half-cast in shadow and his eyes narrow, his brow creased. Claire had the feeling that he was almost as worried about his farm as he was about himself. He was a farmer because he liked the way it made him feel at the end of the day. Claire tried to remember the last time she had felt that way. "Tell me what I don't know."

He never moved a muscle, just kept looking out the window. She was about to ask him again when he spoke. "Whoever killed them, knew them," he said.

"That's it? That's always been the assumption."

He turned. "But you also assumed they were killed by somebody who had it in for them. They weren't. They were both killed by somebody they trusted. That's the key. Think about it—somebody walked up to a guy Dupree's size and drove a steel shaft into his heart, and he just let them? There was no struggle in that sand trap, right? And Comstock is armed to the teeth and still somebody shoots him six times with his own gun."

"With Dupree, he was whacked in the head first. Probably with the golf club that killed him."

"From the front or the back?"

"Front."

"Same thing then. He wasn't afraid of the guy."

Claire thought for a moment. "And if it had been you who showed up, they wouldn't have let you get close."

"Yeah."

"So this theory exonerates you? At least to your way of thinking."

"To my way of thinking, I had already exonerated me. It's you people I need to work on."

Claire smiled at that. He turned away, glancing out the window again, watching the trough as it filled.

"Tell me what happened in Quebec. Who was the woman who lost her house?"

He kept his eyes on the pipe gushing water outside, and she could tell he was deciding whether to tell her the story. "Her name was Madeleine Jones," he began. "She raised me. Small town south of Montreal that you've never heard of. She had a little bungalow on ten acres on the edge of town. Used to be an orchard but the trees were all dead by the time I got there. Place was overgrown."

"Where were your parents?"

"My old man split. My mother was killed in a plane crash. Going on vacation to Mexico with some guy."

"So Madeleine Jones adopted you?"

"Yeah, something like that," he said, dismissing the details. "Anyway, after I left home they started developing the area. Town was a bedroom community for people who worked in the city. Typical stuff. This lawyer Finley kept trying to buy the property so he could turn it into a subdivision. Madeleine wouldn't sell. She didn't have two nickels to rub together but she wouldn't sell. She didn't want it all bulldozed. One thing led to another and then she met up with this guy, allegedly some handyman or something, and they started seeing each other. Romantically, you know? He was quite a bit younger than her. She was getting up there, and her mind was starting to go, I guess, and somehow this handyman ended up with the title to the property. Well, you can figure it out. The handyman was working for Finley. Next thing you know, Madeleine is out on the street. They basically stole the place out from under her. I was playing ball in Toledo at the time, or maybe I could have stopped it. She filed charges against Finley and the handyman, but they had their bases covered. She lived the last couple years of her life in a little apartment in town, over a Chinese restaurant. After she died I ran into Finley one day and well, again, one thing led to another. As it sometimes does."

"And you went to jail and he didn't?"

"That's right."

He turned to look at her then. He shrugged and at that moment Claire's cell phone rang. She pulled it from her pocket and answered.

"It's me," she heard Todd say. "I just wanted to tell you . . . I needed to tell you that . . . that I was happier with you than I ever was at any other time in my life."

"Not now," she said into the phone and hung up. She looked at Virgil and almost smiled. He and Todd were roughly the same age, with similar backgrounds. However, they might as well have been from different planets. Todd wouldn't know how to fix the old pump, and he wouldn't have the inclination to learn. Instead, he'd pay somebody a thousand dollars to come out and install a new one. And he'd put the thousand on his credit card.

She saw a flash of light in her peripheral vision and turned to see a vehicle pull in the drive up by the house. It was the county police.

"Shit."

"What?" Virgil asked.

"There's a cruiser here."

Virgil had a look. "Well, you called them."

"No, I didn't."

"You didn't?"

"Shit," she said again. "They must have been doing a drive-by and saw the house lights were on." She bit her bottom lip, struggling with something. Then she turned to him, and after a moment she put the Beretta in her coat pocket and walked over and unlocked the cuffs.

"You just got done telling me how dumb you are. Well, I'm giving you a run for your money, doing this. But I know if they lock you up again, it's going to be case closed, at least to people like Joe. We don't have the budget to be investigating murders that have already been solved."

She took her card from her jacket and put it in his shirt pocket. "My cell's on there. You find anything, I'd better be the first to know."

Virgil rubbed his wrists and nodded to her. It seemed he was too surprised to speak. "Get going. You got three days."

"The trough isn't full."

"I'll fill the damn trough. Go."

So he went, out through the door and toward the barn, where the darkness soon took him in. Claire stood alone in the little shed, stunned by what she had just done.

And already regretting it.

TWENTY-FIVE

It appeared one of the horses had attempted to eat the new fedora. Apparently it hadn't proved as tasty as it looked. It was lying crumpled in the dirt of the Boddington corral, with teeth marks in the brim and the crown trampled by the horses' hooves.

Miller Boddington was twenty feet or so from his hat. He was in a seated position, with his back against the wood fencing. His linen suit was streaked with dirt, and draped across his lap was the bridle that had presumably been used to strangle him. His expensive Italian loafers were a few feet away; he must have kicked them off while struggling to stay alive.

His thoroughbred broodmares were milling about in the corral, unnerved by all the police and forensics people on the scene. One of the uniforms was holding the mares back from the body. Julie Hansen was taking pictures while Claire stood just inside the gate, looking at the dirt of the corral, still damp from the recent rain.

"Any footprints?" she asked.

"Lots," Julie said. "All wearing horseshoes."

"Maybe that's who killed him," Claire said.

"Would you call that justifiable homicide?"

"I might. And we could all go home." Realizing there were no human footprints to obliterate, Claire walked closer to the body and had a look. Miller Boddington did not appear as arrogant now. His face was pale blue, his eyes half-open.

"Any idea of time?" Claire asked.

"Nothing close," Julie said. "But I would ballpark it as last night. See the color of his fingertips? Been a while."

"What about cause?" Claire asked.

"Marks on his neck, I'd say strangulation," Julie said. "Too early to say, though. But those reins would have done the job."

"Oh, the symbolism," Claire said.

"He who lives by the horse, dies by the horse?" Julie said.

"Something like that."

"I heard he had all those charges dismissed yesterday," Julie said. "And this happens less than twenty-four hours later? That's a little too coincidental."

"That's what bothers me," Claire said. "It's *too* coincidental."

Claire wanted to talk to the groom who found the body that morning, but apparently he was tending to some horses on another part of the estate. Claire doubted he could tell her any more than she could see by looking at the corpse. She left the forensics unit to their work and walked up the hill to the Boddington house, a huge redwood mansion on a rise above the farm. Claire had heard over the years that it was a Frank Lloyd Wright design but had always assumed that was a Miller Boddington falsehood, like so many others.

A state trooper was standing on a side porch, talking to a skinny guy with a reddish soul patch. The guy's name was Henri, Claire learned, and he was the Boddingtons' chef. He had arrived at eight thirty to an empty house, he said.

"Where's the wife?" Claire asked. "What's her name again?"

"Suzanne," the chef said. "She leaves me a note, says she has gone to the city. She spends many nights there. Some days I come to cook, I have no one to cook for."

"When did she go?"

"The note does not say. It is just a note."

"I'll need to see it," Claire said. "Were you here yesterday afternoon? Or evening?"

"No. I arrived in the morning and the madame sends me to the farmers market. For the fish and the chicken. She tells me I am okay to come this morning. Not last night."

"But she didn't tell you she was going to the city."

"*No*," the chef said emphatically. "I tell you already, the note tells me this."

"Settle down," Claire told him. "What, you need to go sauté something?"

"But I already tell you. Do you not listen to me?"

"Let me run this my way," Claire said. "You're lucky I haven't asked to see your green card yet."

Claire meant the comment as a joke but apparently it hit close to home, because Henri was suddenly very accommodating.

"When was the last time you saw Miller Boddington?" she asked.

"For breakfast yesterday."

"With his wife?"

"Yes. And the Spaniard, Rafael de Costa."

Spaniard, my ass, Claire thought. She asked Henri a few more questions, but the chef didn't have much more to add to the case. He seemed rather vague on the comings and goings of his employers in general, probably an occupational quirk. Protect the people who sign the checks. Claire finished with him by asking for a phone number in New York City where she might reach Suzanne Boddington.

Telling someone a family member was dead was never easy. There was an added level of intensity in telling someone that their spouse had been murdered, because in most instances the partner would be included on a short list of suspects. So their initial reaction was usually of great interest. For that reason, it was preferable to do it in person, but Claire didn't have that luxury in this instance.

As it was, she didn't get much of a read from Suzanne Boddington. There were no histrionics, to be certain. There was surprise, quite naturally. Whether it qualified as shock, Claire couldn't determine. She couldn't even say for certain that the surprise was genuine. Having the exchange over the telephone was not conducive to much evaluation. But there was something else in the woman's voice, something Claire would describe as fatalism.

Coming to that conclusion at home that night, Claire wondered if such resignation was inherent to Suzanne Boddington's nature, or if it was something she had acquired having been married to her husband for many years. Because it seemed to Claire only natural that at some point somebody would want to kill a sonofabitch like Miller Boddington.

The phone conversation ended with Suzanne Boddington saying she would be leaving for home within the hour. Claire hung up and then, after telling the now-groveling Henri she did not want him to scramble some eggs for her, she walked down the hill to the barn, where she found that Joe Brady had arrived on the scene.

Joe was standing off to the side of the corral, talking to the trooper Claire had dismissed from questioning the chef earlier. One of Boddington's workers had turned the broodmares out to pasture while Claire was gone. Seeing them grazing made her think of Virgil Cain's farm, of the rescued horses there.

Then she was required to think about Virgil Cain, something she had been avoiding since she'd received the call saying that Miller Boddington was dead. There was no connection between the two men. If Claire had decided that Virgil was innocent in the killings of Mickey Dupree and Alan Comstock, then why would she even think he might be involved in this?

She was quite sure she hadn't mentioned to him that Boddington had just yesterday walked on his animal cruelty charges. But he could have heard it anywhere. On the radio. In a bar, although it was unlikely he was frequenting bars these days. Claire would have remembered telling him. But the time she had spent with him, the conversation itself, was something of a blur. When she had awoke that morning, a minute or so passed before she remembered that she had cut him loose. She was hit with a sudden and acute stab of remorse. It was like waking with a hangover and then slowly recalling regrettable deeds committed the night before. Even the story she'd told the patrolman in the cruiser had been lame. She had said that her car had broken down on her way to Cain's farm to check on things and that she'd had the vehicle towed and continued on foot.

But Virgil Cain wouldn't be concerned with Miller Boddington. He had made a pretty convincing case last night that he was just a simple man who wasn't interested in exacting revenge on anyone. Not on Alan Comstock, and not on Mickey Dupree. So there was no logical reason for him to go after Miller Boddington. He had definitely persuaded Claire of that, or she would never have let him go. If he had been acting, he was very good at it.

But then she had to consider his friendship with Mary Nelson. The woman was extremely interested in Boddington, and Virgil was in her corner. Dirk Hopman had received abused horses from Boddington, and Virgil had taken it upon himself a few nights earlier to beat the hell out of Hopman. That was hardly minding his own business.

Shit.

Virgil Cain, you'd better not have been interested in Boddington, Claire thought as she approached Joe Brady and the trooper. I might have to shoot you after all.

She was hoping his name wouldn't come up at all regarding Boddington's demise. It was an unreasonable expectation and one that died a quick death.

"I can say one thing about this Cain," the trooper was saying to Joe when Claire walked up. "He only kills people that nobody likes anyway."

"This wasn't Cain," Joe said at once. "Trust me, I'm an expert on the man. Virgil Cain killed Comstock and Dupree because of what happened to his wife. Boddington doesn't figure in that scenario. Besides, I happen to know that Cain is hiding out in Quebec. I have people on his trail night and day. He pops out of his hole for a pack of cigarettes and his ass is grass. I guarantee you he didn't sneak back over the border in the middle of the night to strangle some dirtbag who forgot to feed his horses."

"Then who do you figure for this?" the trooper asked.

"Some wacked animal lover who couldn't handle the news that our judicial system gave Boddington a free pass," Joe said. "The timing is everything here. A blind man could see it."

Claire kept walking. For once she was happy to let Joe talk, even if he didn't know what he was talking about. Although this time, the gist of what he was saying just might be true.

At least Claire hoped it was.

She waited until they had loaded Boddington's body into the van and taken it away before she did the rounds of the local neighbors. Nobody reported anything out of the ordinary. The Boddington house and barns sat well back from the road and for the most part were hidden from view. In addition, due to the nature of the horse business, there was apparently a fairly constant stream of traffic in and out of the farm. Nobody paid particular notice. A woman walking an Airedale along the shoulder of the road out front told Claire that she had seen Suzanne Boddington drive off in her SUV at around four the previous afternoon. A couple hundred yards down the same road, a man drinking coffee on his front porch claimed he had seen Suzanne arriving back at the farm at roughly the same time. But it could have been the day before yesterday, he admitted.

When Claire got back to the farm, the forensics unit was still at work. The groom, whose name was Tuttle, had identified the bridle as being from the stable, and so they were dusting the tack room for prints. Claire walked Tuttle around to the side of the barn to have a talk with him. The man was maybe fifty-five, paunchy, and stoop-shouldered, and wore a denim shirt and brown twill pants, cowboy boots and a tooled leather belt with a *T* etched into the buckle.

"I know you've been over this already," she said by way of apology. "What time did you leave yesterday?"

"Four minutes past five," he said. "We punch a clock."

A time clock on a farm, Claire thought. Virgil Cain wouldn't last a day here. "And Miller Boddington wasn't here then?" she asked.

"He wasn't down here. He coulda been at the house but I didn't see his car. He never came down to the barn much."

"No?"

"Not much. Especially lately."

"Why lately?"

"He wasn't too much interested in the horses anymore," Tuttle said. Claire could hear traces of an accent now. Tennessee maybe. Or Kentucky. Thinking about it, Kentucky would make sense. Horse country.

"Because of the charges against him?" Claire asked.

"I wouldn't say that was it. By the way, so you know, those animals were not on this farm. They were over at the other place, upstate. I never mistreated a horse in my life. My daddy would rise up from the grave if I did."

"I believe you. What about Boddington?"

"Just your typical stuff. These rich guys always get into the game thinking they can buy a winner. Miller wanted a Derby winner. All he talked about at first. Well, it ain't that easy. There's guys over there in Dubai, or wherever they're from, got more money than the Pope, and they can't do it neither. Only God can pick out a Derby winner, and he only does it once a year. And it's usually got nothing to do with money."

"So he got bored with it?" Claire asked.

"I guess maybe. Or he got mad 'cuz he couldn't have what he wanted. Guy like that is used to getting his way."

"You don't sound as if you're going to miss him."

Tuttle shrugged but didn't answer. The truth might incriminate him. And he didn't seem like the type who would bother to lie.

"Boddington and his wife get along okay?" Claire asked.

"I couldn't say."

"Well, did they spend a lot of time together?"

"Didn't seem like it. He was gone, she was here. But she never come down to the barn too much neither. She used to. But that stopped, oh, a couple years ago."

"Why did it stop?"

"Don't know."

Claire sensed something. "Yes, you do."

Tuttle hesitated. "There were rumors. You looking for rumors?"

"Sometimes rumors turn out to be true."

Tuttle took a moment. "Story was she was having a fling with Miller's foreman at the time. Guy named Stevens. Miller fired him, right around the time you guys busted him for the horse abuse. Put the blame on Stevens and sent him on his way. Killing two birds with one stone, you know?"

"Yeah." Claire said. She had heard the rumor about the foreman back when she'd been investigating Boddington the first time. She had dismissed it at the time as being irrelevant, whether it held any truth or not. "And then Suzanne stopped coming around?"

"Yup," Tuttle said. "But I got the impression she didn't want to leave, though," he added.

"What do you mean?"

"The boss has been talking about moving full-time to California. Getting out of the thoroughbred game and into the wine business. I hear the missus didn't want to go." Tuttle hesitated, even longer this time, before continuing. "That little French guy up at the house was telling the cleaning lady that the missus wasn't too happy that the boss skipped on the abuse charges. Like maybe she was hoping he'd go to jail."

"Oh?" Claire asked. "And the cleaning lady told you?"

Tuttle actually blushed. "Yeah, we're friends."

I have a feeling you're more than friends, Claire thought. Women and cowboys. She turned and looked toward the house on the hill. She glanced at her watch. Suzanne Boddington wouldn't be home for a couple of hours, at the earliest.

"Thanks for your time," she said to Tuttle.

"No problem," he said and walked away.

Claire watched him and then got into her car and headed back to Kingston. The bodies were piling up, and she didn't have anyone who even slightly resembled a suspect.

Other than the guy she had let go the night before.

TWENTY-SIX

When Virgil left the farm, he drove west and got a room for the night at Kate's Lazy Meadow Motel on Route 28. Tucked in an overgrown grove of trees, the place was barely visible from the highway. Driving there, he wondered what the hell had just happened back in the pump house.

There had been a moment, upstairs in the bathroom, when he had considered the possibility that Claire Marchand might actually shoot him. An hour later, she had let him go. He wondered what had happened in that time to make her change her mind. But it seemed to him, even when she was pointing the gun at him, that she wasn't all that convinced he was guilty. Still, turning him loose was an awfully big leap of faith on her part. He wondered who had called her on her cell phone just minutes before and if that had anything to do with it. He didn't have any answers by the time he reached the motel. He signed in under the name William Bonney.

In the morning he got up early and had breakfast at a truck stop a few hundred yards away. There was a fancier place next to the motel, but it looked as if it catered to the tourist trade. He was more at home with the truckers.

After he ate he went back to his room and had a shower before checking out. Coming out of the bathroom he turned on the TV to the sports channel and caught the baseball scores. Wanting to hear the weather too, he changed to the local news. He didn't learn anything about the barometric pressure, but he did find out that Miller Boddington was dead. It wasn't yet nine o'clock and the story had just broken. A camera crew at the Boddington horse farm was filming various police and emergency vehicles as they arrived on the scene.

Virgil sat on the edge of the bed and watched, thinking he might see Claire. At one point there was someone in the background that might be her, but he couldn't be certain. When the news anchor mentioned that Boddington's death came on the heels of the "vicious murders" of Mickey Dupree and Alan Comstock in recent days, Virgil got to his feet. When he heard his own name mentioned, he turned the set off. He didn't need to hear the speculation. He didn't need for Claire to hear it either, but there was nothing to be done about that.

He left the key on the dresser and got into the Dodge and went to find Buddy Townes.

He drove east into Kingston on 28, got off on Washington Avenue, and swung down by Rondout Creek, past the museum. From a block away he could see that Buddy's Cadillac was not parked in front of the house. When he pulled up to the curb, he saw the reason why. The house looked deserted and there was a FOR RENT sign in the window.

Virgil sat looking at the place for a time and then got out of the truck and started up the walkway. At once the front door of the adjacent house opened and a man walked out onto the stoop. He was short and thick, with a torso like a forty-five-gallon drum, and wore a wife beater with coffee stains down the front. He had a half-eaten fried-egg sandwich in his hand.

"You looking to rent?" he asked.

"I'm looking for Buddy Townes."

"Buddy's gone."

Virgil walked across the lawn toward the man. "Gone where?"

RED MEANS RUN

"Florida. You not looking to rent?"

"No. You own the place?"

"I'm the one looks after it." Behind the man a TV was blaring. Virgil could see it through the doorway. "Guy who owns it lives in Jersey," the man said. "Indian. From India, not a casino Indian."

Virgil looked at the sign in the window. "So Buddy's not coming back?"

"Nope. All he took was a suitcase. Said he won the lottery and he was going fishing. You interested in any furniture? He gave me . . . er, I bought the contents of the house."

"No," Virgil said, and he thought. "You know, maybe I'll have a look. I might see something I need."

"I gotta get the key."

The man went inside. Virgil took his Mud Hens cap off and pushed his hair back from his forehead. He wondered what Buddy meant, saying he won the lottery. Maybe he actually did win the lottery. But Virgil didn't think so. Inside the house next door, someone was now flipping the TV from channel to channel, and then they stopped. Virgil heard a news announcer talking about Miller Boddington's murder.

The man returned, carrying a ring of keys. He came down from the stoop and crossed the lawn, walking splay-legged, his chest puffed out under the dirty shirt. Virgil noticed movement in one of the windows behind him and saw a woman there, staring out from between the blinds. Virgil put the cap back on and pulled it down.

"I don't own the place," the man said again. "An Indian from India bought it a few years ago. People are buying up the whole goddamn country."

Inside the house were what Virgil assumed to be the worldly possessions of Buddy Townes. It seemed as if Buddy had left

256

in a hurry. There were still clothes hanging in the closet, toiletries in the bathroom. The house had two bedrooms, one of which had evidently served as Buddy's office. A computer sat on a scarred metal desk. There was a printer alongside and several books, most of them on legal procedures and case histories. Virgil hoped he might see a filing cabinet but there was none. The man in the dirty shirt stood in the doorway, watching Virgil.

"That's a good computer. Brand name. You can have it for a hundred bucks."

"I wouldn't know what to do with it."

"Well, the wife's nephew says it's not all that new. Take the computer and the desk for a buck fifty."

Virgil shook his head and walked out of the room. He went into the kitchen and looked around. "You say all he took was a suitcase?"

"Yeah."

"He have any visitors before he left?" Virgil opened the fridge, thinking he could keep the man talking if it appeared he was in the market for something.

"Nope. He left here about five o'clock, came back maybe six or so and then he was out of here for good a half an hour later. That's a good fridge."

Virgil closed the door. "You figure he really won the lottery?"

"He won something," the man said. "Said when he got to the Keys he was gonna drive his Cadillac into the ocean and buy himself a brand-new one. You know what a new Caddy's worth?"

"I can guess," Virgil said.

"So you want any of this stuff? Oh, don't fall in love with that TV. It's not for sale. I'm taking it. You wouldn't want to carry it next door for me, would you? I got a bad back. Doc says I can't lift anything heavier than my prick."

Virgil thought about the woman watching him through the blinds. "My doctor told me the same thing," he said. He started for the door and stopped. "I don't suppose Buddy said anything about forwarding his mail . . . ?"

"I asked him," the man said. "He told me to cash the checks and burn the bills. Said he was done with this town."

Outside Virgil walked along the cracked sidewalk toward the Dodge. He stopped and turned back. The man was standing on the stoop of the former home of Buddy Townes.

"You know what?" Virgil said.

"What?"

Claire caught up with Joe Brady back at the station. It was a little past one o'clock and Joe was sitting at his desk eating fried chicken and fries from a greasy cardboard box with a picture of a red rooster on the lid. He had his feet up and Claire could see horse manure on the sole of his right shoe. She could smell it too but maybe she just imagined that, after seeing it.

"I need to take a look at that list of license plate numbers from the park," she told him. "From the day Dupree was killed."

Joe glanced around the desk, as if the list in question might be lying there under his chicken. "I don't know where it is," he said. "This minute, anyway."

"I need to see it."

"Why?"

"Why?" Claire asked. "Because I want to know who was in the park that day. None of the names jumped out at you?"

"I wasn't expecting anything to jump out at me," Joe said. "I was looking for Cain's plate number. We've been over this, Claire. Either he told them a story at the gate or he walked in along that ravine. Why do you always want to complicate things?"

"Did you look at the list, Joe?"

"I had Marina check the list for Cain's plate. I didn't have time to search every plate number that drove in the damn park that day. You might recall that right around that time I was out with the dogs, looking for a killer who had escaped custody. You figure I should have been back here, checking out license plate numbers of fly fishermen from Pennsylvania?"

"Where's the list, Joe?"

"That would be a question for Marina, wouldn't it?" Joe took a handful of fries and shoved them in his mouth. He nodded in the direction of the front desk. "And here she comes right now."

Claire turned to see Marina approaching. She had a piece of paper in her hand and was heading toward Joe. Claire intercepted her.

"Marina, those plate numbers you got from the park the day that Dupree bought it? I know it's a lot of work but I'm going to need the names."

Marina shrugged. "No problem," she said. She made a point of looking at Joe. "I offered to do it before but I was told it wasn't necessary."

Joe glared at her, munching on his fries. He swallowed and took a drink of his soda. "That's because it wasn't."

"I can have it in a couple hours," Marina told Claire.

"I'll be back shortly," Claire said and got to her feet. "By the way, Joe, you got manure on your shoe. Seems like you got shit coming out of you from every direction."

Joe watched as she left, then looked at his shoes, one after the other. Marina started to walk away but then remembered why she'd come over. She came back and put the sheet of paper down in front of Joe.

"Another Virgil Cain sighting," she said.

Joe didn't bother to look at the paper. "Yeah, where was he this time?"

"Woman said he was looking at a house to rent here in town. Over on Sycamore Street."

"Right here in Kingston?" Joe asked. "Imagine that. And here we've been looking north of the border. What makes her think it was Cain?"

"She said she was watching the news about Boddington and they showed Cain's picture, and she looked out and he was standing in the yard, talking to her husband about this house for rent. The husband is the landlord, I guess. She said it was Cain, no question. He went in and looked at the house."

"Was she drunk?"

"It was ten o'clock in the morning."

Joe laughed. "I don't think Virgil Cain is looking to rent a house in Kingston."

"Actually, she was a little fuzzy on that part. First she said he was wanting to rent the house . . ."

"Yeah?"

"But then she said he was looking for Buddy Townes."

When Claire got back from lunch Marina already had cross-referenced the plate numbers and had the list of names ready for her. Joe was gone and Claire didn't ask where he went. She sat at her desk and went over the printout and then got up and left.

The forensics unit was still at the horse farm when Claire got there. She drove past the barns and up to the house, where a silver Mercedes SUV was now parked in the driveway. She found Suzanne Boddington in the kitchen, drinking a Bloody Mary and talking to Henri the chef. Claire introduced herself to Suzanne and then turned to the Frenchman.

"I need a couple of minutes with your boss," she said.

Henri looked to Suzanne for guidance. She nodded and he

left, casting a nervous glance toward Claire as he departed. Suzanne watched him, then turned to Claire.

"He thinks you want to deport him."

"I really don't care who you hire to flip your burgers," Claire said. "Strange thing for him to be worrying about, though. Given the circumstances."

"He's a little on the neurotic side. He can cook, though."

On the drive out there, Claire had been thinking it was odd that—despite the fact she had personally arrested Miller Boddington on the animal cruelty charges and had appeared in a courtroom with the man on several occasions—she had never actually been in the presence of Suzanne Boddington. Unlike a lot of wives married to rich guys with a propensity for fucking up, Suzanne was not one to stand by her man, at least in a literal sense, in his times of trouble.

Now Claire was face-to-face with her. The woman was tall and curvy, very tanned. She wore a number of bracelets on both wrists and a heavy gold necklace. No wedding ring, though. She had on a summer dress, rather short, and sandals. Her toenails were painted bright red.

And she was as dry-eyed as any woman Claire had ever encountered on the day of her husband's demise. Claire was certain Suzanne had been discussing dinner with the chef when she had interrupted them. Now she asked if Claire would like a Bloody Mary.

"No thanks. I'm working."

"There's coffee," Suzanne said. "It's fresh."

"Sure."

They sat at the table, Claire with the cup of coffee, which was possibly the best coffee she had ever tasted, and Suzanne with the vodka mix. Suzanne sat watching Claire patiently, her finger absently tapping the side of her glass, as if Claire was keeping her from something but she was too polite to mention it. Claire kept quiet for the moment, sipping from the cup while pretending to be interested in the ongoing activity around the barns down the hill. She wanted to see if Suzanne had anything unsolicited to offer. When the woman finally spoke, though, there was little to suggest she had anything to hide. It seemed as if she wanted to get on with things, maybe because her mind really was on dinner. For someone who'd just become a widow a few hours earlier, she oozed confidence.

"So," she said. "Does anyone have a theory on this?"

"None so far," Claire said. "They're still looking for prints. Any physical evidence."

"He was strangled?"

"Who told you that?" Claire asked.

"Nobody has told *me* anything," Suzanne said. "One of the troopers was talking to Henri."

"They won't have a definitive cause of death until they do an autopsy." Claire drank her coffee. "But strangulation is a possibility. Do you have any idea who might want to kill your husband?"

Suzanne didn't hesitate. "Somebody who didn't like the fact that he was exonerated yesterday from the charges that he abused a bunch of thoroughbreds?"

"He wasn't exactly exonerated."

"No, but he did walk. Didn't he?"

"Yes, he did."

"I recognize your name," Suzanne said. "You're the one who arrested Miller on those charges in the first place. So I assume you weren't a very happy woman yesterday." She paused and then smiled. "Now that I think of it, how unhappy were you? You didn't kill my husband, did you?"

"No, I didn't," Claire said. She looked at the woman for a moment. "I have to say—you have a strange way of grieving."

"Do you bare your soul to strangers? Believe me, I'm crying on the inside."

She had a point. Claire nodded.

"Who do you think did it?" Suzanne asked. "If it really was some horse lover, it sort of seems contrary to the whole notion of being a proponent of animal rights."

"It does, doesn't it?"

"Now, as I was driving home, all I kept hearing on the news is that someone is on a killing spree in Upstate New York. And this Virgil Cain character keeps getting mentioned. The guy your department arrested and then, what, forgot to lock up or something?"

"Something like that."

"But Cain killed Mickey Dupree and Alan Comstock because of the situation with his wife. Isn't that the theory? Miller had nothing to do with that. So how can anybody tie Cain to my husband's murder?"

"No one has," Claire said. "Except maybe the media. That's why I tend to listen to CDs when I drive."

"Right. I'll keep that in mind."

"Did you know Mickey Dupree?"

"I knew him," Suzanne said. "He was Miller's lawyer, which of course you know. He'd been here to the house lots of times. He and Miller were buddies, I guess. They went to the track together. They got drunk together. And I know Miller gave him a lot of money in attorney's fees over the past couple years. I didn't care for him all that much, if you want to know the truth."

"Why not?"

"He was a pig."

"That's it?"

"That's enough."

Claire had another sip of coffee. She wanted to ask the brand name. "Did you know Alan Comstock?"

"Yeah. He was a nut."

"I like these one-word appraisals," Claire said. "How did you know him?"

"Jane and I are good friends." Suzanne paused for a moment. "I have to wonder how much you guys already know when you're questioning people. I suspect you know Jane and I are friends, and you're just fishing around for something."

"I might not be as clever as you think."

"Is that supposed to inspire confidence? After all, you're investigating my husband's murder."

"I'll do my best," Claire assured her. "So you're friends with Jane Comstock but you didn't like her husband."

"It has nothing to do with whether I liked him or not," Suzanne said. "When I said that Alan was a nut, I wasn't being flip. He was fucking insane. Guns and drugs and paranoia were his daily bread. How do you think that girl ended up dead?"

"Why did his wife stay with him?"

"We never talked about it but I think she knew that if she left, he'd either kill her or himself. Or both. So she stuck it out."

"Nice way to live," Claire said.

"Oh, she could handle it. She's very smart. Not only that, but she loves her life here. She loves the community, and she shows it. That's how we met, over that landfill proposal a few years ago. Which we defeated, I might add."

"The power of grassroots," Claire said. She looked out the window again, over the impressive property. "Does she think Cain killed her husband?"

"Well, yeah. Didn't he?"

"That seems to be the prevailing theory," Claire said. "To tell you the truth, it's just about all theory, though. There's not a lot of evidence that says he did it."

"Do you have somebody else in mind?"

Claire looked at her now and shrugged. "I hear that Jane Comstock is a runner. You too?"

"Yeah. I jump in my SUV and run to the liquor store. Two, three times a week."

"You ever run at Coopers Falls Park?" Claire asked. "I was told a lot of runners train there because of the hills."

"I don't run."

"Have you ever been to the park, though?"

"No."

"Are you sure?"

Suzanne's eyes narrowed. "I beg your pardon?"

Claire took her notebook from her pocket. "I just wondered if you could be mistaken. Because an SUV registered in your name was at Coopers Falls Park a week ago Tuesday. And I just double-checked the plate when I walked by that Mercedes in your driveway."

"I'm not mistaken," Suzanne said, speaking slowly now. "I have never been there. So, somebody's mistaken but it's not me."

"You're saying someone wrote down the wrong plate number?"

"That would be my guess," Suzanne said. She stood up and walked across the room to where a calendar hung beside a wall phone. "You're talking about the ninth? I was in Boston that night, having dinner."

"Where?"

"Little Vito's."

"Alone?"

"You're asking me if I flew to Boston to have dinner by

myself? That would be very suspicious, wouldn't it?" She stared at Claire, as if she was expecting a reply. "No, it was my sister's birthday. I was with her and her boyfriend."

"I'll need their names and contact numbers," Claire said.

"All right," Suzanne said. "I don't know what this is about, but I can tell you that you're confused. Either that or somebody is leading you astray."

"Well, you know what Davy Crockett said," Claire told her as she got to her feet. "He was never lost, but one time he was mixed up for a week. Or something like that."

"I beg your pardon?"

Claire smiled. "I'll still need those names."

TWENTY-SEVEN

Jane was weeding the flower beds along the drive late in the afternoon. It was a job that she usually left to the gardener, but he had been off all week with a recurring bug, one that Jane suspected he kept encountering at the bottom of a bottle.

Jane didn't mind the work, though. It was mindless and simple, and therefore therapeutic. The baptisia along the drive had finished flowering so she trimmed it back. She weeded the black-eyed Susans, now in full bloom, and pruned away some dead growth on the Japanese maples along the front walk. She was pushing a wheelbarrow full of cedar mulch around the corner of the house when she heard a vehicle slow down out front, and she looked up to see Joe Brady pulling into the drive. Jane straightened up and watched as the cop slid his belly out from under the wheel and got out. He said hello in a voice like that of a country auctioneer. Presumably he knew what she thought of him.

"What can I do for you?" she asked.

"I'm just here to give you a heads-up," he said, approaching her. "I guess you heard about that situation with Miller Boddington."

"Yes. I heard."

"I couldn't know for sure."

"It's sad news," Jane said. "But I don't see what it has to do with me."

"I would have said nothing. But it turns out that Virgil Cain is back in the area."

"But I thought he was in Canada."

"He's back. And that makes him a prime suspect for this Boddington killing. Apparently this thing runs a lot deeper than we thought. I need to know that you have security out here."

"Why would I need security?"

"Because this guy's a loose cannon. There was a certain logic to him going after Mickey Dupree and, all due respect, your husband. But this latest, well, he's either off the deep end or he's got grievances we don't know about. We know he keeps rescued horses out at his farm, so maybe that's the connection. Either way, I'm trying to stay one step ahead of him. I know you're out here alone. What also bothers me is all the guns your husband owned. Cain knows they're here. They were in plain sight the night he . . . well, you know."

"I've turned those guns over to my lawyer. He's going to consign them to an auction house in Albany."

"That's good."

Jane removed her cloth gloves and folded them together. "Do you think I'm in danger?"

"I'm not saying that. I'm trying to cover all bases at this point. Had I known Cain was back, I could have given Boddington a heads-up."

"But why would you have?"

"Mickey Dupree is the common denominator here. He's the thread that's been running through this from the get-go. It's obvious that there's more to this than just Cain looking for revenge for his wife being killed. But I haven't fit it together yet. Until I do, I'm following the Mickey Dupree through line. And you're part of that, because of your husband."

"How do you know Cain is in the area?"

"He was spotted in Kingston this morning. And he was looking for Buddy Townes. The same Buddy Townes who worked for Dupree all these years. See how this thing goes round and round? Cain was in Buddy's house. We lifted a fingerprint off the fridge door."

Brady was getting all worked up just telling the story. His face was flush and he was perspiring.

"I thought you should know that the man who killed your husband is back. Be vigilant. Just so you know, he was spotted driving a brown Dodge pickup truck with 'Ulster Veterinary Service' on the door."

"I don't understand."

Brady shrugged. "It's a long story. He got it from a friend of his, this lady vet. She's playing cute right now, but she has an accessory charge coming her way. I'm holding her in custody until she decides to talk."

Jane nodded and turned to look at the house. She exhaled. "I can have the security people send someone over. But I still don't know what he would want with me."

"He knows there were guns here. Better safe than sorry."

"Where's his farm again? Is it near here?"

"Windecker Road, over towards Saugerties. Close enough."

"Yes, it is close enough." Jane turned to Brady. "I still don't understand how Cain escaped custody in the first place. And now you say he's driving around in a truck with a sign on the door and yet you can't seem to find him."

Brady chafed at the accusation. "I give you my word he won't get away again." Jane watched in disbelief as he pulled his revolver from his shoulder holster and checked the cylinder loads before putting it back. "This thing is nearing epidemic proportions. It's apparent that I'm going to have to take this man down. It's dead or alive now."

"Well," Jane said. "I'm going to go in and call the security company."

"Ten-four," Joe Brady said.

Claire sat at the bar in Fat Phil's, waiting until the afternoon bartender came on shift. She'd hit all the usual watering holes in Kingston and nobody had remembered seeing Buddy Townes yesterday. Phil's was her last chance. It was actually her best chance, as Buddy was known to frequent the place. Claire had been there earlier but the bartender said he'd been off the day before. The other bartender, who had worked a double yesterday, came on shift at five. He was running late.

Virgil had called her cell while she was driving back from her talk with Suzanne Boddington, and he'd told her that Buddy had apparently skipped town. Claire wasn't buying the lottery story either, and when Virgil said that it seemed as if Buddy had met with somebody the previous afternoon, Claire decided to check out his usual haunts. Buddy had become, at least in recent years, a predictable guy.

She sat at the bar and drank a coffee and watched the Cubs and the Dodgers on the flat screen above the liquor display. When her cell rang she answered on the first ring. It was Marina.

"Joe told me to find you."

"What's up?"

"Virgil Cain was in Kingston this morning. Looking for Buddy Townes."

"You sure?"

"They found a print."

"Okay," Claire said, her mind working. "So what's the plan?"

"Well, Joe's got everybody out except the Girl Scouts. Cain is driving a pickup registered to a Mary Nelson. Joe's got the woman in custody, putting the heat on her."

She gave Claire the vehicle's details and Claire pretended to write them down.

"It's all on the down low for now," Marina said. "Joe doesn't want the media to know because he's afraid Cain will go to ground again."

"Go to ground?"

"Joe's words."

"What is Buddy Townes saying?"

"Nobody can find him. His landlord claims he left town."

"Okay," Claire said then. "Tell Joe you found me."

"He's acting all Wild West," Marina said. "You know?"

"Yeah. I know."

Claire hung up and sipped her coffee, thinking about what to do. She needed to find Virgil Cain. More specifically, she needed to find him before Joe Brady did. She didn't care for Marina's description of Joe's mind-set. Wild West and Joe Brady sounded like a bad combination. Joe was running a long losing streak in the courtroom and Claire suspected he was looking to settle one without a judge and jury. And without a lawyer telling the world that he was an idiot. There was one way for Joe to do that.

So she needed to find Virgil Cain, and she had no idea how to do that. She shouldn't have let him go. She'd been thinking at the time that doing so could turn out badly for her. Now she had to consider that it might turn out very badly for him. She was growing more antsy by the minute, and then the bartender came in. She recognized the guy from the few times she'd been there but didn't know his name. He was young, maybe twenty-two or so, and obviously worked out a lot, judging by the size of the biceps that bulged out of his too-small T-shirt. Claire showed him her badge and he gave her a flirtatious smile. He said his name was Cujo. Of course it is, Claire thought.

"Buddy was here yesterday," the kid said. "I remember because it was weird."

"In what way?"

"First of all, he only stayed for one drink. That's not Buddy. And he was with a woman. At least he met this woman."

"What's strange about that?" Claire asked. "Buddy was always a ladies' man."

"Not this woman. She walks in here and gives the place the once-over, and she's got this look on her face, like, who farted? You know? Then she ordered a Bloody Mary and sat over there, waiting for Buddy. He showed a couple minutes later."

"What did she look like?"

"Pretty good-looking. For her age, anyway. Tall, kind of like an athlete, or used to be an athlete."

"Blonde?"

"She wore a cap."

"Any logo on it?"

The kid, who'd caught a glimpse of himself in the mirror behind the bar, was only half paying attention.

"Shit, I don't know. It was just a cap, like a ball cap."

"How old was she?"

"I don't know. You women, after a certain age, I can never tell." He was still admiring his arms.

"How'd you like a smack on the head?" Claire asked.

"She was older than you," the kid said quickly, turning to her. "I'm thinking fifty maybe. Shit, I don't know."

Claire got off the stool and put a couple of dollars on the bar for her coffee. "Did she give him anything?" she asked.

"I don't know. I guess she could've."

"I'm guessing she did."

*   *   *

Claire crossed the street, got into her car, and started to drive without knowing where she was going. She had to determine who Buddy Townes had met with, although she was pretty sure she knew who it was; but first she had to locate Virgil Cain. And she was very aware that a whole bunch of people were out there trying to do the same thing. People with guns and somewhat different agendas than hers. She started for the station but didn't want to run into Joe if he was there. It was too early for her to tell him anything and there was always a chance he would fuck everything up if she did. So she turned around and headed home, thinking she would change and head out to Virgil's farm. He might be there.

Her cell phone was ringing when she walked in the door. She took it from her pocket.

"Hey," he said.

"You've been made," she told him.

"What?"

"Somebody put you at Buddy's place. Where are you?"

"On the road."

"Good luck with that. That truck is as hot as you are. Listen, I think I'm onto something here. But you have to turn yourself in. Now."

"No."

"Virgil, listen to me. They've got you down for three killings and now Joe's got everybody's blood up. They pull you over and you as much as scratch your elbow and they're going to start shooting."

"Then I'll lay low."

Claire threw her purse on the table. "Chrissake, Virgil. Are you even listening to me?"

He didn't say anything.

"Where are you?" she asked. "If you won't turn yourself in, then come here." She waited, imagining that he was considering it. Or hoping he was.

"I don't know. Why would I come there?"

"Because nobody's going to shoot you here, for starters," she said. "Get over here and we'll figure out what to do."

"Okay."

His tone was reluctant and she hurried to give him directions before he changed his mind. "Park in the garage. I'll move my car out."

"Can I bring anything?"

"What?"

"You know. Bottle of wine. Dessert."

"Laugh it up. See how funny it is when the shooting starts." She hung up.

Claire was in need of a shower. She had left the house in a rush that morning as soon as she'd received the call about Boddington. After she moved her car, she went upstairs and had a shower, and as she was stepping out of the tub she heard him pull in the driveway. Under the spray she'd been trying to decide what to wear. It wasn't something she should be thinking about, but she was, and it bothered her. It was like a question on some lame magazine cover—what to wear when welcoming a fugitive into one's home? Virgil showing up so quick eliminated her concern. She threw on jeans and a T-shirt and went down to meet him, drying her hair with a towel as she did.

She had left the back door ajar and when he knocked she told him to come in. Claire stood by the island counter that separated the kitchen from the dining room, the towel still in her hand. He smiled at her. She had been thinking about that smile since she'd let him go at the farm. It was a good smile, and Claire was pretty sure he used it to deflect the seriousness of the shit he was in. He wasn't as oblivious to certain things as he let on.

"Hey."

"Mr. Cain," Claire said. "You close the garage door?"

"Yeah."

"Sit down. You want a beer?"

"Sure."

Virgil sat down on a stool at the counter, and Claire opened the fridge and brought out two bottles of Bud Light. He looked doubtfully at the offering.

"Got any real beer?"

"Beggars can't be choosers," she told him as she put the beer on the counter. She walked around to sit across from him, the towel draped around her neck now, like a prizefighter.

"You're not going to like this but I think you should know. Joe Brady picked up Mary Nelson earlier. He's holding her at the station, hoping she spills the beans on you."

"She's got nothing to spill."

"She wouldn't even if she did. She wouldn't give you up at Hopman's that night."

"What makes you think I was there?"

"Maybe you should start giving me some credit. I'm the only one in Upstate New York who thinks you *might* be innocent, cowboy."

"Okay," Virgil said and had another drink. "You said you were onto something."

"Yeah. Operating on the assumption that somebody paid Buddy off."

"Maybe he did win the lottery. People do, you know."

"I checked it out with New York Lotto. His name isn't in their database, not as of last night. Somebody bought him."

"Who?"

"He met with a woman at Fat Phil's around five yesterday afternoon. They had a conversation and a drink."

"And an hour later he blows town."

"Yeah."

"So who was the woman?"

Claire got up and went into a kitchen cupboard, rummaged around until she found a package of peanuts. She put them in a bowl and brought them over, grabbing a handful for herself.

"You had a theory that whoever killed Mickey Dupree went through Coopers Falls Park," she said. "And you figured that the victims knew the killer. And that they wouldn't have feared him."

"Yeah."

"Or her."

"Did you say her?"

Claire took a drink of beer and wiped her mouth with the back of her hand. "Boddington's wife was in the park that day. They had her license plate number at the gate. And she knew Dupree, and Comstock. And you know what? She didn't like either one of them."

"How do you know that?" Virgil asked.

"She told me."

"She told you? Why would she do that?"

"I'm not sure. Maybe she's trying to throw me off with her candor. She's an intelligent woman. She claims she's never been to the park, says she was in Boston at the time, but I'm still checking that out." Claire took another drink. "Two things have always bothered me. One, that Mickey Dupree's killer took time to rake the sand trap afterwards. That sand is fine, you could never distinguish one tread from another. But you could tell the *size* of a footprint, the difference between a woman and a man. So she raked it over. That never made sense until now."

"What else?"

"This one just came to me the other night, when I was laying awake trying to figure out how to catch you." Claire paused and had another drink. "The night Comstock was killed, somebody called him and told him that the cops had picked you up. Which meant he could send the security guard home. But they just hired the guard that day. How would anybody know? And if it was you who killed Comstock, how would you know?"

"So tell me."

"Suzanne Boddington was with Comstock's wife that night, down in the city. She would have known."

Virgil reached for a handful of peanuts. "What's her motive? So she didn't like Comstock and Dupree. That's not a reason to kill them. And even if she did, are you saying she killed her husband? Why would she do that, just to muddy the stream?"

"The husband," Claire said. "Shit, I have a feeling that might have been the easy one for her. I had coffee with her today, a couple hours after she got the news. You could find more emotion in that bowl of peanuts."

"That doesn't mean she killed him."

"Story is, he wanted to sell out and move to California. She didn't. And look what she's got now—a fancy house, a large fortune, and no sociopathic husband to share it all with."

Virgil thought about it. "You still don't have a motive for the other two. Or is she just your run-of-the-mill serial killer?"

"I don't think so. Like you said, Buddy Townes is the key. Joe Brady's been acting all along like these are revenge killings. But they're not about revenge. They're about keeping people quiet. I don't know what this woman is hiding but whatever it is, Buddy must have found it. And Buddy told Dupree and Dupree told . . . well, he obviously told somebody something.

Otherwise he'd still be alive. I'm thinking he told Miller something about his wife that even Miller didn't know."

"It would have to be something big," Virgil said. "To start killing people."

"Yeah, but she saw her chance. You were the perfect fall guy. Why wouldn't you want Comstock and Dupree dead after what happened?"

Virgil took a long drink of beer, considering what she was saying. "But why pay Buddy off? Why not kill him too?"

"Because Buddy wouldn't be easy to kill. Not like the others. For one thing, Buddy carried a gun every day of his life."

"I know that," Virgil said. "Firsthand."

"That would be Buddy," Claire said. "He would be hard to kill, but easy to buy. And his leaving doesn't necessarily mean he can't help us out. I applied for a search warrant for the house, should have it in the morning. I don't know what he left behind but maybe there's something there. We know he left in a hurry so maybe he got careless."

"What if he left his computer?" Virgil asked.

"There was a computer there?"

"There was. Not now."

"Where is it?"

"In that Dodge pickup parked in your garage."

TWENTY-EIGHT

Virgil knew nothing about computers, other than he had purchased this one earlier today for fifty dollars. He sipped his beer and sat on Claire's couch and watched her make the connections at the back of the PC that had recently been the property of Buddy Townes. They were in the living room and she had the components spread across her coffee table.

"This thing is an antique," Claire said. "What did you pay for it?"

"Fifty bucks."

"You got ripped off. You country boys." Claire plugged the tower in and powered it on. After a long time the desktop finally came up and an icon appeared, requesting a password. "Yeah," she said. "I figured that."

Virgil watched as she tried typing in different variations of Buddy's names, first and last. She muttered to herself as she worked. "Buddy, what the hell was your real name? Something old-fashioned, I think. Arnold? Yeah. Arnold. Arnie. Shit, nothing."

"Did he have a dog?" Virgil asked.

"A dog?"

"Yeah. They made me get one of those cards down at the bank when I opened an account. You know those cards, you see kids using them to buy a bottle of pop. Anyway, I needed a password so I used the name of a dog I had when I was a kid. Skippy."

"Unfortunately I don't know the names of any dogs Buddy might have had when he was a kid."

"You don't have to be sarcastic."

Claire sat back and pushed her hair away from her face with both hands. "We'll have to leave it until morning. We've got a guy at the station who'll crack it." She looked at his empty bottle. "Grab another beer."

Virgil stood up. "You want one?"

"Yeah."

She waited until he walked into the kitchen and then leaned forward and typed "Skippy" into the password request. Nothing happened. She shut the computer down before he came back.

"Are you hungry?" she asked.

"I am, you know."

Claire took the beer from him and stood up. "Do you know how to make an omelet?"

"I think so."

She gestured toward the refrigerator. "Have at it. I'm going to go dry my hair."

They ate at the counter. Virgil had found onions and mushrooms and some sliced ham to put in the omelet. Claire opened a bottle of red wine and poured for them both.

"So you can scramble an egg," she said to him.

"Can't you?"

"Of course I can."

"But you're surprised that I can?" Virgil asked. "You seem to have this preconceived notion that I'm some sort of dumb hick."

"Not true," Claire said. "I do have a notion that you're a pain in the ass. But it wasn't preconceived. I got to know you and then came to that conclusion. But you're not dumb. You're probably too damn smart for your own good."

"I could never figure out what that means."

"It means you're a smart guy capable of very stupid behavior," she said.

"Yeah?"

"Yeah. Beating up that guy in Quebec, the one you went to jail for. That wasn't real bright."

"No, it wasn't."

"So I assume you regret it?"

"No, I don't."

She gave him a look, as if checking to see if he was joking. He wasn't.

"How come a woman like you lives alone?" he asked her.

"What do you mean by a woman like me?"

Virgil had lifted a forkful of eggs but stopped before eating it. "Okay, I want to retract that part. But why do you? Buddy said you were married."

"Buddy's a one-man knitting circle."

"What happened?"

"To my marriage? Well, it's a long story and as a rule I don't share it with every escaped convict that shows up at my door."

Virgil nodded and had another mouthful.

"Let's just say he was a pain in the ass," she said.

"Like me, then."

"Oh no," Claire said. "Nothing like you. You two are barely even of the same species. Shit, that jail you broke out of in Kesselberg? Todd couldn't have thought his way out of there in a hundred years."

"So you divorced him because he couldn't do stuff like escape jail?"

"Yeah. That's exactly what the papers said when I filed." Claire had a drink of wine. "No, I divorced him after fifteen years because I was too stupid to do it after ten. Or five. He's an okay guy. He's just a lost soul in constant need of a savior. And I'm no savior."

Virgil finished his eggs and reached for the wine.

"Your turn," Claire said. "Was the sham marriage to con the US government your only trip down the aisle?"

"You have a way with words. But yeah."

"How come?"

Virgil smiled. "A guy like me?"

"All right, all right," she said. She picked up the plates and carried them over to the sink. "You want anything else?" she asked.

"No. Thanks."

She came back and sat down. "Tell me about Kirstie. I sat in on the trial a couple of days. Mickey Dupree really did a number on her."

"He made up lies about a dead girl," Virgil said flatly. It was the first time Claire had seen any sign of anger in him. "He tore her to shreds, just to get Comstock off. And he did it for money. He ripped her to pieces for money."

Claire didn't say anything for a moment. Virgil had a drink of wine and looked over.

"So what was she like?" Claire asked.

Virgil hesitated, then he smiled. "Well, I can tell you that *she* couldn't cook an egg. Not that I ever saw. She was naive and she was . . . she was kind. She lost her mother when she was just little and I don't know if that was part of it or what. She thought the best of everybody. I know that sounds like an admirable thing but sooner or later an attitude like that is going to get you in trouble. And maybe it's not your fault but it's trouble just the same."

"She thought the best of Alan Comstock?"

"Yeah, and he didn't have any best in him."

"Was she talented?" Claire asked. "As a musician?"

"Oh yeah," Virgil said. "But I don't know if that's worth anything nowadays. I don't know if she could have made it in the music business. Turn on the radio and listen to what's out there. Listen to what they call country nowadays. That music would gag a buzzard."

"Was Kirstie a country singer?"

"No. Kinda rock and roll, I guess. She loved Neil Young. Her idea, I mean what she wanted Comstock to produce, was a whole record of Neil Young songs. Like that woman did with Leonard Cohen that time."

"Jennifer Warnes. I have it here."

"Yeah. Kirstie had a favorite Neil Young album. *Rust Never Sleeps*. There's this song 'Powderfinger,' she used to play all the time. It's got this great first line and sometimes when I came in from the barn she'd be sitting on the back porch with her guitar, and she'd sing it to me while I was walking across the lawn. You know the song?"

"I don't think so. How's it go?"

Virgil laughed. "I start singing and you *will* turn me in." He poured more wine for both of them. "It's this song, I guess it takes place back on the frontier. About this young guy left in charge of the homestead. And I guess his father's dead, and there's somebody named John, maybe an uncle or something, and his wife drowned, so he's taken to the bottle."

As he talked, Claire got to her feet and walked to a computer on a desk in the living room. Virgil turned to watch her as she powered it on.

"I'm listening," she said.

"Well, that's about it. Just a song, but there was something about it that she was drawn to. Maybe because it was from a different time, or maybe she identified with the kid, this young guy bucking the odds. It's a good song."

"What's it called again?" Claire asked.

"'Powderfinger.'"

Claire began to type and within a half a minute Virgil heard the song he'd been describing.

Look out, Mama, there's a white boat comin' up the river,
With a big red beacon and a flag and a man on the rail—

Virgil walked over, and there was Neil Young on the computer screen, a live clip from somewhere, Neil wearing a straw cowboy hat and playing the shit out of an old electric Gibson guitar.

Claire sat on the desk chair and using the mouse started the song again.

Look out, Mama, there's a white boat comin' up the river—

"That's the line?" she asked.

"Yeah."

They listened to the song all the way through this time, Virgil standing beside the chair, watching the computer screen at first, and then watching Claire. She was smiling, her eyes on the screen.

Daddy's rifle in my hand, felt reassurin'
He told me, red means run, son, numbers add up to nothin'.

Virgil noticed a strand of still-damp hair tucked behind Claire's ear. He saw her breasts rise under the T-shirt with each breath as she watched Young and his band on the screen. She had a tiny scar at the corner of her eye he hadn't noticed before. When the song finished he gave into impulse and reached out to touch the hair at the nape of her neck.

"Your hair's still wet," he said.

He felt a jolt go through her and pulled his hand away at once. Embarrassed, he walked over to the counter to retrieve his wine. When he looked back, she was turned in the chair, watching him. If she was upset that he had touched her, she wasn't showing it.

Virgil indicated the computer. "How did you find that song so quick?"

"It's something called the Internet. You ever hear of it?"

"Yeah, I've heard of it."

"But you don't use it."

"No."

"You do have electricity out there at the farm . . . ?"

"I got everything I need out there."

Claire got to her feet. "Do you?"

"Yeah."

Now she was standing just a few feet from him. "So you like being alone?" she asked.

Virgil indicated the house. "How am I any more alone than you?"

"I have a social life. I have friends."

"Me too."

"Horses."

He shrugged.

"Or do you have women stopping by? Spending the night?"

"Why do you want to know that?"

"I'm a cop."

Virgil stepped forward, cutting the distance between them

in half. He could smell the soap she had used in the shower. Her breath was growing quicker but now her eyes narrowed and she pulled back, just slightly.

"You can't kiss me," she said.

"Why not?"

"Because this isn't what's going on here," she said. "I'm a police officer trying to protect you. I'm trying to do my job here and what you need to understand is—"

"Shut up."

"Okay."

He put his hand on the side of her neck and kissed her softly. She put her arms around his neck and kissed him back, not so softly. She pushed him a couple of steps backward and onto the couch. He sat and she straddled him, their lips still together, his hand still on her neck, pulling her in. Finally they broke away and she ran her fingers down the side of his cheek.

"Are you going to shave when this is over?"

"I thought you were going to stop talking."

"I am."

And he kissed her again.

When she awoke it was pitch-black in the room. The candle she had lit earlier, before they had fallen into bed, had burned down. The clock said five after four. He was sitting on the edge of the bed, buttoning his shirt.

"What are you doing?"

"You said Brady arrested Mary," he said. "That means nobody's tended to my stock."

"She might have arranged something."

"But I don't know that."

Claire sat up. The sheet fell away from her breasts and she saw him turn to look at her. He smiled and that made her happy. She was actually pretty happy even before he smiled. It had been a while since she'd been naked in bed with a man.

And she had never been naked in bed with a man who chose to leave her at four in the morning to go water his horses.

"Take my car," she said, knowing she couldn't convince him to stay. "You won't make it five blocks driving that truck."

He looked at her, and she could see that he knew she was right. He nodded.

"Hide the car and stay out of sight. Can you do that, just for the day? Joe's not going to figure you to be at the farm but there could be somebody checking it anyway. So lay low, okay?"

"Okay."

"You were going to leave without saying good-bye?"

"I'm not exactly going to China," he said. But he knew what she meant. "I didn't want to wake you."

"You fell asleep before I did," she said. "I lay here for a while and I had that song in my head. 'Powderfinger.' What does 'Powderfinger' mean?"

"I'm not sure."

"What happens at the end? When his face flashed in the sky? Does it mean he gets killed?"

Virgil stood up and leaned over the bed. He pushed her hair from her face and gave her a long kiss, his mouth full on hers. When she tried to put her arms around his neck, he pulled away.

"I think it does," he said, and he left.

TWENTY-NINE

When Suzanne pulled in the driveway, Jane was walking across the lawn to her SUV, a gym bag in her hand. Suzanne parked behind the BMW, beneath the shade of a sprawling white oak, and got out. The morning was growing warm, and she took off her jacket and tossed it back in the car before turning to Jane, who was watching her, her expression flat.

"Hey," Suzanne said.

She was looking at the bag in Jane's hand, and now Jane glanced down at it, as if remembering it was there. She opened the back of the SUV and put the bag inside before closing the hatch and turning to Suzanne. Her eyes were red, the lids heavy, as if from lack of sleep. She seemed spaced-out, moving on instinct.

"I was going to stop by later," she said absently. "I would have called yesterday but I assume it was a madhouse over there. I know the scene. Unfortunately."

"Yeah," Suzanne said. "We can start a club, you and I. The Widows of Woodstock. Where you heading?"

"Um . . . go for a run."

Jane was wearing khakis and sandals, not her typical running gear. "You usually run here," Suzanne said.

"Maybe I feel like a little variety," Jane said. "Is that all right?"

Suzanne shrugged. "Well, it's a good day for it. You want some company?"

288

Jane smiled. "Right. Last time you ran, you were in high school."

"Might be a good time to start." Suzanne hesitated. "You okay?"

"I'm fine."

"You look a little . . . wired."

"Yeah, well I've been going through a rough patch," Jane said. "You know I have. But I'm just about finished with it now. What doesn't kill you makes you stronger, you know?" She turned and looked down the winding road, as if she could almost see her way to the far side of her troubles. "The shit we put up with, right?"

"What do you mean?" Suzanne asked.

"I mean the shit we put up with to get where we want to go. You start out thinking that things will get better if you stick it out, and when they don't, you just end up sticking it out anyway. At some point you get too old to move on. Too old to start over again."

"I guess."

"You *guess*? You know what I'm talking about, Suzanne. You know better than anybody. The only difference between you and me is that you don't have a plan. You don't need a plan. You're happy with what you've got, Suzanne. You don't have a restless bone in your body."

Jane was still looking down the road as she spoke. Suzanne glanced that way, wondering if something was out there, something she was expecting. Or feared.

"If you're saying I don't want to run for congress, you're right," Suzanne said. "Looks to me like it costs too much."

Jane turned to her. "That's not true. It costs what it costs."

"And what's that, Jane?"

"You don't need to know." Jane walked over to open the door of the SUV.

"Where are you going?" Suzanne asked. "I hear that Coopers Falls Park is a popular spot for runners."

Jane stopped and looked at her, but said nothing.

"You're not going to deny anything, are you?" Suzanne asked.

"Deny. Confirm. What the fuck does it matter?"

"Christ. At least tell me it was just Dupree. He was the one telling tales."

"It was just Dupree. I had no choice, Suzanne." She put the heel of her hand against her forehead, as if she was attempting to settle her thoughts.

Suzanne took off her shades. "I have no way of knowing if you're lying or not. But I have some cop asking me questions about Coopers Falls Park. You didn't see that happening?"

"I knew you had an alibi. They can't touch you."

"What the fuck are you doing, Jane? Nobody cares about Manson. It was a hundred years ago."

Jane flinched when she heard the name.

"What—did you think Miller knew and I didn't?" Suzanne asked. "Pour two drinks into Mickey Dupree and he would tell you everything he ever knew. Nice attribute for a lawyer." She paused. "You have nothing to say?"

"You want details all of a sudden?" Jane asked. "You never cared about details in your entire life, and now you start asking questions. Tell me—which of these three guys would you bring back if you could?"

Suzanne didn't say anything.

"No answer?" Jane asked.

"There are other considerations here," Suzanne said. "Besides, do you think they won't figure things out? Do you think the police are stupid?"

"I think that some of them are. And if one of them takes Virgil Cain down, then it's all over. Right now, he's the only person they're looking at. And Joe Brady told me he was going to get him."

Suzanne indicated the BMW. "So where are you heading? And don't say you're going for a run."

"I thought I might lend a helping hand," Jane said. "You know, as a civic-minded person. I'm so close to where I want to be, Suzanne. Can't you see that? You, of all people, I thought would understand. I just need to tie up a few loose ends and then I'm home. You wouldn't happen to know where Windecker Road is, would you?"

"No idea."

Jane shrugged. "I'll find it." She half smiled, a dreamy look on her face. "Remember when you were a kid, when you used to count down the days until Christmas? That feeling, as it got closer and closer? That's how I feel, Suzanne. I feel as if I'm just a day away. You remember the feeling."

"No, I don't. Christmas sucked at my house."

"Well, I don't want to be rude but—" Jane gestured at the Mercedes, indicating it was in her way.

"I'll go," Suzanne said. "I'm not sure about turning my back on you."

"Oh, come on," Jane said. "We're birds of a feather." She paused. "You know, I really believe I can make a difference. Do you understand that at least?"

"I believe that you believe it," Suzanne said.

"That's good enough," Jane told her. "Now move your car."

Claire sat at her desk looking at the monitor. A couple of hours earlier all of Buddy Townes's files had been uploaded onto her computer. For all his human failings, Buddy was very good with details, and he had enough information on the residents of Upstate New York—from the ragged lowlifes to the people who passed for high society and everybody in between—to start his own tabloid newspaper. Some of it was enough to make Claire blush, and she hadn't blushed since, well, since a few hours ago at her house.

When she started thinking about Virgil, she lost focus on the monitor and had to will herself back to the task at hand. She had been at it for two hours. Buddy's computer files were as disheveled as Buddy himself, and because of that, it had taken her a while to get to the pertinent information. And there was plenty to find. Buddy was sloppy, but he was extremely thorough.

Claire suddenly realized that someone was standing at her desk, and when she looked up she saw that it was Suzanne Boddington. She was wearing faded jeans and a worn T-shirt with a very young Kris Kristofferson smiling across her breasts.

"I got tired of waiting for you to come out and arrest me," she said.

"I had every intention of doing just that when I got up this morning," Claire told her. She looked at the monitor. "But you're a square peg and I'm not having any luck fitting you in a round hole."

"I hear you talked to my sister."

"Yeah," Claire said. She indicated a chair. "Sit down if you like."

Suzanne sat.

"I talked to your sister," Claire said. "And she tells me you were indeed in Boston at the time somebody pierced Mickey Dupree's black heart. And Northwest has you on a plane for Boston that afternoon. Your sister says you paid for dinner and put it on your credit card. I've asked Amex for a copy of that receipt, but I have to tell you that I've pretty much decided to believe you on that count."

"I'm so sorry."

"Buck up," Claire told her. "So now I'm looking through Buddy Townes's extremely comprehensive files for somebody else who might fit that round hole. Somebody who roughly fits your physical description."

"What's that got to do with it?"

"Because Buddy met with a woman of a certain age in a bar just before he blew this pop stand yesterday. Bragging that he won the lottery. A woman that *maybe* kind of looked like you. A woman who in all likelihood paid Buddy off." Claire hit a key. "So what other women were on the periphery of this thing? Well, Mickey Dupree was dating a waitress just before he died and not treating her particularly well. But she was twenty-five."

"Imagine that."

"I think we can rule her out. Who else do we have? I know that Sally Fairchild threatened Mickey the day he was killed, but Sally Fairchild is a blowhard who threatens people on a weekly basis. I've got nothing to tie her to Alan Comstock or your husband. On and on down the line, until I come to Jane Comstock. Actually, I passed her by once because it made no sense, but then I went back because nobody else makes sense either. And I have to admit that physically you and her are not all that close but your age is within a decade, which might be close enough for a dim-witted bartender on steroids. And I also discover that Buddy has a lot of information on Jane Comstock. By the way, Buddy has a lot of information on you too, Suzanne. Were you aware that your first husband is doing time in Florida for embezzling retirement funds from naive snowbirds?"

"We all have our secrets," Suzanne said. "You ever been married?"

Claire smiled. "Moving on," she said and hit another key. "Jane Comstock has an interesting past. Born Mary Jane Simmons, raised in the West, never knew her father, left home and ended up hitchhiking to California when she was only fourteen years old. She was a Haight-Ashbury child who went by the name Janey Julep for a time. Arrested for vagrancy. Shipped home to Montana and then ran away again, straight back to San Francisco. Pretty standard stuff for the time. But you know what else she did in California?"

"Yeah," Suzanne said. "She lived on the ranch with Charles Manson."

Claire looked from the monitor to Suzanne for a moment, then smiled. "Yeah. She lived on the ranch with Manson. Now that's a fascinating little tidbit and one that Buddy surely would have shared with Mickey Dupree. But who did Mickey tell? And more importantly, why would it matter? It's a pretty insignificant thing after all these years. She was only seventeen at the time, and she wasn't there when the murders went down. There were dozens of teenagers who passed through the ranch. Outside of the usual pharmaceutical abuses of the time, there's nothing to suggest she did anything illegal. By the time she met Comstock twenty-some years ago, her name was Jane Fitzgerald and she was working as a publicist for Columbia Records. She buried her past. So Jane Comstock is like you, another square peg that I can't fit anywhere." Claire straightened in her chair and tapped a couple of keys again. "So where do I go from here?"

Suzanne sat running her fingers back and forth across her chin, as if deliberating on something. Claire watched her quietly. She thought she could smell a whiff of pot emanating from the woman.

"All right," Suzanne said. "There's something that Buddy Townes wouldn't have in his files. Mainly because nobody knows about it yet. Well, hardly anybody. Edie Bryant isn't going to run for congress again. She's finished next year."

"So?"

"She wants Jane to take her seat."

Claire took a moment to digest the information. "And Jane is open to this?"

"I think Jane has been angling for this for years."

"Okay," Claire said. She paused again to think. "For your average citizen, being a Manson follower is barely a footnote. Especially forty years after the fact. But if you're running for public office, and a US congresswoman is pretty damn public, then it's a big deal."

"It's a game changer."

"Yeah, I would say so," Claire said. Looking at the screen, she exhaled heavily. "So tell me why your car was in the park."

"She drove me to the airport. I don't like to leave my car in the lot there. She said she'd give me a ride then called at the last minute and said her car wouldn't start, so I drove to her place and we went in mine."

"And then she keeps on going, to the park," Claire said. "What about the night Alan Comstock was killed? You guys were both in New York City."

"I don't know about that," Suzanne said. "We took separate vehicles. But I remember she begged off right after the theater, said she had a headache. However, we did have breakfast the next morning."

"But she could've driven upstate, called Alan on the way on the burn phone to tell him that they caught Cain. That's why Alan didn't question it; he heard it from his wife. And that's also why he didn't fight back. She could've walked up, kissed him on the cheek, picked up the gun, and started shooting. And then drove back to the city. Which sets Cain up as the fall guy."

"It does more than that."

"Oh?"

"It gets rid of a husband who was going to be a huge liability in an election campaign."

"Ah, yes," Claire said. "I never thought of that." She sat silently for a moment. "Okay then, what about your husband?"

"Miller knew about the Manson connection. In fact, he mocked her about it just a few days ago. They didn't like each other, and, believe me, he would not have kept quiet if she ran for office."

"And then he has his charges dropped and she sees her chance."

"Maybe."

Claire looked at the screen again. "Well, it's an interesting theory. I'm not sure it all fits or not." She glanced at Suzanne. "Why are you here?"

"Just being a good citizen?" Suzanne suggested.

"Okay," Claire said. "With maybe a dash of self-preservation thrown in there?"

"Possibly. I went to see her this morning. Up until now she's held everything in check, but I think she's off the rails. Your guy Brady told her that Cain is back in the area, *and* that he's going to kill him if he gets the chance. Jane knows that solves everything. She referred to it as tying up loose ends. I actually think she sees herself helping out."

"How?"

"I'm not sure," Suzanne said. "But like I said, she knows that if Cain is dead, then everything is wiped clean. She told me to get out of her way."

"What else did she say?"

"She asked me where Windecker Road was."

THIRTY

It was still dark when Virgil arrived at the farm. He parked Claire's Honda in the brush at the back of the woods and walked along the lane to the barns. The moon was out and nearly full, showing his way. The Neil Young song was playing in his head, like a constant loop.

Look out, Mama, there's a white boat comin' up the river.

The water tank was down to its last couple of inches. Virgil started the pump and, while the water ran, walked over to the house and had a look around. It didn't appear that anybody had been there since the night Claire had arrested him and then let him go, but he couldn't be sure. He had to assume the police were watching the place to some extent.

After he shut off the pump he headed back to the woods, walking along the fencerow just as the sun was rising behind him. There was enough light that he could check out his cattle. He found a spot in the fence that they had nearly succeeded in knocking down while trying to get to the grass on the other side. He would have to fix it soon.

He was suddenly tired and realized he'd only slept for a couple of hours during the night. He found a blanket in the back of Claire's car and carried it to his spot in the cedars and rolled himself up in it. He closed his eyes but didn't go to sleep for thinking of Claire. He saw her sitting at the counter, the towel around her neck, and he saw her at the computer listening to Neil Young, and he saw her in bed, naked on the cool sheets. He could still smell the scent of her, in his hair, on his mouth, on his fingers.

He hadn't been expecting any of this. The past couple of years, since Kirstie had died, he'd been on autopilot, running the farm, staying a step ahead of the bank, keeping to himself for the most part. Once in a while he'd go into Saugerties for a few beers and some chicken wings, usually at Donny's Downtown Bar. But he had managed to eliminate the drama from his life. It had always served him poorly in the past, and while he hadn't made any conscious effort to rid himself of it, it seemed that he had done so. Maybe it was a subconscious thing or maybe it was just the luck of the draw. Whatever the reason, he had been glad to leave it behind.

But it had found him again. He hadn't seen it coming but then how could he have? He'd been in trouble in the past but it had always been of his own volition. And while he hadn't always been happy with the outcome, he'd always accepted it for what it was. Reap what you sow. This time was different. This time he didn't see it coming.

Or Claire either, for that matter.

He didn't want to think about her, not now anyway. He needed sleep and he knew he wouldn't get any as long as she was on his mind. So, to push her from his thoughts, he forced himself to think about what needed to be done around the farm. The fence fixed, for one. The rest of the hay to come off. There was a tractor with a U-joint that had been clunking for a month. He went through the tasks one by one and finally his mind rested.

When he awoke the sun was high in the sky and the song was still rambling in his head. He got to his feet and shook the blanket out. He wanted a closer look at the house and barns, but he'd left the binoculars in the Dodge pickup in Claire's garage.

He watched for half an hour but saw only a couple of vehicles pass by on the main road and none pull into the drive. He decided to risk walking up to the machine shed to grab pliers and a roll of wire to fix the fence where the cattle had breached it. He couldn't spend the day sitting in the cedars.

Walking quickly, he kept close to the fence line, thinking he could take partial cover by a post if a vehicle appeared. None did and he went into the machine shed through the door at the back. He was surprised to see that the big doors of the shed were open. He hadn't opened them. Maybe Mary Nelson had, but he couldn't imagine why. He gathered what he needed and put everything in an eleven-quart basket, and, just as he was about to head out, he heard tires on gravel. He walked to the front of the shed and looked out the dirty window. A navy-blue SUV was coming in the drive, idling along. The windows were tinted dark and he couldn't see who, or how many, were inside. The vehicle got closer and he saw then that it was a BMW. When did the cops start driving BMWs?

He looked around. If he went out the back door and started to run, he'd be seen at once. He remembered what Claire had said. For all he knew, Joe Brady was in the BMW. Virgil didn't think Joe would shoot him down in cold blood, but he wasn't interested in finding out he was wrong. He would wait. If they went into the house for a look around, he might be able to slip out the back door and make his way to the barn. If he could climb up into the haymow, he could hide there in the bales.

However, the BMW didn't stop. It had come in the lane leading to the barns and then completed the horseshoe and driven out the other lane by the house.

In the machine shed, Virgil watched until the car was out of sight. It had just been a drive-by. Maybe it wasn't the cops after all. A real estate agent had been after the place off and on since

Tom Stempler had died. Maybe this was another one, having heard that Virgil would be going to prison for twenty or thirty years. Real estate agents were more likely to drive BMWs than were cops.

But he couldn't assume that it wasn't the police. Maybe they hadn't stopped because they were looking for the Dodge pickup. And maybe that was why the door to the machine shed was open. The cops had done it earlier, checking for the truck. Virgil couldn't risk walking back to the woods in the daylight, not knowing when they might return. He would have to wait for dusk.

Look out, Mama, there's a white boat comin' up the river,
With a big red beacon and a flag and a man on the rail.

It was going to be a long day unless he could find something to do. He could remove the U-joint from the tractor but the new parts were still on order. Then he remembered the bearings that he'd bought for the pump. He put some sockets and wrenches and screwdrivers in a toolbox and then, after checking to see that no vehicles were approaching, he headed across the yard to the pump house.

I think you'd better call John,
'Cause it don't look like they're here to deliver the mail

There were two windows in the pump house, one facing the road and the other, by the door, that gave a view of the house. Virgil would be able to see a car approaching from either lane. Not that it would do him any good—if anyone stopped, he would have no place to go. But they hadn't checked the buildings the last time. They were looking for the truck, it seemed.

He unbolted the pump from the base and lifted it onto a shelf that he'd used as a workbench in the past. He removed the motor from the pump and then took the end plate off. It took him a while, with a ball peen and a drift, to hammer the old bearing free. As he was sliding it from the shaft, he heard a car in the drive.

He ducked down and moved toward the window by the door, listening for the car to go past the shed before sneaking a peek.

It was the Dodge pickup. From where he stood he couldn't see the driver but he knew it was Claire. Virgil felt a little tingle in his chest, like he was a goddamn teenager and his girlfriend had stopped by.

He immediately heard another vehicle in the drive and looked out the front window to see the BMW returning. It drove by the pump house as well and parked just a few feet away, twenty yards or so behind the pickup. He realized it had been following the pickup. Of course, whoever was driving the BMW would assume that Virgil was driving the truck. They were about to get a surprise when they saw Claire get out.

Virgil resigned himself to the fact that he was about to be arrested again.

Daddy's gone, my brother's out hunting in the mountains,
Big John's been drinkin' since the river took Emmy-Lou.

The door to the BMW opened and Jane Comstock got out. Virgil knew her on sight; he had watched her sitting behind her husband every day during the trial. But what the hell was she doing here?

Her motions seemed robotic as she walked around to the back of the car and opened the hatch to take out a gym bag.

Claire got out of the truck then, talking on her cell phone. When she saw Jane Comstock, she reacted and shut the phone off. She walked with purpose toward the BMW. The vehicle was blocking her view and she couldn't see what the woman was doing.

But Virgil could. He saw Jane Comstock hesitate upon seeing Claire. Obviously she had been expecting Virgil to step out of the truck. And then Virgil saw a strange look cross the woman's face, something between resignation and resolve. She pulled a handgun from the bag.

Red means run, son, numbers add up to nothin'—

Virgil kicked open the pump house door and, like the song advised, started running.

"She's got a gun!"

Claire hit the ground, scrambling backward toward the truck. Jane stepped away from the SUV and fired a couple of rounds at her, kicking up the gravel in the driveway, but then seemed to realize that Virgil was coming hard on her flank. She turned the gun on him and fired it point-blank and, as he heard the roar of the gunshot, Virgil lowered his shoulder and barreled into her. He felt something tug at his ear, like a finger flicking it, and then his shoulder hit the woman full in the chest, knocking her heavily to the ground. Virgil reached wildly for her right hand, but when he found it, the gun was gone. The woman rolled away from him.

Then he heard Claire's voice, shouting. He looked up to see her driving Jane Comstock facedown into the gravel, her knee on the woman's back, the muzzle of her Beretta against her head.

"What the fuck are you doing?" Jane demanded. "That's Virgil Cain! That's the guy you're after."

302

"We're going to have to talk about that," Claire said calmly. She fumbled for her handcuffs and shackled Jane's hands behind her. She read the woman her rights.

Then she told Virgil he was an idiot.

The first cop to arrive after the fact was Sal Delano. Claire had put Jane Comstock in the front seat of the BMW and was giving Virgil the condensed version of the woman's alleged involvement in the killings. Virgil had pulled something in his right shoulder and kept trying to work it out. His ear was bleeding where the bullet had clipped him. Claire had looked at it and given him a tissue to stop the bleeding.

"Take Mrs. Comstock back with you," Claire told Sal.

"What's she charged with?"

"Shit, I can't even begin to tell you," Claire said. "But I think it'll make the six o'clock news."

She watched as Sal took Jane to the cruiser and put her in the back. Sal walked around to the driver's door and looked back at Claire.

"You all right here?"

"Yeah," she told him.

He backed around and drove off. Claire watched him until he was on the road and then turned to Virgil.

"You're probably going to need a couple stitches in that ear," she said. "We can stop at emergency on the way to the station."

"Why are we going to the station?" Virgil asked.

"Because I'm arresting you," Claire said. "Escape custody. You forget about that?"

"You can't arrest me right now," he said. He gestured over his shoulder. "I've got a pump apart in there and if I don't get it back together, I won't be able to water my horses."

"You and your damn horses."

Taking another tissue from her pocket, she walked over to him. She gently wiped the blood from his ear and had a look at the wound. Then she kissed him on the lips, her mouth full on his.

"Come on and fix it," she said and walked toward the pump house.

"And then what?"

"And then you're under arrest."

"And then what?"

"We'll see," she told him, and she went inside.

ACKNOWLEDGMENTS

A wise person once observed that it takes a village to raise a novel.

Or words to that effect.

With that in mind, I would be remiss if I didn't thank the people who helped out along the way with *Red Means Run*. Their contributions vary in size but not in significance.

For editorial input, sage advice, and enduring friendship, I would like to mention Lorraine Sommerfeld, Jennifer Barclay, Donna Morrissey, and Linda Muir.

Thanks to Mitch Bowden, for showing me the difference between a Gibson and a Fender.

From Simon & Schuster Canada, my gratitude to Kevin Hanson, Alison Clarke, and my friend Lorraine Kelly.

Thanks to Adam Vollick—a Canfield boy—who lighted the winding path that led to Neil Young.

I owe a debt (and a pint or two) to Mike Murphy and Herb Schilling of Kingston, New York.

My endearing gratitude to Wendy Sharko and Julie Casper Maynard, from Canada's best little bookstore, The Avid Reader.

A bushel basket of thanks to my editor at Scribner, Anna deVries, who loves books and the Yankees unconditionally.

And a bushel more to my agent, the tenacious and loquacious Victoria Sturnick.

APACK

3/12